The In
Contract

by Scott Burdick

"And the Lord God said, 'Behold, the man is become as one of us, to know good and evil: and now, lest he put forth his hand, and take also of the tree of life, and eat, and live forever . . .'"

Genesis 3:22

Chapter 1

The lies we tell ourselves about ourselves—about the seen and the unseen, about the mysteries of life and death—come as natural and unconscious as dreams. None are free of such self-deceptions.

Empires rise and fall on them.

We wear our delusions on golden chains around our necks, on flags, bumper stickers, and even mount them to the tops of buildings for the world to see. We laugh at the delusions of others, and rage when someone laughs at our own.

Some delusions are harmless, some inspiring, some comforting.

Some can kill.

Has it really been eleven years since that day?

The man from the embassy had called in the middle of the night. "I'm sorry to inform you that your wife and daughter have been slaughtered like pigs," he'd said.

Not really in those words. The ambassador had been subtle and compassionate, but there had been no hiding the brutal truth.

From that moment on, revenge became the North Star of existence, the founding fact and justification for living on. Revenge—not only on the ones who wielded the knives, but especially on the mastermind behind the assassination. A serial killer so dangerous and powerful, entire nations bowed before him.

It had taken over a decade, but the trap was finally set.

Today, I will avenge you, my loves.

Theon gripped the armrest of the hated wheelchair and levered his atrophied body forward. The familiar pain flowed along his spine like molten lead into a fractured mold. With arthritic slowness, he pressed gnarled fingers against the cool surface of the polished steel door. Within its sheen, a stranger glared back at him. The deep wrinkles crisscrossing the eighty-seven-year-old visage resembled the desiccated remains of a mummy—except for the fierce slate-gray eyes.

He eased the door open a crack.

Dozens of reporters waited in the opulent lobby, the snow-topped peaks of the Continental Divide framed in the towering windows behind. An aura of stale alcohol and cigar smoke clung to the gathering from the previous night's New Year's Eve celebrations. A few yawned.

Investigative journalists, my ass.

Theon glanced at Helena, her youthful radiance all the more striking beside his withered carcass. A rail-straight posture registered her disapproval, but she'd made her pledge and would play the appointed role.

Helena's emerald eyes met his with a final plea. Her delicate fingers cupped his gnarled and liver-spotted hand as if in prayer. The expressive grace of the gesture echoed a sculpture of the Virgin Mother his grandfather donated to their neighborhood church. As a child, he'd gazed upon it with awe every Sunday, while the priest droned on and on.

Francesco Torano—Grandpa Frank to him—spent two years carving the statue. Wracked with lung cancer, the family patriarch hoped it would be his ticket to Heaven, an offering to cleanse a sin that haunted him from the old country. What act required such radical atonement, Grandpa Frank never shared with any outside the confessional.

At the funeral, Father O'Malley assured them that Grandpa was in a better place. For a time, he believed the soothing lie.

"Please don't do this," Helena said.

Theon withdrew his hand from her unblemished fingers—his own masterpiece of sorts. "No more argument. I've made my decision."

Her full lips compressed into a tight line. "This is madness."

"You know this is necessary," he said.

"I'm not as certain as you."

"So you're an agnostic, then?"

"Keep your labels to yourself. I'm not interested." She resumed her post behind the wheelchair like a soldier preparing for a suicide mission.

In time, she'll realize I'm right.

Last-minute preparations swirled about them like a well-choreographed musical.

A large number of his company's staff were disabled to various degrees. Gloria—Down Syndrome—stood ready with press releases. Eddie—his feet twisted backward from a birth defect—sat at a desk monitoring the Web. A dozen other employees sat at laptops, ready to respond to media requests after the announcement. Some were blind, some without limbs, and others with impairments not obvious to the eye.

Most were eligible for government disability, but they preferred to work, earn their own living, and contribute to a cause greater than themselves.

No different than anyone else.

Lamarr—big, black, and a year older than Theon at eighty-eight—rumbled toward them. The onetime heavyweight contender teetered side to side on his busted knee. A well-aimed brick had shattered it during a march with Martin Luther King, a badge of honor he wore with pride.

Lamarr jerked to a stop beside them, rubbed his frosty mess of a beard, and studied Helena from the top of her fiery hair, to the tips of her high heels.

"Ready for your big moment, Miss Helena?"

Lamarr adjusted the folds of her skirt as if preparing a store-front mannequin for a window display.

Helena slapped his massive hands, but the former pugilist paid no mind.

When Lamarr first showed her the dress, she expressed contempt and suggested her customary lab coat instead.

"Viral news requires cleavage," was all he said, and that was that.

Helena sighed and submitted to the primping. "Theon tells me you two met in the boxing ring during high school."

"I boxed, that's true enough," Lamarr said, "though I'm not too sure what the boss man here was doing."

Theon laughed for the first time in weeks. "If memory serves, I was lying on the canvas crapping my pants after you literally knocked the shit out of me! That cured any notion I had of entering Golden Gloves again, let alone going pro like you."

Lamarr's chuckle might have been the rumble of a winter thunderstorm. "Would have saved me a lot of trouble if you'd knocked the shit out of me, instead. You should thank me for doing you a favor."

"Remind me to send a cow pie and flowers."

Lamarr stepped back and surveyed his work. "We sure fixed you up good, didn't we, Miss Helena?"

"You surely did, Lamarr."

Her sarcasm fell flat as a diminutive Japanese woman in her mid-seventies waved a clipboard in front of Lamarr's bushy face. "Stop impersonating a fashion designer! We have work to do!"

"I know, I know," Lamarr said defensively. "We've rehearsed this a thousand times, Kyoko."

"And I don't remember any of them including you pawing girls' dresses!"

Despite Kyoko yanking on his tree-trunk of an arm, Lamarr couldn't seem to abandon his masterpiece.

Suddenly, his eyes widened. "I forgot the perfume!"

Kyoko threw her hands in the air. "Television cameras can't record smells!"

"Oh . . . right," Lamarr said. "Where's Anna?"

"Down here, King Kong," Anna said from her motorized wheelchair. She had no legs, and her torso was squashed downward and outward from what she called *God's punishment for my sins as a wayward fetus*. A pair of oversize glasses with dark rims obscured much of her face. Lamarr once suggested contact lenses, which caused her to laugh for a full minute.

"Sorry, Anna, I didn't see you there."

"No shit?" Anna said in mock surprise. "First time that's happened."

"Is everything ready?" the former boxer asked.

"As ready as I am to stick my tongue down Elizabeth Warren's throat."

"Anna!" Kyoko said.

The crippled girl shrugged. "I would have said Sarah Palin, but that seemed too obvious. She is hot!"

"So I can take that as a yes?" Lamarr asked.

Anna saluted. "Tube's flooded and torpedoes ready to fire, Captain."

Lamarr turned to Theon. "All set, Boss?"

"Put me in, Coach."

Lamarr placed a hand against the door and smiled with the mischievous glee of an altar boy preparing to toss a water balloon onto an Easter procession. "Yes, siree, we're gonna shake things up!" He glanced at Helena. "Remember, shoulders back and chest out. Think Beyoncé."

She groaned as Lamarr swung the gleaming door wide.

Theon's wheelchair rolled forward with his red-haired goddess at the helm.

The eyes of the news vultures tracked Helena's every step. The glory of her youthful splendor accentuated the horror of his own wasted senescence—a stark reminder of what Nature had in store for them all.

From the front row, Reverend Cyril Doberson rotated his pudgy face toward them. A white Armani suit swathed his bulky form, while a golden crucifix shielded his heart like a celestial sheriff's badge. Beneath this, fuchsia embroidery read: *Giveth to the Lord and Prosper.*

"Should I have security escort him out?" Helena asked through clenched teeth.

"I'd enjoy that as much as you, except the reverend is here at my invitation."

"Of course you'd choose the most extreme straw man you could find," she said. "You do know there are moderate believers as well?"

"Merely a difference of degree, my dear."

The famed televangelist rose from his seat and approached with surprising fluidity for such a large man.

Helena brought the wheelchair to a halt before the self-proclaimed *Moral Conscience of America.*

"Welcome, Reverend," Theon said.

"Call me Cyril," the reverend said in his Appalachian drawl. He engulfed Theon's hand in both of his own and shook as if still campaigning in his failed presidential run. A scent of lilac suffused the space around him. "I was quite pleased with your invitation, Doctor Torano."

I'm sure you were, you blood-sucking parasite.

Out loud, he said, "Call me Theon, and the pleasure is mine."

Cyril's face expanded into a broad smile. "Might I presume, Brother Theon, that you're interested in joining our fellowship?"

"I thought you knew I was an atheist, Cyril?"

"I did, but many experience epiphanies as their mortal end approaches."

Theon chuckled. "I'm not that feeble-minded yet, Cyril."

The evangelist's smile shriveled. "Why invite me here, then?"

"You are an acclaimed faith healer, are you not?"

"I am but a conduit through which the Holy Spirit and God's Grace heals those in need."

"Could you cure me?" Theon asked.

"The Lord's power to heal is without bounds," Cyril said. "But only if you first accept Jesus as your personal Savior."

"So I'd need to profess my faith in your God to be cured?"

"It's not me who makes the rules, you understand?"

"Indeed, I do."

The reverend's smile returned. "I could offer you my personal attention—"

"Can't you see you're being set up?" Helena asked.

Cyril spluttered, but no words came out.

Theon coughed to cover a laugh. "Forgive my nurse. She forgets her place."

Helena jerked the wheelchair, sending a stab of pain into his spine. "The reporters are growing restless," she said.

As Helena rolled him past the evangelist, Theon said, "I think you and your congregation will find my announcement of great interest."

Cyril retreated to his seat with a relaxed smile aimed at the cameras. His self-control was masterful.

I almost feel sorry for him.

Helena pushed Theon to the podium and stepped onto her prearranged mark.

Theon raised a hand, and the room stilled.

A few of the reporters glanced at their watches.

Not one of them realizes they're about to witness history.

He took a deep breath and began. "Science, Reason, and the pursuit of Truth. I've navigated by the light of these stars since entering the field of molecular biology sixty-five years ago."

Shutters snapped here and there, while the reporters fidgeted without making a single note. Reverend Cyril glanced at his smartphone, no doubt waiting for the right moment to exit.

"The scientific breakthrough I'm here to announce is the culmination of research begun half a century ago by my late wife, and fellow scientist, Taslima Saud."

A few reporters nodded, probably having covered her murder.

"Taslima wondered why a mouse lives only a few years, dogs no more than twenty, and some tortoise species several centuries. The Prometheus Tree, the self-regenerative Hydra, and many bacterial colonies, have no upper limit at all. Scientists call such creatures *functionally immortal*—meaning they would live forever if not for predation or accident."

A spark of interest ignited within the faces of his audience. Even Reverend Cyril glanced up from his phone.

"The cells in our body perform identically to these organisms for the early part of our lives, until something happens, some epigenetic switch halting regeneration in individual cells. It's as if a mysterious biological referee blows some telomeric whistle and declares that a cell's DNA can no longer renew itself through reproduction.

"As the proportion of underperforming cells mount, waste products accumulate. Our bodies, minds, and general health deteriorate as a consequence. We become less able to repulse infection, repair damage, and replace worn-out cells with new ones. This is what we mean by the term *aging*, and what my wife set out to cure, like any other disease."

Four lab assistants rolled an aquarium next to the podium. Half a dozen mushroom-like forms floated within the water, their translucent bodies illuminated by lights in the bottom of the tank.

Helena took her place behind the glass, the bright orange creatures reflected in her green eyes.

"These are Turritopsis dohrnii," Theon said, "commonly known as *the Immortal Jellyfish*. When stressed by a lack of food, these hydrozoans age—in reverse—back to their polyp state. In some ways, it can be seen as an efficient form of hibernation. Once environmental conditions normalize, these extraordinary creatures grow back to their adult form and resume reproduction."

I've got their attention now.

"Thirty-five years ago, Taslima collected these specimens off the coast of Japan. Since then, they've completed fifty-seven cycles of regression and restoration."

The staccato of shutters paid tribute to Lamarr's stagecraft. The older reporters scribbled in their notebooks, while the younger ones held audio devices aloft to capture every word.

"Taslima never finished—" Theon's throat constricted, and he fought tears.

The Saudi police had found his twelve-year-old granddaughter curled in a fetal position beside her dead mother and grandmother. They'd been stabbed a combined fifty-nine times, and their heads nearly decapitated.

Taslima's elderly mother and the servants described three masked men shouting Jihadi slogans. None were ever captured.

His granddaughter remained mute for a year. When the words finally came, her story was fantasy. Reality had become too much for her psyche to deal with, so it created its own.

Stay focused! I owe it to them to do this right.

He cleared his throat. "Since my wife and daughter were murdered, I've spent every waking hour, and more than half of my seventy-billion-dollar fortune, completing Taslima's research."

Every eye locked onto him in anticipation. Cyril's pudgy fingers blanched as he gripped his cell phone.

"Today, I am pleased to announce that Amara Pharmaceuticals has cured the condition known as aging."

Cyril's mouth fell open.

Dozens of voices erupted with questions.

Theon raised a hand for silence and pointed to the AP reporter, a somewhat mousy woman in her twenties—a fellow science-nerd.

"What is the mechanism of this procedure?"

"While the details are proprietary, my laboratory has developed a monthly pill that restores every cell in one's body to optimal functionality. The patient will age in reverse at ten years per month, until reaching their prime—for humans this is the equivalent of twenty to twenty-five years old. As long as one continues taking the pill each month, they will stay young, essentially forever."

"Does this reversion process erase one's memories since that age?"

"The neural connections remain intact, so there is no memory loss, but the brain cells gain the ability to regenerate and repair the damage of aging, dementia, stroke, cancer, etc."

A grizzled old *New York Times* reporter raised his hand. "What if someone changes their mind about living forever?"

Theon spread his hands wide. "Simply stop taking my Fountain of Youth Pill, and you will decline ten years per month until reaching your natural age. Then you will resume the inglorious march toward death, as nature intended."

He paused, letting this sink in. "The question isn't if you want to be immortal, but whether you want to live healthy for another day, month, or year, until you've had enough of life. It isn't much different from a heart surgery, knee replacement, or any other medical procedure to extend life and improve its quality."

The *Wall Street Journal* raised a hand. "What will you charge for this miracle pill?"

Theon smiled. "Since I own my company outright and have no stockholders to please, I've decided to give my discovery to the world free of monetary compensation."

He pointed to a young NPR reporter.

"If you're giving this drug away for free, why not release the formula on the Internet?"

"I said free of *monetary* compensation."

"What else could you want besides money?"

Of course they would think that's all that matters.

Theon reached beneath the podium and removed a single sheet of paper. "This is my *Immortality Contract*. It is a terms-of-use agreement required to receive my drug."

☐Theon settled a pair of glasses atop his nose. "In exchange for Amara Pharmaceutical's Fountain of Youth treatment, I affirm that science and human reason alone created this drug. Whatever my spiritual views, I pledge to forswear public support of all supernatural systems of belief. This includes, but is not limited to, financial donations to churches and/or governments that espouse, endorse, or promote such beliefs. I understand that any public declaration of faith in the supernatural, be it verbal, written, or by any other means, will cause the absolute and irrevocable disqualification of my ever receiving this drug again."

Reverend Cyril surged to his feet. "What do you hope to accomplish with such a vile document?"

Theon set the paper aside and smiled. "Isn't it obvious, Cyril? I intend to utterly and completely destroy the global institutions of organized religion."

Stunned silence.

Several camera crews dragged their equipment to the side for better framing of the age-old confrontation between science and religion. Conflict equaled ratings.

"That is not only immoral, but illegal!" shouted Cyril.

"Reverend Doberson, didn't you tell me just a few minutes ago that you reserve your healing powers for those who publicly endorse your beliefs? I am merely doing the same, except that I will offer scientific proof that my claims are true."

"God and Heaven are no lie."

"In that case, why would your followers delay their reward in the next life by taking my pill in the first place? Or do you fear that—deep within some hidden recess of their minds—they doubt your claims?"

Reverend Cyril spluttered, and beads of sweat inch-wormed down his face. "Would the Constitution allow the inventor of a heart valve to deny it to Jews or Muslims? This is religious discrimination."

"And yet, you encourage Christian businesses to refuse service to gay couples. Not to mention defending the right of Christian pharmacists to deny contraception to women based on their religious beliefs."

"You're talking about killing people!"

"Don't you believe dying of old age is God's doing?"

Reverend Cyril's jowls trembled with fury. "You're a demon."

"To continue providing ever more powerful technologies to a species lacking the rational tools necessary to control them would be the height of irresponsibility."

The BBC asked, "How can you police people's private thoughts?"

"Consumers of my Fountain of Youth Drug are free to pray to Thor, Minerva, Tinkerbell, Jesus, or whatever nonsense they choose in the privacy of their own minds and homes. They simply may not publicly promote or finance such views."

NPR raised a hand. "I notice you mentioned governments in your contract. Are citizens of Islamic theocracies ineligible for your drug based simply on geography?"

"You're assuming I'm giving Israel a pass for its religious bias, or Britain's constitutional entanglement with the Church of England, or our own country's bias. When you add up the United States' income tax exemptions for donations to churches, property tax subsidies, and parsonage tax exemptions, we're talking an estimated seventy billion dollars a year in lost tax revenues. Isn't it time we took God off the government dole and let him pay his own way?"

"Churches are the fabric of our society," Cyril said. "They deserve government support just as much as science does."

"Just as much?" Theon asked. "The combined budget of NASA, the National Science Foundation, and the National Institutes of Health's is forty-seven billion dollars a year—nearly half of the tax subsidies given to religion. How many diseases has religion cured? How many galaxies have divine revelation discovered? Imagine if those tax breaks were ended and that money spent on education, research, or job creation?"

Cyril faced the cameras. "You are witnessing a farce. A hoax by a bitter old man who blames God for the murder of his wife and daughter."

"I'm shocked at your skepticism, Reverend," Theon said. "What if I told you that Jesus gave me the formula in a miraculous vision? Would that inspire more faith?"

"You see, he can't prove it," Cyril said with a smirk. "He's a liar and a fraud."

Theon clapped his hands in mock applause. "Well done, Cyril. You are capable of doubt, after all. As you correctly point out, I have not submitted the evidence supporting such an extraordinary claim—but I must point out that your claims are even more extraordinary."

Laughter spread through the room.

"You nearly had us!" called out the *New York Times*.

After a moment, Theon raised his hand, and the room settled. "This is no publicity stunt. While I shall present more conclusive proof at the time and place of the government's choosing, here is a taste."

Helena stepped from behind the tank of jellyfish. She faced the room like a defiant slave on the auction block.

"When were you born, my dear?" Theon asked.

"During The Great Depression. I'm eighty-five-years-old"

Several reporters laughed.

"Come on, Doctor Torano," the grizzled old BBC correspondent shouted. "I think you're pushing this joke a bit far."

Cyril shook his head in disgust and headed for the exit.

Helena's voice rose above the tumult. "It's no joke!"

They laughed harder. A few started packing their equipment.

Helena snatched a magazine from beneath the podium and strode forward, stopping in front of a female reporter in the first row. "You wrote a profile on me for *Time* magazine three years ago." Helena raised the magazine for everyone to see. A stately woman in her eighties graced the cover. The caption read: "The Grande Dame of Venture Capital."

The reporter took the magazine and opened it to a photo of Helena in her twenties. On cue, a screen behind the podium displayed the same image.

In the photograph, a youthful Helena stood beside a young Theon and his future wife, Taslima. The caption read, "Helena Mueller, Theon Torano, and Taslima Saud—the Three Musketeers of science in their student days."

A tear slid down Theon's cheek at the sight of his wife.

No pill will restore you.

"It can't be," Judith said. "I spoke to Helena after her cancer diagnosis. She had only months to live."

"You mentioned your husband's false diagnosis, and suggested I seek a second opinion."

Judith's eyes widened. "I never told anyone about that phone call."

Helena nodded. "I took your advice, but a second doctor confirmed that the cancer had migrated throughout my body."

Helena turned to Theon. "I thought I was at peace with death—until you made your offer."

"I'm glad I reached you in time, my dear friend."

"This is ridiculous!" Cyril shouted from the back of the room. "She's an impostor coached to play a part."

Helena resumed her station behind the wheelchair with the air of an actor completing a monologue.

"Doubt is the lifeblood of the scientific method, Cyril," Theon said. "I salute your skepticism."

He addressed the reporters. "Lend Cyril some of your skill as journalists. How might I have faked this evidence?"

The *BBC* correspondent scratched his chin. "Maybe you planned this stunt before the article and simply Photoshopped this woman's face over the real Helena Mueller's."

"Excellent theory!" Theon said. "You see how this works, Cyril?"

The famed evangelist strode forward within camera range. "Then you admit this is a publicity stunt?"

"Not at all. This photo has been used in dozens of articles for the last fifty years," Theon said. "But even so, I admit that such an extraordinary claim requires a great deal more evidence than a single photograph."

Cyril's upper lip curled in contempt. "This is nothing but an elaborate game to prove a theological point."

"It is no game, Reverend. I intend to destroy you and your kind once and for all."

The evangelist pointed an accusing finger at Theon and addressed the cameras. "His own decrepitude proves he's lying. It's exactly what you'd expect from an atheist with no morals."

Theon's eyes narrowed to slits. "Thomas Edison was also maligned for his rejection of an afterlife—even while everyone enjoyed the gifts of his rational mind. I'm here to tell the world that the free ride is over."

Theon raised a white pill in the manner of a priest blessing a communion wafer. "Here it is—the key to life. The ultimate product of the human capacity to reason, and the greatest challenge religion has ever faced. In the coming weeks and months, you will witness my transformation with your own eyes."

He lowered the pill toward his mouth. "In the coming days, every person on the planet must ask themselves if they have more faith in science and life here on Earth, or God and life after death."

Theon placed the pill on his tongue, closed his mouth, and swallowed.

Chapter 2

The demon was back. Gnawing at her insides with its demand of sustenance.

Feed me, it whispered, like that infernal plant from that play her mother took her to in third grade. She'd laughed and clapped along with the rest of the audience as the monster grew.

As the night stretched, the need tore at her with increasing violence. *Feed me!*

Panic mounted alongside the torment. Vomit rose from the pain in her gut, but she forced it down and smiled into the blinding darkness. The headlights flowed in an incessant torrent, illuminating her like a stiletto-heeled lightning bug advertising for a mate.

What a cliché I've become. The junky prostitute. Star of a thousand cheap TV crime dramas. The excuse for the sexy dead body lying half-naked in the alley, while the detectives shake their heads at the tragic waste.

Please stop, please . . .

Despite the desert chill, a clammy sheen of sweat clung to her. The shivers began at midnight. Her nipples thrust against her shirt as if drawn to the diminishing lights.

FEED ME!

She plucked a compact mirror from her purse and added a fresh layer of bait to her lips. Her brown eyes resembled prisoners banished to purgatory—the same eyes that had watched blood ooze from her mother's severed head.

Mom had been an artist.

A self-portrait of her mother used to hang in Alma's bedroom. The painting was dated six months before her daughter's birth.

A double portrait, then.

The image always calmed her—knowing each stroke came from her mother's hand. She'd run her fingers over the ridges of paint, feeling the connection.

The gallery bought the rare self-portrait outright, since prices skyrocketed after the artist's shocking murder.

Better for someone else to protect this last piece of her mother. At least, that's what the demon told her.

A beat-up Ford Escort stopped. At the old age of twenty-three, Alma's BMW days were long passed. What demon made him stop for something like her?

It didn't matter. Nothing did. There was no room left for shame. If the demon made him hit her, or piss on her, or whatever else, she deserved it. She got into the car and pulled off her meager clothes. He smelled of popcorn and cigars. A carnie?

Stop thinking. Life is an illusion. Consciousness a trick played by quantum mechanics. All the science books say so.

Ten minutes later, clutching the wad of crumpled bills, she stumbled away from the river of light, down an embankment, and under the cover of an overpass. Here and there fires guttered, fed by trash and illuminating the graffiti on the ribs of concrete and steel. Huddled forms sprawled across the rubble like the remnants of a tribe of hunter-gatherers. The twisted remains of a rusting bus substituted for the butchered carcass of a mammoth.

The mixed odor of rotting garbage, urine, and smoke recalled the camps of those first immigrants. Only the added scent of exhaust fumes from the road above marked the advance of civilization.

She stumbled to the nearest group of cave dwellers and exchanged the paper in her fist for something real. Everything except the four tiny bags was an illusion.

Sandi lay curled in a ball at the top of the slope. JoJo must have beaten her again.

"Is that you, Alma?" Sandi's breath came in a straggled rasp. Her once glorious black hair lay matted into clumps, and her exotic dark eyes stared through swollen lids like hunted refugees.

"It's me, sweetie." Alma stroked her friend's cheek, and Sandi leaned into her.

She removed the serving spoon pocketed from Golden Corral, emptied two of the bags of powder into it, and then flicked her lighter beneath. When the powder bubbled into liquid, she sucked it into a syringe.

"That's too much," Sandi said. "You'll overdose if you—"

"Half for me, and half for you." She motioned to the other two baggies in her purse. "And two for later."

"You shouldn't waste it on me."

"Enough of that." She tied off Sandi's arm and injected half the syringe into a vein. "You'd do the same for me."

Then she repeated the process on herself.

Within seconds, the demon slithered into its lair and left her in peace. Sandi's hand found hers and held it just as her mother used to do. The light of the fires danced across the walls. A coyote howled, answered by silence. Another lonely soul searching . . . searching . . .

"The world is shit," Sandi said. "Even MacDonald's is selling those crappy Egg McMuffins all day now."

"Out of everything, that's the example you choose?"

"It ain't right, that's all. You wouldn't eat cake for breakfast."

"Okay, Miss Manners, what about that waffle topped with ice cream and cool whip you scarfed down at IHop yesterday?"

"Exactly what I'm sayin'. Waffles are for breakfast and cake is for dinner."

Alma laughed. "Bedouins eat buttered locust for breakfast."

"I saw a bum eat a pigeon for breakfast, but that don't make it normal." Sandi grimaced. "The dude yanked that poor bird's head clean off, and then—"

Alma's vision filled with stars, and a queasy knot expanded in her gut.

"Oh, shit," Sandi said. "I'm sorry—"

"Forget it." Alma forced her gaze toward the fire until the nausea subsided.

At least I didn't pass out this time.

As if to change the subject, Sandi pulled a crumpled page of newspaper from her pocket. "I saved this for you." She flicked on her lighter and revealed the headline: Is the Immortality Drug a Hoax?

Alma shrugged. "Why would I care about that shit? Who wants to live longer than they have to in this crappy world, anyway?"

"Not that BS." Sandi pointed to a picture of a man in a wheelchair, speaking to reporters. "Isn't he the old dude that bailed you out of jail a couple years ago?"

Alma's heart jolted, and she snatched the page from Sandi. It was him—the fucker. With a violent shriek, she shredded the paper and flung it away.

Sandi flinched and covered her ears, until Alma's rage passed. After a few moments, she removed her hands from her ears and asked, "Was he a john?"

"He's my grandfather."

"No shit? Maybe he could—"

"I hate that fucking asshole!" Alma shouted with such vehemence that Sandi cowered into a fetal ball.

Alma cradled Sandi's head in her lap, rocking her back and forth. "I'm sorry, San." The girl trembled and muttered like a child after a beating.

Eventually, Sandi calmed and opened her eyes as much as the bruises allowed. "I didn't mean to upset you. The article said he's rich, so I thought—"

"I made that mistake once," Alma said. "He bailed me out and convinced the judge to imprison me in a mental hospital for three months. Ninety days without smack to shut out my nightmares. It almost drove me over the edge, but I wouldn't give them the satisfaction. I wouldn't let *him* win."

"How did you get out?"

"They released me when their tests proved I was sane, which shows how useless they are. After that, I made sure he couldn't find me."

She became a child again, holding Grandpa's hand as they walked through the forests surrounding her house. Amidst the Oaks, Sycamore, and Lilac, he taught her the secret workings of nature—the intricate relationships between every living creature on the planet. Being the sister of a butterfly and cousin to a daisy filled her with wonder.

On one walk, they came upon an earthworm. Grandpa explained its primitive nervous system, lack of eyes, and reproductive cycle—all contained in that tiny twig of a body.

"So it lives in complete darkness, eats, has babies, then dies?" she asked.

"For an earthworm, that's a full life."

"And its children do the same thing over and over for millions of years? What's the point?"

He'd looked into her eyes and smiled. "Life is its own justification. Your life continues your parents, grandparents, and each of your ancestors, extending backward to the first prokaryote founder of life on the planet."

As the vision faded, Alma wiped her eyes and glanced at Sandi resting in her lap.

An earthworm made its way through the trash beside her. A living perpetual motion machine seeking the soil it craved without knowing why. The worm never questioned its purpose. It followed its programming as its parents had before it, and as its children's children would until the end of time.

Am I any different?

Alma placed her thumb on top of the earthworm's body. The eyeless, brainless creature thrashed to free itself. It wasn't afraid—how could it be? It reacted to stimuli like an algorithm. How many trillions of mindless ancestors dodged every predator and disaster to shuttle its immortal genes through time to this moment?

All that work—for nothing.

It took the slightest effort, a minuscule amount of pressure, and the fragile body compressed into oblivion. The worm's guts spurted beneath her gargantuan finger like a burst water balloon.

Sandi flinched. "Why'd you kill it?"

Alma stared at the mess of lifeless goo on her thumb. "I did it a favor."

As a child, she'd caught flies and spiders to set them free outside. She imagined each life she rescued starting a vast dynasty tracing back to her heroic act.

All an illusion. A pointless gesture by a pointless machine perpetuating another pointless machine's pointless replication. Why feel guilty about unplugging a copy machine endlessly reproducing a page of random numbers?

That must have been her father's conclusion when he placed the shotgun in his mouth on the fifth anniversary of her mother's death.

"I don't think you're crazy," Sandi said.

Alma wiped the remains of the worm onto the concrete. The atoms remained, but the sum of the parts no longer equaled something greater. Entropy, her grandfather called it.

"You're a terrible liar," she said.

"Well, not completely crazy," Sandi said, then pointed. "Who's that?"

The form of a man in a dark suit, white shirt, and black tie made his way toward the first fire. He carried something in his right hand.

"Is he a cop?" Sandi asked.

"They'd have scattered by now."

The man stopped beside the figures huddled around the fire and seemed to speak. For all the response he aroused, he might have been invisible.

"Maybe he's one of those artists or photographers?" Sandi said. "The last one paid two bucks a photo."

"And sold the prints for a thousand dollars each in that fucking gallery downtown. The asshole told stories of his harrowing expeditions into the dark underworld of the city to document the strange and pathetic natives."

The man walked to the second fire, with the same result.

"He's holding a book," Sandi whispered.

Alma spat onto the ground. "Son-of-a-bitch. I know what he is."

"What?"

"He's infected with a disease."

Sandi's eyes bulged. "You mean like rabies?"

"Worse. He's infected with a god-virus."

The missionary looked toward them.

"Shit, I think he spotted us." Alma pulled her knees toward herself and hugged them. "Ignore him and he'll go away."

Alma tilted her head forward, letting her hair veil her face. She could see out, but none could see in.

The missionary was tall and lanky, with a boyish face not long out of high school. Never tasted alcohol in his life. Probably a virgin. Pathetic.

He held the Bible in both hands as he mounted the slope. His pale blue eyes glowed with an inner illumination. Or was it a trick of the light?

Sandi clutched Alma's hand tighter as the boy came to a stop near them.

"My name's David."

Sandi's grip became painful.

I shouldn't have made that virus comment. Now she's terrified of the asshole.

"Do you believe in God?" he asked.

Alma snorted, despite her resolve to ignore the dimwit.

"I pray to God," Sandi said in a tremulous voice.

Alma turned on her with a furious glare.

Sandi shrank back with a whimper. "But I do, Alma. I believe God helps us all the time."

"Where the hell was God when that drunk driver killed your mom and baby brother? Where the fuck was he when your asshole father ditched you at eleven? Or when Jojo beat you two days ago?"

"Remember that earthquake?" Sandi asked. "They pulled that baby from the rubble after five days. Everyone said it was a miracle. Only God could do that."

They called me a miracle once. Until I remembered. Then they called me insane.

"Thirty people died in that building, and you give God credit for saving *one* of them? If I could save thirty people's lives, but chose to saved only one, what would you think of me?"

Sandi averted her gaze. "I need to believe there's more out there— otherwise, what's the point?"

"Jehovah loves us all," David said. "Sometimes it's hard to see the purpose—"

Alma sprang to her feet and glared at the fresh-faced missionary. "Listen, you fucking retard. There is no Santa Clause, no Easter Bunny, and no goddamn Jehovah! I won't let you sink your claws into my friend because she's easy prey."

His unworldly eyes gazed at her with a maddening calm. "I want to help you."

Alma took a step closer, her face reflected within those pale eyes. "I'm infected by my own parasite, and there's no room for another one."

Alma shoved him, and he stumbled back.

"We're all sinners," David said, "but Jesus died on the cross to forgive—"

Heat surged through her veins, and her vision flamed red. She snatched a broken wine bottle at her feet and pressed it against the missionary's throat.

"Don't do it!" Sandi screamed.

"You're not afraid, are you?" Alma held his narrow black tie in her left fist like a leash, pressing the jagged glass harder into the side of his neck. A single drop of blood trickled down and bloomed into a rose on his starched collar. "I'd be doing you a favor, wouldn't I? You'd die a martyr and get your reward in Heaven early."

He didn't flinch. A true zealot. She'd seen eyes like that once before, except that they'd been dark. They'd also been certain of what God commanded.

"I'm not afraid for myself," he said.

Alma threw the bottle, and it shattered on the rubble. "Leave me alone!" she screamed.

He placed a hand on her shoulder. "Let me help you."

She slapped the hand away and retreated. "I don't want your fucking pity!"

"Is this asshole bothering you?" Crow was shorter than David, but his scarred and tattooed face held a lifetime of battle. Gang symbols covered his shaved head and muscular arms.

"It's okay, Crow," Sandi said, heading him off. "He's harmless."

Alma stared into the missionary's eyes for some hint of hypocrisy, but they remained pools of certainty and purpose.

"Yeah, he's bothering me," Alma said.

Crow moved Sandi aside as if shooing away a midnight moth. His hand settled on David's shoulder. Crow smiled. Two of his lower teeth were missing. "Didn't your mama teach you not to bother girls?"

David said nothing, and Crow's eyes narrowed to slits. He drove his fist into the missionary's stomach, and David doubled over. Then his knee smashed into the boy's face. He crumpled to the ground, a broken nose spurting blood.

Alma spat on him. "Where's your god now?"

Crow kicked him in the ribs.

David cried out and then vomited.

"Stop it," Sandi pleaded. "He didn't do anything."

"He killed my mother and grandma!" Alma shrieked.

"It wasn't him. You know it wasn't him," Sandi begged. "You're hallucinating again!"

"They're all the same!" Alma shouted.

David struggled to his feet and faced her. Blood, dirt, and vomit smeared his face. But those demon-possessed eyes bore into her.

"Let the Lord help you," he said through swollen lips.

Alma covered her ears and ran to her hovel. For the thousandth time, she watched the man with the dark eyes put the knife to her mother's throat.

"Kill him, Crow!" she shouted. "Kill him, please!"

Crow dragged the boy down the incline toward the nearest fire. All the while, Sandi begged him to let him go, but he ignored her. That's when the real beating started. The others formed a circle—a wolf-pack watching the alpha discipline an invader. The mob mocked, spat on, and taunted the missionary. Some threatened rape, burning, or injecting him with AIDS-infected blood.

"Where's your god now?" Alma whispered.

The lifeless remains of the earthworm lay at peace beside the two baggies of heroin. Why put off the inevitable? Why prolong the pain?

Alma went through her ritual a second time.

By the time Sandi arrived back at her side, time had slowed and distorted.

"She's OOOODDDD'dddd!" Sandi's voice stretched and overlapped into an ethereal choir.

"I love you so much," Alma said.

Her friend's lips moved, but the sounds splintered into a million crystals, each the color of a dewdrop reflecting infinity.

The missionary's face appeared above her. Blood coated most of it, but those hypnotic eyes remained.

The boy lifted her in his arms. Was he a demon in human form? How else could he survive Crow? In her previous life—before becoming a filthy junkie whore—she'd read that the word "demon" came from the Greek "daemon." Sometimes special daemons transported humans to the gods. The priestess Diotima told Socrates that love was the greatest of all daemons.

A light grew within the strange purple-blue eyes and enveloped her. Untethered from the world, she flew toward a constellation encircling Orion. As she neared, the stars transformed into dancing figures of light, their colors more intense than any rainbow. Each color emanated scent, taste, and sound. Peppermint, chocolate, and cinnamon mingled with a thousand notes in a profound symphony.

An infinitely tentacled creature of energy pulsed at the center of the universe. Brighter than a million suns, but soothing to look upon. The radiance washed through her with wave upon wave of well-being.

It fractured her defenses and healed her inner wounds with a suddenness that left her gasping. A love almost unbearable. She wept with joy unblemished by desire or physical sensation. The essence of her being transcended atoms.

She swallowed a supernova. It spoke inside her, saying, "I Am Truth."

Beams of light coalesced into a glowing female figure.

"Mother?"

Her Life-Giver embraced her. "I've missed you, my darling."

Alma became a little girl again. She wore her favorite pink dress with the bow. "Will you take me with you, Mama?"

Her mother smiled. "When your task is complete, you may join us." Behind her mother, floated her grandmother, then her great-grandmother, and onward through the generations to the source of it all.

"What are you?" Alma asked the glowing being at the heart of creation.

"I am Truth. I am Life. I am You." The voice was coming from inside her. "I will lead you to the Truth, if you choose to follow."

Something tugged her back from the loving embrace of his energy.

An antiseptic odor inserted an off-key note into the magnificent symphony of sensations. She fought it, but was powerless to resist. "Don't leave me!"

"We'll await your return," said a million voices in tandem.

She was in a room, hovering near the ceiling. A naked girl lay on a table beneath her like a human sacrifice on an altar. White-clad priests moved in a ritual of technology. A nurse held a mask over the girl's face, while a doctor pumped her bare chest up and down—up and down—up and down.

"It's been fifteen minutes, Doctor."

"Okay, I'll call it," said the white-haired physician. "Time of death is 2:17 am."

The figures retreated from the inert form, their science-god having failed.

A terrible pressure built within her.

"Cause of death is diacetylmorphine overdose."

Some force drew her toward the repulsive thing on the table. She fought against it.

That's not me!

Darkness enveloped her. Trapped in her mortal prison, Alma surged upward, eyes opening wide.

A nurse screamed and toppled a tray of medical instruments.

"Jesus Christ!" shouted the doctor.

Someone covered her face with an oxygen mask, but she shoved it away, gasping for real air.

"Nurse, prepare another dose of naltrexone, in case she relapses."

"It was so . . . beautiful," Alma said between gasps.

The doctor studied her, a half-filled syringe at the ready. "What was beautiful?"

Her breathing slowed. She looked around the emergency room. A team of four doctors and nurses stared in amazement.

"Heart rate approaching normal."

"Blood pressure stabilizing."

Alma looked at her naked body.

Is that me?

"What was beautiful?" the doctor asked again, his eyes intense. "What did you see?"

Alma's gaze rose toward the ceiling, the blinding operating room lights a pale imitation of Him.

"I saw . . . God."

Chapter 3

Theon pointed a remote control at the flat-screen television and pressed the power button. Light expanded in a sudden burst of electrons, forming the image of a middle-aged man in a blue suit, Brooks Brothers white shirt, and purple tie.

A few centuries ago, this simple act would have seemed like magic. Now it was accepted as routine—not magic, but science.

Science is magic that actually works.

"This is Brent Billings reporting from CNN's news center," the reporter said. "Thank you for joining day three of what we're calling Immortality Mania. For the latest political fallout, let's check in with Allison Mayer outside the capitol building."

The image cut to a blonde in her mid-twenties holding a microphone amidst a sea of people. Behind her loomed the iconic dome of Congress. "Great to join you, Brent."

A smaller window in the upper left corner of the screen displayed a live shot of Brent. "What can you tell us of congressional response to Doctor Torano's demands?"

"So far, the Republicans won't discuss eliminating church tax breaks or changing the national motto."

As she spoke, the camera panned 360 degrees, revealing the national mall packed with elderly protesters. The group of seniors surrounding her chanted, "Don't wait until it's too late!" Here and there, smaller groups of counter-protesters lifted signs reading *The Pill is a Hoax.*

Allison approached an elderly woman in a wheelchair. She held a sign reading: *My life is worth more than tax breaks for preachers.*

"Could you tell us your name?" Allison asked, placing the microphone near the white-haired woman's mouth.

"I'm Abigail Sheets, and I'm ninety-one years old."

"Have you signed the Immortality Contract, Abigail?"

The old woman nodded. "My granddaughter helped me get on the website and sign it the day of the announcement, so I'll be at the front of the list."

"You think Theon's pill will make you young again?"

"He proved it by making that red-haired woman young. I hope our worthless politicians get off their keesters and do their job before it's too late for people like me!"

Theon grinned at the television. "You tell 'em, Abigail!"

The reporter turned to a thirty-something man with a goatee holding a sign reading *Trust in the Lord*.

Not waiting for a question, the man said, "The Immortality Contract is nothing but a sick stunt to trick people into denouncing their faith."

"So you don't believe the drug will work?"

"It's a lie, plain and simple. Everyone knows the Fountain of Youth is a myth."

This from someone who telepathically prays to an invisible creature in the sky.

An elderly man beside him asked, "What if it's true?"

"Would you abandon Christ even then?" goatee man asked.

Abigail said, "You'll change your tune when you're my age."

The reporter turned to a college-aged girl standing behind Abigail's wheelchair. "You're too young to need the Fountain of Youth pill. Does this give you a different perspective?"

"My guess is that it's a hoax," the girl said, "but I hope I'm wrong, since I don't want to lose my Granny." The girl patted the old woman's shoulder.

"Wait until I'm young again," her grandmother said. "I was a knockout in college!"

"Do you still believe in God?" the reporter asked Abigail.

"I told you I signed the Immortality Contract—are you trying to get me killed?" The old woman's face puckered. "My beliefs are my business alone."

Theon grinned.

It's already working.

The reporter faced the camera. "There are mixed viewpoints out here, but from what I've seen, the majority of people want Congress to make the changes demanded by Theon."

Brent's face filled the screen once more. "Thank you for that report, Allison. We now go to Allen Howell, CNN's Middle East Bureau Chief, reporting live from Islamabad, Pakistan."

A man with a graying beard filled the screen. He stood on the balcony of a hotel, with a mosque visible in the distance. Thousands of chanting protesters overflowed the streets below. "Here in Pakistan, protests against Theon continue around the clock."

"Is this because of the secular demand in the Immortality Contract?" Brent asked.

Allen nodded. "Article two of Pakistan's constitution names Islam the state religion. Blasphemy, apostasy, and insulting the Prophet Mohammad are illegal."

"Is the mere act of signing the contract considered blasphemy there?"

"That's what the courts ruled earlier today. Because the names on the website are public, mobs have executed dozens who signed."

"That's chilling news," Brent said.

Allen consulted a notepad. "By my count, thirty-two countries criminalize blasphemy, eight of them in Europe."

"Have other governments in the region issued statements?"

"Iran's Grand Ayatollah declared a fatwa calling for Theon's Torano's assassination, and a dozen Islamic states have banned their citizens from signing the Immortality Contract."

"So they take Theon's claims of eternal youth seriously?"

"The common feeling here is that it's a CIA plot to—"

A glass jar with a burning rag stuffed in the top sailed through the window and exploded against the wall. Flames erupted and the image went black.

Brent cringed. "Our satellite feed has gone down. We will keep you posted on Allen and his crew as information becomes available."

Brent looked off-camera, visibly shaken. Then he put his finger to his ear and nodded. "In the meantime, we have evolutionary biologist Richard Dawkins joining us from Oxford University via satellite."

The screen split to show the famed atheist next to the television anchorman.

"Professor Dawkins, this Immortality Contract seems predicated on the idea that religion itself poses a threat to humanity."

"When atomic weapons were first invented," the atheist biologist said, "only the most technologically advanced nations were capable of developing them. As this becomes progressively easier, nuclear and biological weapons could fall into the hands of fanatics who actually want to die."

Richard cocked his head to the left. "On the one hand, we have Christians obsessed with the Book of Revelation, who see the conflict in Israel as necessary to happen before the final return of Jesus. Those people would not have the normal deterrence against releasing a horrible apocalypse. They *want* an apocalypse."

The biologist tilted his head to the right. "On the other hand, we have people in the Islamic world who, for their own reasons, want to die a martyr's death and go to a martyr's heaven. The normal restraint against unleashing Armageddon doesn't apply to such people."

"But how likely are such scenarios?" Brent asked.

"Martin Reese, onetime president of the Royal Society and still Astronomer Royal, thinks we may go extinct in the twenty-first century because of a weapon of genuine mass destruction falling into the hands of a religious nut who—he doesn't put it exactly this way—who actively wants to die."

"And you think this Immortality Contract will solve this?"

"I don't know, but it seems we must try something before it's too late."

"In your book *The God Delusion,* you write about—"

The television blinked off.

"Hey, I was watching that!" Theon said.

Helena tossed the TV remote into a trash can. "People have died because of this."

"In the long run, it's for the greater good," he said.

"Spoken like a true Jihadist."

"You can't seriously compare—"

"What do you think Taslima would say about your Immortality Contract?"

How dare she use her to win an argument!

"My wife and daughter aren't in Heaven, Hell, Purgatory, or any other fantasy land. Nothing I do will affect them."

Helena remained silent for several heartbeats. Then she sighed. "They're here."

"Who?"

"They say they're Secret Service."

"What are you waiting for? Let them in!"

She shook her head and opened the door.

Two men in dark suits entered.

Their height differential reminded him of Poncho and Cisco from the old television show *The Cisco Kid.*

Cisco said, "I'm agent Ralph Oberg, and this is my partner, Matt Smith."

"Thank you for seeing us, Doctor Torano," Poncho said.

"You say that like I have a choice."

"The president is only requesting a meeting."

"And if I refuse?"

"This isn't an arrest."

Theon studied them. "In that case, thanks for the invitation, but I'll stay here."

Cisco glanced at Helena and she shrugged.

"Please give my regards to the president." Theon folded his hands in his lap and waited.

Why should I go easy on them?

"Fine," Poncho said. "You don't have a choice. We will call backup if necessary."

Theon leaned forward. "Are we talking tanks, helicopters, assault teams?"

The two agents said nothing.

Helena scowled. "Should I get a tape measure so you can compare genitalia?"

Theon laughed. "I'm certain your balls are the biggest in the room."

"Nice of you to notice," Helena said.

"My one request is that Helena accompany me."

Cisco nodded. "That's fine, Doctor Torano. May we assist you to your wheelchair?"

"I think I can manage on my own." With the help of a wooden cane, he levered himself upright. He'd been six foot two in his youth, but age had twisted his spine and stunted his bones. "Hope you don't mind the glacial pace, but it has been two years since I walked unaided."

He took a few steps, leaning heavily on the cane.

Poncho's stoic expression melted. "It's only been a few days since you took the pill."

"It works fast on basic functionality, but full recovery takes months."

Cisco's face remained impassive. "You could have faked your disability at the news conference."

"True," Theon said. "Let's see what you think in a couple weeks."

"I assume you have a ride?" Helena asked.

"There's a tilt-rotor Osprey parked outside your gate," Poncho said.

"Now you're talking!" Theon led the way, with Helena's help. "Isn't President Kane in Russia, meeting with his favorite dictator?"

"He'll return this evening and see you tomorrow morning."

"I look forward to hearing what the leader of the free world has to say."

Chapter 4

The makeup girl powdered his face, and Cyril sneezed. Annoying, but crucial for the most important broadcast of his career.

In the three days since Theon's press conference, his childhood nightmares returned—the man from the bank with his polished shoes, the sobs from his mother, his own tears.

Amazing how one mule kick can destroy a family.

He'd been ten. The humiliation of their meager possessions laid out on the scorched lawn filled him with the old shame. Even the bicycle he'd worked so hard to restore went on the auction block. Wesley Carroll's father had bought it for his son, as a birthday present.

Months later, he crept into the Carrolls' barn in the middle of the night and smashed the bike to pieces. Wesley didn't accuse him, but they never spoke again.

With his crippled leg, his father abandoned farming and became a moonshiner—drinking more than he sold. In and out of jail, he withered away until little remained for the coffin.

"Do you think the Fountain of Youth Pill works?" the makeup girl asked. He'd forgotten her name.

"The Bible relegates the power of life and death to God alone," he said. "It's nothing but a publicity stunt by a bitter atheist facing his mortality."

"I told my pawpaw it was a trick of Satan," she said, and applied his lipstick. "But nothing could stop him from signing that blasphemous contract with the Devil." The scent of youth followed her. She needed no Fountain of Youth pill—yet.

The smell of moldy paper invaded the air. Did that cursed accountant ever wash his suit?

"You know I don't talk business before a sermon," Cyril said as the pallid face appeared in front of him.

The accountant's thick spectacles magnified his bloodshot eyes into a caricature of a caricature. "The situation is deteriorating," he said. Even his pathetic comb-over had gone askew.

Cyril sighed. "I know donations are lagging—"

"Revenues are down by half!"

The nameless makeup girl left with a farewell smile and wink.

If only I could be young again.

He faced the accountant. "There's no doubt in my mind this is a hoax. Once Theon fails to prove—"

"That could take months!"

Cyril's assistant handed him a towering cup of his customary extra-large dark chocolate mocha Frappuccino topped with whipped cream.

"I don't think you appreciate the danger," the accountant said in his usual shortsighted manner.

Such men could never grasp the glorious nature of his calling. They lacked the imagination and faith.

Cyril sipped the wondrous combination of flavors through a straw, to keep his lipstick intact. "If money is that tight, sell the jet to bridge the gap."

"We used the plane and your other assets as collateral, so you can't use them to make your payments."

Cyril stopped sipping. "Surely they'll allow us more time, given the circumstances."

The accountant shook his head. "The Immortality Contract threatens the entire business model of religion. Revenues are plunging everywhere, forcing banks to seize shaky assets before they depreciate."

"What remains if they called in my loan?"

The accountant shied from his gaze. "I warned you of this possibility when you—"

"Tell me," Cyril said.

"You'd be left with nothing. Less than nothing, in accounting terms."

The Frappuccino slipped from Cyril's fingers and landed on the shelf of his expansive belly. Dark liquid geysered onto his white shirt, jacket, and pants.

Two assistants flew into motion. They stripped his clothes with practiced efficiency and replaced them with fresh versions. The makeup girl applied emergency touch-ups on the splashes on his face.

Cyril sat utterly still. His wealth and success displayed God's endorsement. The pin on his lapel said it all: *Giveth to the Lord and Prosper.* Without such evidence . . .

His assistant thrust a phone into his hand. "It's Reba," she said.

Hope bloomed like a dying ember tasting a breeze. "My dear Reba! Did you get the flowers I sent after the Grammys?"

"Oh, my lord, yes," purred the voice of the superstar singer. "You have been such a blessing, Reverend. My children grew up watching your show."

"We're so excited about your performance next week for the ministry fundraiser. My makeup artist has spoken of nothing else."

"That's why I'm calling," Reba said. "You know I've battled cancer several times."

"How could I forget, since you credited the prayers of this church for your recovery?"

"And I'm still thankful . . . but prayers can only do so much. My children and grandchildren depend on me."

Cyril's heart sank. "You've signed the Immortality Contract."

"Please understand that I still pray in the privacy of my own—"

"But you won't perform next week at our service."

"It violates the contract."

Cyril handed the phone to his assistant. Reba had dedicated her last album of spirituals to him and was a top contributor. If he could lose even her . . .

"What will you do?" the accountant asked.

Cyril gazed at him with such fierceness that the little man took a half-step backward.

"I will do what I've always done when things seem darkest," he said. "I will turn to the Lord."

Ten minutes later, he stood in the dim light beneath the main stage, the familiar calm suffusing his mind. Greatness comes to those who overcome great odds. This was his moment, his destiny.

Lord, let me be your mouthpiece.

A circular hole slid open in the low ceiling. Cyril stretched his arms toward the light as if embracing the whole of creation—and rose on the pneumatic platform beneath his feet.

As he ascended to the main stage, choral music bloomed from the ten-foot-tall speakers mounted at regular intervals throughout the great hall. The sounds engulfed him and reverberated to the core of his soul.

Thousands of voices erupted as the lift brought him level with the stage floor. The blinding spotlights transformed him from a man to an angelic apparition—a prophet reflecting the divine light of God's Word.

The music stilled, and the cheering faded. Cyril let his arms drop to his sides. His gaze fell to the congregation before him. They sat with faces transfixed with awe, love, and hope.

In the years since opening, not a single seat had gone unfilled—until today.

His ushers had corralled everyone to the center of the vast room so the television cameras could mask the deficit, but those attending knew. The bankers holding his loan would also find out.

Translucent wires levitated an oak crucifix twenty feet above the altar in tribute to Christ's ascension—a reminder of the everlasting life awaiting them all in the next world.

The stadium-like hall bristled with the latest gizmos, gadgets, and whatnots—creating a vast technological megaphone projecting God's commands across the globe.

"The Lord welcomes you, my brothers and sisters in Christ!"

"Amen!" shouted the crowd in response.

His voice deepened. "Who is our enemy?"

"Satan!" came the reply.

"Who is our savior from evil?"

"Jesus!"

He paced the stage, chanting the call-and-response like a general.

"Whom do we pledge our lives to serve?"

"Jesus!"

"Who died for our sins?"

"Jesus!"

"Who has conquered death?"

"Jesus!"

With each response, the volume grew. Those overcome with the spirit gesticulated with a palsy of religious fervor, their faces pointed upward toward the heavens. A few babbled in tongues as their souls interfaced with the Holy Spirit.

The exact words he called out were secondary. The alternating from hate to love, fear to relief, laughter to tears, this opened a direct pathway to their emotional core.

"Have you sinned?"

"Yes!"

"Do you want to burn for eternity?"

"No!"

"Who will forgive your sins?"

"Jesus!"

"What fate awaits blasphemers?"

"Damnation!"

"What is the reward for accepting Christ into your heart?"

"Eternal life!"

The music crescendoed and fell silent.

The moment stretched as he gazed on the sea of flushed faces. Humans were instinctually tribal. Once united by a shared emotional experience, the mind submitted to the group and its leader, even to the point of self-sacrifice for the larger whole.

"Brothers and Sisters, I want to tell you a deeply personal story."

It didn't matter that they'd heard it already. As any parent learns, a child's mind craves repetition and predictability. The same is true for adults. They not only want to believe—they need to.

If I don't give it to them, they'll find it somewhere else.

"I was twelve when my Grandpappy passed," he said. "The inevitability of death struck terror in my young mind. I was in a helpless and hopeless state."

He thrust his index finger toward the congregation. "Every minute, a hundred people die. Every day, a hundred and fifty-four thousand people are yanked off the face of this Earth. Every year, fifty-six million people plunge over this cliff we call death!"

"Save us, Lord!" someone shouted.

"Every one of those people loved life, because their Creator endowed them with a will to live. Yet this same Creator allows death to stalk us all, good and evil alike. My young mind cried out at this injustice. Life seemed futile if death loomed at the end no matter what I did."

Everyone sat motionless, eyes wide with the same fear.

Cyril stopped at the edge of the stage, gazing past the sea of faces to a point high above. His eyes widened.

"Then it happened," he said in a hushed tone. "That was the first time the Lord spoke to me." He shielded his face with both forearms. "A thunderous voice shook me to the core. It said, 'I proclaimed a death sentence on you and every son of Adam and daughter of Eve because of your sins!' "

The crowd gasped, their eyes following his gaze to the ceiling as if expecting God to appear. People wanted to believe. All they needed was permission.

"In the presence of my judge, I did what any sinner on death row would. I begged for mercy."

"Save us, Lord!" the congregation cried out.

"Despite my sins, despite having disobeyed my Creator, the Lord said, 'Because I love you, I provided you a Savior. My only son has given his life in a sacred blood offering to pay the fine of your sins. If you acknowledge this sacrifice and follow my commands, your sins will be forgiven, and everlasting life will be yours.' "

"Praise be to the Lord Jesus!"

"Then and there, I accepted Jesus into my heart and was born again. My fears vanished. I realized this life was nothing but a temporary testing ground for a far more glorious existence."

As one, they shouted, "Praise be to our Savior Jesus Christ!"

Cyril raised a hand, and the room stilled.

"Almighty God said to me, 'Cyril, son of Noah, I choose you for my messenger.' "

Not a single person stirred.

"What did I do when the Lord gave me my orders?" Cyril's head slumped forward in shame. "Obstinate sinner that I was, I complained that no one would listen to a poor boy from Appalachia." Cyril clasped his hands in front of him and gazed upward. "I begged the Lord to find someone else."

Cyril's eyebrows flexed inward. "Do you know what the Lord did when I questioned His judgment?"

"Tell us, Brother!" someone shouted.

"The Lord of Creation struck me dumb, blind, and deaf right there on the spot!"

Someone cried out at the horror of it.

"My poor parents took me to the doctor, but they proclaimed my ailment a mystery beyond scientific explanation or cure. For three whole days I lay in my bed, out of my wits, unable to see, unable to hear. Three days! And then, as sudden as the parting of the Red Sea, my eyes, ears, and mind simply healed."

He looked at his fingers as if witnessing a miracle. He cupped his hand to his ear, and the choral symphony rose, then settled to silence once more.

"How can we grasp the miracle of creation? In those three days of separation from God and all his gifts, I finally appreciated the enormity of God's love."

"Praise be to Jesus!" shouted multiple voices.

Cyril held his hands at his side in a pose of surrender with his palms exposed. "When the Lord spoke to me again, I did not question him a second time."

He paced the length of the stage, scanning the eager faces. "When the Lord ordered me to preach, I preached! When the Lord told me to mortgage my house to start this ministry, I did not question!"

His pace quickened as he strode the stage, voice rising with each exclamation of faith. "When the Lord told me to sell the holy anointing oil that has healed so many hundreds of thousands of you watching, I didn't ask the Lord why, or debate the details, I followed every one of his commands WITHOUT QUESTION!"

"Amen!" shouted the crowd.

Cyril halted, breathing hard. His voice dropped to a whisper, magnified by the microphone and carried into the hall like a disembodied spirit. "When the Lord spoke to me this very day and told me to tear up the sermon I'd prepared, I tore it to shreds."

"Tell us!" someone shouted from the balcony. "Be a witness to the Lord!"

" 'Brother Cyril,' the Lord said, 'There is a message I want you to deliver. I want you to tell my followers that the Devil is the greatest temptress of all. Lucifer will lie and cheat and use any trick to sway the weak from the path of righteousness.' "

"Praise the Word!" a woman shrieked.

" 'Warn the world that Theon Torano is in league with the Prince of Evil!' "

The crowd erupted in angry shouts of "Blasphemer!" "Atheist!" and "Antichrist!"

When the crowd settled, Cyril reached forward, as if inviting them to take his hands. He spoke directly toward the main camera broadcasting his words to the world. "Death is a blessed sacrament. Would you purchase a few extra years in this world for the price of an eternity in Hell?"

The faces of his followers reflected their fear.

Silence stretched, until a single voice drifted into the breach. "We'll follow you, Reverend!" It was the voice of one of his employees, sprinkled through the hall for just such a lull.

"What should we do?" shouted a member of the congregation. Soon everyone joined in, chanting, "Guide us, guide us, guide us!"

A rush of adrenaline surged through him. He was Peter spreading God's Word to the world. He was Joshua bringing down the walls of Jericho. He was King David vanquishing the Canaanites.

Music exploded through the million-dollar amplifiers, while a fifty-member choir—all volunteers—led the old-time hymn. As they sang, many congregants raised their fists, while others sobbed.

We are soldiers in God's army.
We have to fight, although we have to cry.
We've got to hold up the bloodstained banner.
We've got to hold it up until we die!

When the music fell silent, goose bumps rose along his neck.

It's time for the harvest.

"Bankers talk about compounding interest, but that's nothing compared to the compounding power of God Almighty!"

"Amen! Praise the Lord!" came the refrain.

"Every cent of the love offerings you tithe to this church will rebound with more interest than any hotshot Wall Street banker can offer. Your tax-deductible pledge to our twenty-four-hour hotline is not a donation, but an investment in your future—in this life and the next!"

He glared at the congregation with the look of a stern father. "If you hold back—if you aren't willing to BELIEVE in the Lord with every ounce of your being, why should He believe in you?"

"We believe!" shouted the crowd.

Give and you will get—it was the founding principle of the Prosperity Doctrine. Only hacks spoke of charity.

Cyril pointed to a middle-aged black man sitting in the second row. "James, tell everyone here what you told me earlier."

The man stood, his skin the color of coal, and his eyes wide with the spirit of God.

An usher handed him a wireless microphone.

"I lost my job at the Chrysler plant last year because I was too old to keep pace. My wife and me was desperate." The man spoke in a slow, simple manner. "When that scientist offer to restore youth to anyone willing to forsake the Lord, I considered it."

Boos sounded from the audience, and James looked around with haunted eyes.

"But then I thought of Lucifer tempting Jesus in the desert, and how our Savior rejected all the kingdoms of the Earth to sacrifice his life to save mine."

"Did you lose faith, Brother James?" Cyril asked.

"No, sir!" James called out. "I went all-in for the Lord. I maxed out my last credit card to pay three times my normal tithe to this here church."

The crowd tensed, waiting for the payoff they'd witnessed a hundred times before.

"And tell us what happened, Brother James," Cyril prompted.

"That was three days ago," James said, the whites of his eyes expanding. "Yesterday, the factory hired me as a foreman at twice my previous salary."

The crowd exploded in applause and shouts of "Praise the Lord!" and "Paid back with INTEREST!"

Cyril raised his arms, and a choir of angelic voices filled the room. Spotlights bathed him until his white clothes glowed with God's grace. "Cast your net wide, and let Jesus fill it with prosperity, just as he did with Brother James!"

Cyril's arms fell to his sides, and the music ebbed to a soothing background choir.

That should get the donations flowing.

In the row behind James, a man in his fifties took the microphone in his large hand. "I'm Phil, and my story is similar."

A flutter of panic rose in Cyril's chest. Damn that sound engineer for not cutting the feed.

"Be a witness, Brother Phil!" multiple voices urged. It was too late now. No choice but to roll the dice and let him speak a few words.

Phil half-turned to the crowd. "Because of my arthritis, I lost my job as an airplane mechanic at Delta. My family has suffered horribly, but I never lost faith. Inspired by stories like this, I also increased my monthly tithe."

"Thank you, Brother Phil," Cyril said quickly. "Your investment of faith will pay great dividends." He prepared to cue the music.

"It already has!" Phil said.

Cyril paused in mid-gesture and smiled. "By all means, share your witness, Brother."

"I used the Reverend's holy anointing oil daily to restore my health and win my job back. I even withdrew my son's college fund and sent it to this ministry."

The man's sunken eyes didn't bode well. A familiar pressure built within Cyril's chest.

Why didn't I cut him off? I know better than to gamble.

"Do you know what I got for my investment?" Phil asked.

"Tell us, Brother!" the congregation replied.

"I lost my house first. Then my wife left, after learning I'd tossed away my son's hope for an education."

Silence filled the hall.

I must end this.

Cyril drew in a breath, but froze as a jolt of pain twisted his heart.

Phil turned to him. "You know what I think, Reverend? I think you are nothing but a con artist."

"How dare you insult Reverend Doberson for your own lack of faith!" a woman called out.

"Blasphemer!"

"Tool of Satan!"

Cyril regained his breath and lifted a hand to calm the unrest. "We all have moments of doubt, but Brother James is proof—"

"How do we know James is telling the truth?" Phil asked. "Has anyone seen him here before today?"

A murmur spread through the hall as people looked for someone to vouch for James. No one did.

At a gesture from Cyril, an usher handed James a microphone.

"I watch on TV with my wife," James said. "I came in person to share my story."

Phil sneered. "Is it any surprise one out of the millions watching got a job this week? What we never hear are the thousands of unanswered prayers. All those that get no return on their investment!"

The pain in Cyril's chest bloomed. Beads of sweat forced their way through the layer of makeup on his face. He reached into his pocket for his heart pills, but it was empty.

They're in the coat I spilled coffee on.

"Don't let the Devil whisper in your ear!" shouted someone from the upper level. He recognized the voice as another of his employees.

Phil made his way into the aisle and limped toward him. "Unlike your worthless Anointing Oil, Theon doesn't ask for money!"

Cyril gasped, the pain spreading into his shoulder. How could he signal his assistant for his pills?

Phil reached the stairs leading to the stage, but an usher blocked his way. Despite his age and arthritis, the mechanic shoved the gatekeeper aside and mounted the steps.

Cyril stumbled back as the man neared. He'd rejected security for fear of projecting a lack of confidence in God.

The audience sat silent, waiting for the Lord to take action against the unbeliever.

"Strike the blasphemer down!"

"The Lord is our protector!"

"I'm putting my faith in Theon!" Phil shouted. "I encourage all of you to join me, and sign the Immortality Contract before it's too late."

A stunned silence filled the church as Phil seized Cyril's white lapels and shook him.

Cyril gasped. "The Lord will—" Pain overwhelmed him and he collapsed.

"Where's your God now?" Phil spat on him and walked away with a look of contempt.

The congregation watched their fallen prophet writhe on the ground beneath the floating crucifix.

One of his aids ran onstage and tried to help him stand.

"Get the nitro glycerin pills out of my dressing room," Cyril whispered. "And end the broadcast."

Some of his followers sobbed, while others bowed their heads in prayer. The rest followed Phil toward the exit.

My God, my God, why hast thou forsaken me?

Chapter 5

Alma shuffled through the bright hallway like a sleepwalking zombie. Each step required a conscious act of mind over body—an empty ritual without purpose.

The hospital slippers dragged across the polished floor with sharp gasps. Her stiletto shoes, purse, and cell phone were lost. A pink *Run for the Cure* T-shirt had replaced her vomit-caked tank top. Only the leather miniskirt marked her true nature.

Her soul, having tasted freedom in its out-of-body exodus, craved release from the crude cage of physical existence. Air rasped through her raw throat in tortured gasps. A heartbeat forced the no longer welcome blood through her veins in a final insult to freewill.

When the doctor interviewed her, she'd said the magic words *accidental overdose*, and secured her release after a twenty-four-hour stay.

Then, the final bombshell. "Did you realize you're five weeks pregnant?" the perky nurse asked when discharging her.

Too exhausted to reply, she simply walked out without a word.

As she continued her odyssey through the endless hallways, the looks of disgust were nothing new. It was the glances of pity that grated against her nerves.

Keep your fucking goodwill off me.

"Coming through!" announced an old woman moving at double the rate of Alma's glacial pace. The white-haired gnome hunched at a forty-five-degree angle over her walker—two tennis balls capping the front supports like a geriatric dragster.

Beside the woman walked a pudgy nurse dressed in pink scrubs. "Have you signed the Immortality Contract, Lois?"

"Are you serious? Of course I have!"

"With all the visits from your minister, I thought—"

"I told Reverend Shaughnessy I was leaving the church the day of the press conference. With his heart condition, it wouldn't surprise me if he does the same."

"Last week you said you welcomed your reward in Heaven."

The old woman stopped, craned her neck to the right, and gazed at the nurse. "I suppose when there's no choice but dying, our minds make the best of it. But now, I'd rather live."

"I suppose I'll lose my job if it's true."

The old woman resumed her rapid progress through the hallway. "Better your job than my life!"

The two were now far ahead of her, their grating voices fading.

Suddenly, the young missionary appeared at the end of the hall. He stepped aside to let the old woman pass.

Alma's heart jolted. His face was swollen and discolored from Crow's beating. A bandage covered his nose, and stitches meandered across his left temple and cheek.

He hasn't seen me. I've got to hide.

Grabbing a handle to her left, Alma stumbled into a dark room. She shut the door and pressed her ear against the smooth surface, listened to footsteps nearing in the hall, and breathed a sigh of relief as they passed.

A whispered voice reached from the darkness. "Hello?"

Alma turned and waited as her eyes adjusted to the dim light filtering through the edges of drawn curtains. A faint smell of corruption suffused the air as if from a long-sealed tomb.

The shadowy outline of someone lying in a bed appeared.

"They keep it dark on account of my eye," a girl's voice whispered.

Alma's slippered feet carried her toward the voice. The body beneath the sheets lacked legs.

A face horribly burned and distorted came into focus. The right eye socket gaped empty. Melted flesh oozed across a flattened nose and into a formless hole of a mouth. The remaining left eye lacked lids and stared at her with the intensity of a lighthouse beacon.

"You're . . . beautiful," the girl said.

Shame twisted through Alma. It burned deeper than any self-pity or self-hatred.

A snore made her start. On the other side of the bed, a woman slumped in a chair.

"That's my mother," the girl said. "She took a sleeping pill and won't wake for at least another hour."

At the word *mother,* Alma's throat constricted.

She'd been twelve when Grandma Taslima took her and Mom to Saudi Arabia. A homecoming of over fifty years. For her and Mom, it was the first time they met anyone from that side of their family.

When they arrived at the house, her Great-grandmother Fatima served tea in gold-leafed cups. She'd been the third of four wives. Married at fifteen, she gave birth to Taslima a year later.

As a distant cousin of the Saudi king, Taslima's father was one of thousands of princes who shared in the vast oil revenues and businesses distributed amongst the House of Saud. He'd fought alongside Abdul-Aziz bin Saud for several decades as they founded the new nation. He was old when he married Fatima, and able to enjoy home and family for the first time.

Taslima's birth—coinciding with the founding of Saudi Arabia—marked her as blessed in his eyes.

After serving tea, the family matriarch shook her head. "Your father spoiled you," she said in English. Her husband admired the British as the most educated and civilized nation in the world, so insisted his family learn their language.

"I knew that accursed English university would fill you with blasphemous ideas," Fatima had said, "but Abdul ignored my warnings."

"Please don't," Grandma had said to her mother. "Can't we enjoy one another's company without opening old wounds?"

"Your father never recovered from the dishonor you brought upon us. It follows our family to this day."

As if at a prearranged signal, five men entered.

Grandma Taslima stood and bowed to them. "Greetings, brothers."

Without a word, the two men grabbed Taslima by the hair and dragged her into the tiled courtyard. The other three seized her and Mom. A fountain gurgled in the center of the garden, and the scent of fig trees filled her nostrils with their sweetness.

They killed Grandma first. The youngest slid the knife across her neck in a crimson waterfall, while the others stabbed her. Then her mother's turn came.

Death was the price their god demanded for being ignored.

The blood had drained into the gutters and carried their lives into the desert sand.

Fatima lied, and told the police that three masked men invaded the house and murdered her daughter and granddaughter.

When Alma finally spoke after a year of silence, the police showed the proof that her uncles had been in Dubai for a meeting during the murder. Two American officials who had attended corroborated their presence. Surveillance footage at the hotel and at the airport proved they could not have killed her mother and grandmother. She was forced to admit that her memories were illusions.

Was that my first psychotic break?

How could anyone know which memories to trust? And why did her mind trick her into accusing five uncles she'd only met over Skype? They'd been polite and excited to meet her when they returned from Dubai a few days later. What did her mind have against them, to invent such a terrible story?

"What's your name?" the burned girl asked.

"Alma. My name is Alma."

"I'm glad to meet you, Alma."

She said nothing in reply. What could she say?

"It was a car crash," the girl said. "A blown tire around a curve. No speeding, alcohol, or texting. Just driving home from high school. People hate when I tell them that. Random shit implies an amoral universe."

The girl raised her shoulders in a half-shrug.

Sandi loved saying karma was a bitch, but what had this girl done to deserve her fate? What had Mom and Gran done? Some of the worst assholes she knew thrived.

"Will you do something for me, Alma?"

"If I can."

"Do you see that small trash can near the bathroom?"

She nodded.

"There's a clean plastic bag inside. I'd be grateful if you'd place it over my head. I'm not asking you to kill me—I'll seal the edge against my throat with these." The girl displayed her hand-stumps. "I wish I didn't have to ask, but you can see my dilemma."

Alma stood motionless, staring into the single eye. Was it brown, or green? Hard to tell in the low light.

"Is there a lot of pain?"

"More than I imagined possible," the girl said. "More than any drug can dull."

"I committed suicide yesterday," Alma said.

The girl fell silent—a hostage negotiating her release with an imbalanced kidnapper.

"How did you do it?" the girl asked.

"I overdosed on heroin."

"You wouldn't happen to have any extra?"

"Sorry, fresh out."

"What was your beef with existence?"

Alma shivered as a chill crept through her.

"There's extra blankets on the chair behind you," the girl said.

Alma took a blanket and wrapped it around her shoulders.

Why did I kill myself? Because of my mother's death? The nightmares?

"The truth is, I don't see the point to life," Alma said.

"Why are you still here, then?"

"I don't know. The nurse said I was dead for over a minute. They'd given up trying to save me."

Should I describe my visions of God?

"A genuine miracle," the girl said. "Don't suppose you have a spare one of those, either?"

She chuckled. "Sorry, I'm out of those too."

For a while they remained silent.

"Will you help me?"

Alma glanced at the trash bag and pulled the blanket tighter around her shoulders. She glanced at the eye sitting in the melted face. "How old were you?"

"Already using the past tense? I guess that's a good sign."

"I didn't mean—"

"I'm sixteen years old. I was top of my class in math and science and a member of the national honor society. I was captain of the swim team and experienced my first and last French kiss three weeks ago, with an exchange student from the Philippines named Rommel de la Torre, after which he dumped me for a cheerleader. Will you help me or not?"

"There's a crazy old guy at Union Rescue Mission that always shouts 'Do unto others as you'd have them do to you.' "

"The Golden Rule," the girl said. "I'm not religious, but I think that pretty much sums up all of morality."

If our places were reversed, what would I want her to do?

"You're not afraid of dying?" Alma asked.

"A strange question coming from someone who tried to kill themselves yesterday, but no, I'm only afraid of being forced to live like this. To me, death is no different than a dreamless sleep."

She had told Sandi she was doing the earthworm a favor.

Will I deny this girl the same gift of oblivion?

Alma shuffled to the corner and removed the clear plastic bag from the trash can. Then she returned to the bed.

I don't even know her name. Had the girl withheld it to make things easier?

"Thank you," the girl said.

Alma slid the garbage bag over the hairless mass of flesh lying on the pillow. The girl groaned as she leaned her bald head upright to allow the plastic behind her neck, then settled back into the pillow.

Without hesitation, the stumps of her hands pressed the edge to her throat, creating an airtight seal. How long had she lain in this bed, tortured by agony, yearning for her chance at escape?

The thin plastic moved in and out as the girl breathed, her lidless eye staring into space.

The woman in the chair stirred, and Alma's heart skipped a beat. What if the girl's mother woke to find her standing over the body of her dead daughter?

"I'm here, my little Edina," the woman moaned, though her eyes remained closed. "Don't worry, darling, Mommy is here."

Edina—her name is Edina.

Edina breathed in desperate gulps, the plastic drawn into her mouth hole with each intake of stagnating air. Her eye bulged outward, and her burned skin became a sickly shade of blue. The stumps of her hands trembled with the effort of holding the thin barrier firm.

Suddenly, a voice filled Alma's mind—the voice from her death-dream—the voice of God. *"The gifts of life and death are mine alone to ordain."*

Alma's hands jerked forward and ripped the bag off Edina's head.

The burned girl erupted in hoarse gasps, her chest heaving and the lidless eye slick with tears. "Why?" she asked.

Alma retreated, her heart throbbing. "I'm sorry, I don't have the right to free you." Her hand found the doorknob.

"Don't leave me here!" Edina shrieked.

The girl's mother woke with a start. "Who are you—?"

Alma stumbled into the hall and ran. When she reached the main entrance, David was there. She slid to a stop, gasping for breath. He limped toward her, favoring his left side.

"Will you let me help you?" he asked.

She lowered her eyes and said nothing, too tired to resist.

As the sun rose, David drove his ancient Ford pickup west out of the city and then north into the foothills of the Sierra Nevada Mountains. The tops of the snow-covered giants glowed against the deep blue of the sky, hinting at an alternate reality beyond the horizon.

The burning concrete gave way to snow, the billboards to trees, and the smog to crisp air.

Alma leaned against the cool glass of the passenger's window and drifted to sleep.

The bump and shimmy of a rough road woke her. A log house sat at the center of a snow-buried farm. Fairy tale mountains surrounded the valley on all sides.

David parked beside a beat-up station wagon and got out. Two children dashed out the front door.

"David's home!" A girl about five years old flung herself into his arms.

He hugged her and winced slightly. "Hello, Maya!"

The boy slid to a stop, his mouth agape. "What's wrong with your face?"

David rumpled the boy's hair. "Just a little accident, Jacob."

"Oh, my God!" a woman in a homemade house dress shouted. Bands of gray streaked her red hair.

"It's all right, Ma." David walked to his mother and smiled.

Her fingers moved toward the wounds, but paused short of contact. "I begged you not to go."

"A Christian must go where the mission fields lie," David said.

"He's a hero, Ma!" a girl around twelve declared. Her hazel eyes gleamed with excitement as she stared at her battle-scarred big brother. "Confronting the Devil face-to-face!"

"It wasn't as dangerous as that, Cassie." He looked around. "Where's Dad?"

"He left early for a cross-country haul," his mother said.

Alma sat silent in the pickup, her heart racing.

Why did I come here?

David walked around the truck and opened her door. His family stared in shock.

"This is Alma. She needs our help."

The young missionary guided her out of the car, and she stood before them in her hospital slippers, black leather miniskirt, and ridiculous pink T-shirt. Then she vomited the meager contents of her stomach onto the snow.

He kept her from falling.

"Take her inside," his mother said, and helped carry her toward the house. As they lifted her into a bed, the tremors started. The children stared through the doorway in wide-eyed astonishment.

"Is she possessed by demons?" Maya asked.

"Hush," her mother said, and shooed them out, including David.

Alma became a rag doll as Merriam stripped her clothes off and tucked quilts around her.

Chapter 6

Theon waited as the secret service officer he'd nicknamed Cisco opened the door to the Oval Office. Poncho stood behind them.

"We scanned for recording devices, Mr. President," Cisco said.

"Send them in," a voice from inside the room commanded.

With the help of his cane and Helena, Theon walked into the most powerful office on the planet.

President Dalton Kane sat behind the famed mahogany desk commissioned by Theodore Roosevelt and used by Richard Nixon to record the famous Watergate Tapes.

The president's icy gaze tracked them as they made their way forward. He didn't offer a seat. His blue eyes, blond hair, and bulky aura of strength perfectly fit the mold of the Aryan chieftain his supporters desired in a president. To his detractors, he was a classic demagogue appealing to the worst desires and prejudices of the mob.

"Leave us," the president said to his secret service officers.

The doors closed with hardly a sound.

Theon cleared his throat. "Mr. President, I—"

"Can you give me one reason why I shouldn't arrest you both as terrorists?"

Helena's grip on Theon's arm tightened.

It was no empty threat. Kane had reinstated torture as a legitimate method of interrogation under the guise of national security.

The president tossed several newspapers to the front of his desk. "Chaos." He gestured out the window at the mob of protesters. "Chaos." He pointed at a globe on a side table. "Chaos!" He leaned forward and skewered them with his eyes. "You haven't distributed a single pill, yet you've brought the world to the verge of anarchy."

Theon's jaw tightened. "Revolutions are judged by conditions at the conclusion, not the start."

"And if you destroy civilization?"

"I'm attempting to rescue us all from Armageddon, before it's too late."

The president slammed his fist onto his desk. "Hospitals, insurance companies, retirement industries—their stocks nose-dived on the possibility of your drug rendering them obsolete. Health care is one-fourth of the entire economy. Do you realize how many jobs that represents?"

"There is certainly a lot of money in death and disease," Theon said.

"Damn right. Dozens of world leaders call every hour to ask if our intelligence services have determined if your claims are true. I'm forced to admit that I don't know. And then there's the religious leaders. If this is a hoax—"

"It's no hoax."

"You should measure what you say here, very carefully," the president said.

Despite two draft deferments, Kane projected a military bearing and defended his strong-man mythos with pathological aggression.

I mustn't betray any weakness in front of this man.

The blue orbs of the president's eyes shifted to Helena. "You don't like me much, do you?"

"I despise all war criminals."

"You have the luxury of slinging your liberal moral judgments because people like me keep your idealistic bubble secure."

"Spoken like a true dictator."

The president eyed her as if sizing up prey. "I read that *Time* magazine article on the woman you're impersonating. How her father lost their farm during the Great Depression and lived off other people's tax dollars for most of his life."

"Since you've avoided paying income taxes for a decade, not a dime of your wealth has financed any programs for the poor."

Kane ran his fingers along the handle of Davy Crockett's bowie knife—bought for a cool million and a half dollars. "The real Helena Mueller was no stranger to wealth. I especially enjoyed her tales of taking dozens of entrance exams at top universities for her wealthy patrons' less-than-astute daughters. Watching those rich fops buy a dream she couldn't afford must have been tough."

Helena shrugged. "I ended up wealthy and educated, but they remained stupid their entire lives, no matter how much money they married or inherited."

"The article failed to mention how Helena Mueller raised enough funds to attend Bryn Mawr, even while her family could barely afford food."

Helena met his gaze with ice, but said nothing.

"The obvious conclusion is that she paid her way by helping one of these wealthy dunces cheat her way through to graduation—in direct violation of the school's Honor Code."

A flush rose into Helena's cheeks.

"Ah, yes," the president said. "Bending rules for oneself is something Helena and I share in common. I imagine the arrangement explains how she afforded the years of post-graduate work at MIT, as well?"

Helena averted her eyes.

He's struck a nerve.

The president opened a file on his desk. "The article doesn't mention the name of the girl who provided this ticket out of poverty."

"Silvia Shore," Helena said without hesitation.

"What was your undergraduate adviser's nickname?"

"Malevolent Maggie."

Kane frowned.

Theon swallowed a smile.

Without warning, the president opened the top drawer of his desk and removed a stainless steel gun.

Helena's grip on Theon's arm tightened.

"It's not loaded," the president said. "Do you recognize it?"

"It's a Ruger Mark III, model 512—the same gun I won the silver medal with at the national championships."

The president tossed the gun across the table, and she caught it in her left hand.

"Field strip it," he said.

Helena pulled the gun apart in seconds and placed the disassembled components on the edge of the desk.

The president frowned. "You've done your homework, I'll give you that."

"It's no act," Theon said. "She is Helena Mueller."

The president pointed at her. "The weed of crime bears bitter fruit! Crime does not pay!"

Helena's mouth curled into a smile. "The Shadow knows."

The president threw his hands in the air in frustration.

"My brother forced me to listen to that radio drama every Sunday evening," Helena said. "It makes sense that you'd admire a noir anti-hero like Kent Allard, since he committed crimes, and even murder, in the name of justice."

"Yes, I did admire the black-caped vigilante growing up," the president said. "He understood the need to put justice above rules."

"I still thought his psychic powers were a lazy cop-out," she said. "Sherlock Holmes was more my bale of hay."

"A naturalist from the beginning," Theon said with a smile.

As she spoke, Helena reassembled the gun and tossed it on the desk. "Ironic that Conan Doyle became ensnared in such supernatural poppycock after his wife and son's death."

President Kane stood. "Are you aware that I'm a Born Again Christian?"

"How could we not be?" Theon asked. "Your campaign was little more than a tent revival."

"You expect me to stand aside as you attack God?"

"Can't we speak frankly, Mr. President?" Theon shifted his cane from his right hand to his left. "Your men made sure we have no recording devices."

The president's upper lip twitched. "Are you calling me a liar?"

"I'm calling you a realist."

The president's eyes narrowed.

Have I miscalculated? What if he actually does believe in God?

A sharp laugh burst from the former businessman-turned-ruler-of-the-world. "Seneca the Younger said it best: 'Religion is regarded by the people as true, by the wise as false, and by the rulers as useful.' "

Theon smiled. "As a man of reason, you must see that religion has outlived its usefulness in the modern age. It's imperative to face truth head-on."

The president shook his head as if at a joke he'd heard a hundred times. "During my freshman-year spring break at Harvard, my father took me on a hunting safari to Africa. At a Himba village, Dad snapped a Polaroid of the tribe's matriarch. What a face! She must have been ninety, at least. Sixteen children and seventy-two grandkids. Never seen such wrinkles in my life.

"When Dad gave the old woman the photo as a gift, she looked at it long and hard. Her sun-weathered face puckered into the deepest frown I've ever seen. 'Am I that ugly?' she asked and flung the photograph into the fire."

The president chuckled. "Those Himba are some warriors. Even survived the German genocide. I don't know what that old woman told her sons, but they informed us in no uncertain terms that if we ever came back, they'd hunt us down like hyenas. In that moment, I learned how dangerous the truth could be."

"I'm only asking for—"

"The impossible." The president rounded his desk and stopped in front of them. "You don't seriously think I'd ask congress to repeal tax breaks for churches? That would be political suicide."

"I wonder how popular you'd be if I announced I was relocating my factories to a country willing to accept my terms?"

The president thrust his face inches from Theon's nose. "I'd seize Amara Pharmaceuticals before allowing that."

"My formula remains hidden outside the US—even from me. It is quite complex, and I couldn't reconstitute the drug on my own in any case. Even if you got the pills themselves, it would be like trying to recreate a steak without ever having seen a cow."

The president's eyes narrowed. "I could arrest you as a national security threat under my Executive Order 14361."

Helena motioned to the window, where the distant crowd of protesters filled the streets. "I don't think that would be popular."

"What other choice have you left me?" the president asked.

He's ready.

"Might I suggest a compromise?" Theon said.

Kane glared for several moments, then slowly walked back behind his desk. He sat in his leather chair and leaned back. "I was waiting for the shakedown. Before you start, I have a question for Helena."

She nodded.

"How long have you loved him?"

"Since the first moment I met him," she said without hesitation.

Theon looked at her in astonishment. "What are you saying?"

Her eyes didn't move from President Kane. "How did you know?"

Kane pulled a cigar from a humidor on his desk, snipped one end, and lit it. After a few generous puffs, he spread his hands wide. "Reading people is my business."

Theon swayed a bit, and Helena took hold of his arm. He looked at her, but she refused to meet his eyes.

"You have as long as this cigar lasts to convince me not to arrest you."

Theon forced his gaze back to the president.

He's trying to rattle me.

Theon took a breath and let it out. Then he said, "Ask Congress to pass a Secularization Bill that is contingent on the outcome of a trial before the Chief Justice of the Supreme Court."

Kane inhaled a lungful of smoke and then expelled it. "Arbitrating what, exactly?"

"I will present my evidence for my drug. If I cannot prove my claim to the satisfaction of the chief justice, it ends there, with me disgraced as a fake and the Secularization Bill not taking effect."

"And if he rules in your favor?"

"Then Reverend Cyril will present his evidence for the existence of God. If the chief justice rules that he's proved his case, I will tear up the Immortality Contract as a condition for my drug."

"A public trial of science versus religion?" The president grinned. "I'd love watching that buffoon of a minister humiliated. I nearly lost the primary when he claimed I faked my conversion."

"You're actually considering this?" Helena asked in disgust.

The president's left eyebrow arched. "I see there's trouble in paradise. Or is this part of the act?"

"It's a straight-forward proposal," Theon said.

Kane puffed on his cigar twice, his eyes following the smoke upward. "The trial is to be broadcast live?"

"That's right," Theon said.

"And the Secularization Bill only goes into effect if Justice Dunn rules you've proven your claim *and* that Cyril has failed to prove his?"

"Correct."

Helen sighed. "You can't prove the existence of God in a court."

"God could appear and settle the matter rather quickly," Theon said.

Helena glared at him.

The president chewed the end of the dying cigar. "It gives everyone political cover under the authority of the chief justice, who doesn't face the threat of re-election."

"No judge will rule against people's most cherished beliefs," Helena said.

She still doesn't understand.

The president leaned back in his chair. "This is clearly nothing but a stunt to gain a global soapbox to preach from."

"Even if that were true," Theon said, "what do you have to lose? If I'm disgraced you will be congratulated on the way you unmasked me without committing to the Secularization Bill."

Theon held his breath.

Everything hinges on this moment.

The president stubbed out his cigar and stared into the ashtray for several seconds. Finally, he looked up. "Okay, you've got a deal. One of my senators will draft the bill." The president chuckled. "After all those dissenting opinions Justice Dunn has written against my Executive Orders, I can't wait to see that so-called judge's face when I tell him."

Chapter 7

A tear traced a path along the wrinkled canyons of Pope Stephen the Tenth's face as he gazed on the sublime grace of Michelangelo's *Pieta.*

The exquisitely carved tableau of a mother's love aroused visions of his own *majka* sitting before the window of their simple stone house. Day after day, she gazed at the lonely expanse of the Adriatic. When a sail appeared on the horizon, her back would stiffen and her fingers falter in her knitting. She'd sit frozen, a mixture of hope and torment—until the sail's markings exposed it for what it was not.

Lost at sea were the three cruelest words spoken in their village. His mother heard them twice—first for a husband and later for the eldest of her two sons.

Their empty graves sat in the churchyard high on the hill, complete with the customary sextant carved into the headstones. Many tombs lay vacant, the bodies claimed by the sea or forgotten wars in distant lands.

His mother opposed both funerals, clinging to the possibility of a shipwreck, or capture by mysterious heathen slave traders, or pirates. She conceded they might lie at the bottom of the ocean, but they were definitely not within the empty coffins in those pointless holes.

When he was six, a boy shoved him at a village gathering. Both fathers agreed that their sons should fight it out, as tradition demanded. The combatants were expected to shake hands afterward, while the adults clapped each other on the backs and recounted their own youthful encounters.

The first punch hit him in the nose, and he collapsed, blood gushing down his face. Papa demanded he fight back, but one look at the crimson splashes on his hands set the world spinning. Stars appeared, and the cheers of encouragement hollowed and stretched. His vision contracted as if looking through a long tube.

When he awoke from the fainting spell, the disappointment carved into his father's sun-weathered visage was more painful than any blow.

A few months later, the sea claimed Papa, cheating his youngest son of any future redemption.

His brother, Juraj, six years his senior, served as father figure from that point forward, protecting his bookish younger brother through the eight years of school required of fisher folk.

He was sixteen when his older brother disappeared in one of the Adriatic's tantrums. Once again, no wreckage or body washed ashore. Like his father, Juraj evaporated from his life overnight.

The next day, his mother informed him he would become a priest. There was no discussion, no explanation, and certainly no question of his obedience. By sending her final child into God's service, she hoped the Lord would restore her lost husband and eldest son.

Call it a bribe, or a sacred offering—was there a difference?

Father Ovčara made the arrangements for his celibate future. The elderly priest gave him two days to mourn his brother before traveling to the seminary in Dubrovnik. As a bounty for his mother's sacrifice, the church granted her a modest pension to keep her from complete destitution.

There may have been a practical side to her plan. Her youngest son's slight physique could never withstand the rigors of a fisherman's life. Only through the wealth and beneficence of the Catholic Church could such a destitute and fatherless boy hope to receive an education commensurate with his oversize intellect.

In later years, he reasoned that she'd sent him away out of concern for his well-being, as much as to enlist God's assistance. Of course, he wouldn't place high odds on his survival if God offered to return his brother or father in exchange for his life

Only one unforeseen obstacle stood in the way of his mother's plan.

Her name was Mira.

Where he was shy and reclusive to the point of invisibility, Mira drew people into her orbit with the sheer radiance of her presence. A born artist in the purest sense of the word, she excelled at all mediums of self-expression. Poetry, singing, painting, dance, or decorating the church for Easter. Her creativity and passion blazed like the cliff-top bonfires the village lit during stormy nights to guide derelict boats home.

He'd spoken no more than a dozen words to her in the years they attended the small schoolhouse together. Why would someone of her splendor take notice of a freak who shunned every form of public sport or celebration?

Even so, he studied her from afar, fascinated by the curve of her graceful neck, the ebony sheen of her long hair, and especially those dark eyes flashing with the boldness so lacking in his own character.

Upon graduating school, it was common for girls to marry older boys who'd proven themselves at sea and saved enough to buy a house. Most in the village thought Mira and Juraj made a perfect match, at least until his brother came calling.

Despite his towering good looks and the fact that Juraj was the best fisherman for miles along the coast, she doubled over in hilarity at his marriage proposal. Soon, he joined in, unable to resist the infectious pull of her spirit.

Juraj selected another girl two days later. A week before his wedding, the sea claimed him, sealing not only his fate, but that of his younger brother.

The day before his departure for the seminary, Mira appeared at their door. "This is for your mother," she said, handing him a bucket of fish from her father's catch. "Can we talk?"

Not trusting his voice, he followed her down the hill toward the shore. She said nothing as they wound through the scrubby olive trees, occasional pomegranate groves, and towering stands of cypress.

By then, he knew her every quirk. The way she tilted her head to the left when pondering a distant bird's song. How she chewed her lower lip when taking math tests. Her gentleness matched her bravery. Armed only with a branch, she once saved a baby goat from a charging bull.

As he walked alongside her, the intoxicating perfume of her skin in the summer heat filled his nostrils with such blunt physicality that he came close to fainting.

She wore her usual calf-length skirt, leather sandals, and unadorned white blouse. Had they been the robes of a queen, he couldn't have worshiped her more.

When they reached the ocean's edge, she faced him and posted her hands on the sides of her hips. He was half a head taller, though so slight in build she probably outweighed him. Her dark, exotic orbs held him frozen in the spotlight of her presence.

"Did I offend you?" he asked.

She expelled her breath in exasperation, took hold of him, and pressed her lips against his.

A rush of contradictory emotions flashed through him. When she stepped back, he steadied himself on a nearby boulder. Had the world gone mad?

Mira's eyes never left his. "Do you remember that day the crow flew into the school window?"

"Yes," he said. "In the third grade." The whole class had gone to look at it, lying motionless on the ground.

"Miss Orson claimed crows were messengers of the Devil."

"A superstitious lie," he said.

"The other boys were about to stomp it, but you stepped in front of them and lifted its limp body in your hands."

Mira's eyes widened. "You spoke to it so softly I couldn't hear the words. After a few moments, the crow's wings twitched. When its eyes opened and looked at the boys, they jumped back as if you'd summoned the Devil himself to come for them."

"It had only been knocked unconscious," he said. "There was no miracle."

"I'm not as smart as you, but I'm no idiot."

"I didn't mean—"

Mira's hand brushed his cheek in the same manner he'd stroked the injured bird. "No one else would save such a despised creature. When you threw it into the air, the other girls screamed, but not me." Her eyes gazed into his. "When that wondrous bird took flight, I knew I loved you."

How was it possible?

Receiving no response, Mira's head drooped. "I figured as much," she said. "You'd paid me so little notice—but now that you're going away, I had to try."

At that moment, his body took over. He gripped both of Mira's shoulders and pulled her toward him. She flung her arms around his neck, her breasts pressed against his chest as he kissed her.

A kiss to haunt his dreams forever after.

He confessed his love in desperate gasps. She begged him to run away with her. They could marry in Dubrovnik. He could teach, and she'd clean rooms in the hotels or paint murals for theaters and restaurants. They could start a family.

But then he hesitated.

What if his mother's celestial bargain could save his father and brother? Didn't he owe it to his family to try? To sacrifice his own life for theirs?

And so he chose God over love—his mother over Mira.

Half a century later, staring through tears at the marble visage of the Virgin Mary in Michelangelo's masterpiece, something gnawed at the back of his mind. Unlike previous depictions of the *Pieta*, Michelangelo portrayed the mother of God as a beautiful young girl, rather than a woman in her fifties mourning the death of her thirty-three-year-old son. This Mary appeared younger than Jesus. Looking at her face and figure, the similarity to the sixteen-year-old Mira was startling.

How could I have missed it?

The statue mirrored Mira's desolation at the moment he chose the church over her. It was only time he saw her cry.

Are my tears for my mother or my lost love?

He studied the face of the virgin. Who had modeled for the sculpture? Was the resemblance to Mira coincidence, or a divine message?

The marble nose was slightly discolored, a testimony to the madman who attacked the famous statue on Pentecost Sunday of 1972.

Shouting, "I am Jesus Christ—I have risen from the dead!" Laszlo Toth, a Hungarian geologist, struck the sculpture twelve times with a hammer. By the time security wrestled him to the ground, part of the virgin's arm, nose, and eyelid lay in pieces on the floor. Onlookers snatched the shards as holy relics. The tip of Mary's nose was never recovered, necessitating a sculptural reconstructive surgery.

A deep voice spoke from behind him. "Theon wields a far more powerful hammer."

Pope Stephen spun around. A massive, barrel-chested man stood a few paces away, his wide face set in its usual half-scowl. The thinning hair atop his solid head counterbalanced a thick mustache extending to the edge of a square jaw. The traditional robes of a Jesuit substituted for his military uniform.

Ignoring protocol, he embraced his comrade in arms.

"How long have you been lurking, Vadic, you old pirate?" he asked in his native Croat.

"Long enough," the giant replied in the same dialect.

"Thank you for coming, my friend."

"You are the successor of Peter. I must obey—but I would come no matter your rank."

"I know."

At seventy, the former colonel in the Croatian Defense Force had lost none of his vitality.

"I think you can guess why I asked you here," Stephen said.

Vadic nodded. "Are the claims of the American scientist true?"

"We don't know yet."

"He strikes our weakest point. Sun Tzu would approve."

"If the drug works, and if this blasphemous contract stands—the church will become a hollow relic, like the temples to Zeus and Aphrodite."

Vadic's muscular brow furrowed. "What do you require of me?"

"I want you to make certain this ridiculous evangelist wins his case in the Supreme Court."

Vadic hesitated. "There is a simpler way."

"I'm not sending you as an assassin."

"We've used extreme measures before."

"That was war."

His old friend grunted. "Is not the Immortality Contract a declaration of war against God?"

Pope Stephen said nothing as he walked away from Michelangelo's masterwork—and from the memory of Mira.

"Do you recall our first meeting?" the pope asked.

"How could I forget the Siege of Vukovar?"

"I mean the first time we spoke."

"You tried stopping me from torturing a captured JNA soldier."

"Do you remember what you told me?" Stephen asked.

Vadic chewed a corner of his mustache for a moment. "I asked you if you wanted to watch this one soldier suffer now, or if you'd rather watch a hundred civilians suffer later from the information this man kept hidden."

They passed the monument to Christina of Sweden in honor of the queen who abdicated her throne to embrace Christianity. Despite that act of sacrifice, she was most famous for inadvertently causing Descartes's death. After a long night of tutoring her in the methods of Cartesian philosophy in her drafty castle, he caught a cold that would prove fatal.

"You confronted me with the reality of war," Stephen said. "I faced Aquinas's double-effect principle in fact, rather than theory."

"The double what?"

"It's a concept first introduced by Thomas Aquinas in his Summa Theologica regarding the morality of violence. The double-effect principle states that any action—however detestable—can be moral if the intended positive effects outweigh the negative short-term ones. It's the same logic the Americans used to justify dropping the atomic bombs on Japan and killing so many civilians. They figured they were saving far more lives in the long run."

"Sounds like the justification used during the Inquisition, when the church argued that the application of pain, and even death, was necessary to save a person's soul."

Stephen nodded. "Though the idea that conversion by force is valid seems rather doubtful in my mind."

"You certainly turned out to be better at *questioning* prisoners than I—after you stopped fainting at the sight of blood, that is."

"My father would have been proud."

"I wonder what the College of Cardinals would think of your participation in torture?" Vadic asked. "Or the fact that you stood shoulder to shoulder with the rest of the defenders of the city, firing your father's rifle like a common infantryman."

"If they'd found out, I would not be Pope, that's certain, but I don't regret my actions."

"Because of the double-effects principle?"

"Because I did what I thought was right."

Vadic glanced at the Monument to Pope Gregory the Fourteenth. "Odd that one of the most unpopular and incompetent popes is memorialized here."

"Despite food shortages, plagues, and lawlessness during his reign, he did ban gambling on papal elections. That's something."

Vadic said nothing as they passed the Gregorian Chapel, the Altar of St. Jerome, and the Statue of St. Helena.

Has time lessened his pain?

During the height of the siege, a Serbian mortar shell hit Vadic's house while he was away fighting. He dug the remains of his wife and daughter out of the rubble, buried them without a word, and vanished for two days. After the war, the colonel knelt before him in the confessional and described the revenge he exacted on the Serbian sentry he caught that night. The double-effect principle hadn't applied in that case.

"I understand the rage of losing a wife and daughter," Vadic said. "Like Theon, I blamed God for a long time."

"The war challenged my own faith," Stephen said. "Vukovar's conquest was the worst destruction of a European city since World War II. I wondered how God could allow such ethnic cleansing."

"We saved those we could," Vadic said. "Though I wonder if God approved of our methods."

After the war, Vadic became a hero of the new Croatian Republic and could have become a general or politician if he'd wanted. Instead, he traded his military uniform for the robes of a monk.

Vadic made the sign of the cross before one of the altars near the front of the basilica. Set into the structure was a mosaic depicting the winged Archangel Michael raising his sword to slay Satan. The artist portrayed Michael as young and beautiful, in contrast to the balding fallen angel with his vestigial black wings.

Stephen pointed to the swarthy face of the Devil. "Reni claimed he modeled Satan on a miraculous vision he had of Lucifer himself."

Vadic stepped closer, studying the face of evil pinned beneath the Archangel's naked foot. "Do you think this is actually what the Devil looks like?"

Stephen chuckled. "Everyone at the time knew of the animosity between Reni and Cardinal Pamphilij, who bears a striking resemblance to the Devil in this painting. It was especially awkward a few years later, when Cardinal Pamphilij was elected Pope Innocent the Tenth."

The soldier-turned-monk laughed. "I've looked at this many times and never realized I was seeing a papal portrait."

"The cardinal complained bitterly when the work was unveiled, but it seems that even a pope can't argue with divine revelation."

They continued toward the Main Tribune of the great basilica. The majestic dome designed by Michelangelo was nearly as large as the dome of the pagan Pantheon built fifteen hundred years before and only a few kilometers south.

"It seems timeless," Vadic said, his face craning upward toward the lip of the dome. Latin letters two meters high proclaimed: *You are Peter, and on this rock I will build my church. I will give you the keys of the kingdom of Heaven.*

"Saint Peter's was built atop dozens of pagan mausoleums and altars," Stephen said. "The shrine of Attis was one of the most popular and dates a thousand years before Christ. His followers believed him born miraculously from a young maiden without sexual intercourse. His death and resurrection were celebrated each year in a symbolic representation of winter's death and spring's rebirth."

Vadic shot him a look. "You sound like that atheist scientist."

Pope Stephen laughed. "Don't get me wrong, my friend. My faith is every bit as strong as your own. I'm merely pointing out that all these"— the pope gestured around him—"are mere rocks. Even some of the stories we tell are less important than feeling the presence of the divine."

Stephen laid a hand on his friend's broad chest. "This is where God truly resides."

Vadic lowered his head. "When I think back to the things I've seen, of those two hundred and sixty patients taken from the Vukovar hospital and murdered after the city fell, of tens of thousands of Muslim women raped and impregnated in a diabolical form of racial cleansing, I'm reminded that the Serbs were Christians as well. They thought they were acting for the greater good as much as we did."

"They probably did."

Vadic's face reflected his inner torment. "I think of Yahweh ordering the Israelites to kill every man, woman, and child of the Canaanites to claim their *Promised Land*. God even orders his chosen people to take the virgin women of Midian as spoils of war. Was that much different from the Serbian war crimes?"

The pope looked at his old friend and frowned.

Have I chosen the wrong person for this task?

Stephen laid a hand on his shoulder. "The difference is that God ordered Saul and Joshua to do those things. Following God's will is the definition of morality. He sees the bigger picture, so we must trust his judgment over our own."

An elderly nun heading their way bowed her head as she passed. She walked with a regal slowness. One of the many visiting servants of the church who'd been rewarded with a personal stay at the Vatican for her lifetime of devotion.

What happens to her, and the millions of others in the orders, the orphanages, schools, and hospitals run by the church if I fail?

Stephen glanced at his friend as they walked. Could he trust him with this assignment? "If God gave you the same orders he issued Joshua or Saul, what would you do?"

Vadic came to a halt before the Altar of the Chair of Saint Peter, the focal point of the Basilica. His eyes moved up along the elaborate sculpture created by Bernini. It held the chair said to be the one Saint Peter used while teaching the Gospel in Rome. During an examination in the 1970s, experts concluded that no part of the wood dated earlier than the sixth century, but that didn't keep Catholics from revering it as the genuine chair of Peter.

Vadic crossed himself and said, "My one goal in life is to serve the Lord and earn the right to see my Raiyana and Tatyana again in Heaven."

Pope Stephen inclined his head.

This is the man I need. A man prepared to do whatever God requires.

Chapter 8

When the demon appeared in the corner of the bedroom, Alma screamed. The creature's glowing eyes watched her with unblinking malevolence. Its blackened flesh resembled charcoal pulled from a fire, with the hint of a reddish glow leaking between the cracks. The reek of sulfur tinged the air.

David's mother, Merriam, assured her the corner was empty, and she smelled nothing odd.

Hallucinations were common when going through withdrawal.

Over the coming days, more demons of every shape and size arrived. Most had horns and wings. Clothing seemed optional.

She'd experienced hallucinations before, but nothing as prolonged as these.

Merriam cared for her around the clock, feeding her small amounts of food in her moments of lucidity. Her filthy hair was so matted, Merriam was forced to cut most of it off. She felt lighter afterward. A fresh start in more ways than one.

Sleeping proved difficult with the continuous cramps, tremors, and vomiting. Through it all, the demons watched, squatting in the corner of the room, or lurking in the rafters like hellish vultures awaiting their chance to feed.

Do they want me to join them?

Merriam recited stories from the Bible. Tales of ancient heroes, magic, angels, and battles between good and evil.

The demons listened with their hideous faces transfixed.

When Alma awoke screaming, Merriam held her in the same way her own mother used to after nightmares.

Now and then, Cassie brought something her mother requested—soup, water, and even some of her own clothes for Alma to wear. David's twelve-year-old sister exuded a wholesomeness reminiscent of a Norman Rockwell painting. Despite this—or maybe because of it—the girl's hazel eyes watched her with suspicion.

Can I blame her?

On her third day at the house, a neighbor needing advice called Merriam away for a few hours. Cassie used the opportunity to slip into the bedroom and confront her.

"It's because of you that David got hurt, isn't it?"

Alma stared at the young girl, a mirror of herself at the same age. Her mother's death shattered that innocence and drove a wedge between her and Dad. She found temporary solace in drugs, while he turned to alcohol. His shotgun eventually provided him with a more permanent release.

"Yes, it's my fault," Alma said.

"Then you admit you're evil?"

A demon the size of a chimpanzee hovered above the girl. It flicked a forked tongue toward Cassie and bared its fangs. An illusion? A side effect of her withdrawal? Or the start of another psychotic break?

Cassie glanced at the ceiling. "What are you looking at?"

"Nothing," she said. "I was just thinking."

"Mama says even the worst sinner can repent. Have you repented?"

Alma turned away from the girl. *I should leave this place before I hurt anyone else.*

"So you refuse to repent?" Cassie leaned close and whispered. "If you harm any of my family, I'll . . . I'll kill you. I swear I will."

The demon shrieked at this invocation of violence. "*Kill, kill, kill,*" it hissed.

So they can talk.

That evening, Merriam helped her leave the bedroom for the first time since her arrival. The cast-iron stove glowed with heat. She sat between Cassie and little Maya at the dining table. David sat beside his father, Abel, who'd just returned from a cross-country trucking assignment. He was tall and clean-shaven, with eyes the same blue as David's.

Thankfully, none of the demons followed her.

"Welcome to our home," Abel said.

Alma nodded and lowered her head, while Abel gave thanks to the Lord.

She kept her gaze from David as they passed the chicken, homemade cheese, bread, and vegetables.

"Cassie said you're a whore," six-year-old Jacob said. "What does that mean?"

Merriam dropped her fork with a clatter. "Jacob!"

Soon the family fell into their routine of chatting and joking. All of it reminded her of her own stolen family.

"Maybe Alma has a story she can share?" Merriam asked.

Every eye turned toward her.

"I . . . um . . ."

"Could you tell us a story with animals?" Maya asked.

"I remember a story my grandpa told about his dog, Barnie."

"I love dogs!" Jacob said. "My friend Daniel has a dog that—"

"Let Alma tell her story," Merriam said.

"Oh, right," Jacob said.

Alma cleared her throat. David's eyes weighed on her, so she concentrated on Jacob and Maya. "My grandfather's neighbor was a widow named Mrs. Thrift. She kept several rabbits and built a miniature bunny village with houses, gardens, and even a tiny bunny church."

"Did you see this village yourself?" Maya asked.

"Oh, yes," Alma said. "Every time I visited my grandpa and grandma, Mrs. Thrift showed me the improvements she'd made—bunny train stations, court houses, and a park with a working merry-go-round. It was a true work of art."

"That sounds awesome!" Jacob said.

"One evening, Barnie showed up with Annie, Mrs. Thrift's white angora rabbit, in its mouth."

"Oh no!" Cassie said.

"There'd been a slight gap under the fence, and Barnie enlarged it into a tunnel."

"Like a prison break!" Jacob said.

"Or a barbarian invasion!" Cassie added.

Alma nodded. "Very similar."

Maya's eyes filled with tears. "I hate thinking of Annie torn to bits by that horrible dog."

"Despite all the dog slobber and mud covering Annie's beautiful white fur, they found no blood or cuts."

"Barnie probably shook her and broke her neck," Jacob said. "My friend's dog does that to squirrels."

"I doubt that made Mrs. Thrift feel better," Cassie said.

"She was in her late seventies and had a bad heart," Alma said, "so my grandparents worried the shock might overwhelm her."

Alma glanced at Merriam and Abel. They looked sorry for encouraging her to tell a story.

What was I thinking? It's too late to stop now.

"Grandpa repaired the hole under the fence, while Grandma shampooed and blow-dried the dead rabbit so it looked as good as new—except that it was dead."

Cassie exchanged a quizzical look with David.

"Grandpa waited until midnight, climbed the fence, and placed Annie in the yard, so it looked like she died in her sleep."

The children's mouths fell open, and Abel chuckled.

Merriam suppressed a grin. "It's wrong to deceive, but I can understand it in this case."

"She must have been sad finding Annie dead," Cassie said, "but not as sad as knowing she'd been dog-murdered."

"The next morning, there was a knock at the door. My grandpa opened it, and there stood Mrs. Thrift, her hair uncombed, and eyes haunted as if she'd seen a ghost. Mrs. Thrift said, 'I wanted to warn you that there's a maniac loose in the neighborhood.' "

Alma paused, letting the suspense build. The children looked confused, as did Merriam and Abel.

" 'You see,' Mrs. Thrift said, 'one of my rabbits died yesterday, and I buried her in the graveyard behind the bunny church. This morning, I found Annie lying next to the train station!' "

The family burst into laughter.

"Oh no!" Merriam said through peals of laughter.

Alma spoke above the noise. "Mrs. Thrift's face was beet red. 'What kind of sick person digs up a dead bunny rabbit, gives it a bath, blow-dries it, and then returns it?' "

Even David joined in the hilarity.

When they regained control of themselves, Merriam wiped her eyes and smiled. "My Lord but that is the funniest story I've ever heard."

"But is it true?" Cassie asked with a skeptical frown.

Merriam shot her daughter a look. "It's not polite suggesting Alma's grandfather is a liar."

"It's okay," Alma said. "I asked the same question when he told me that story."

Cassie beamed, but Merriam looked shocked. "You doubted your own grandfather's honesty?"

"Well, Grandpa sometimes used stories to teach me important lessons, even if not literally true."

"Like Jesus with his parables," Abel said.

"Exactly," Alma said. "Grandpa asked me if lying to Mrs. Thrift was the right or wrong decision."

"It's never right to lie," Jacob said.

Cassie scowled at her younger brother. "They kept the bunny lady from knowing something that might hurt her. It's like when Mamma stops me from telling you the truth about how stupid you are."

"You're stupid!" Jacob said.

"No name-calling," Merriam said.

Alma suppressed a laugh. "Grandpa pointed out that despite their good intentions, it backfired."

"Your grandfather has an excellent way of illustrating the need for truth," Abel said.

"But was the story true?" Cassie asked in exasperation. "Or did he make it up to teach you a lesson?"

"He wouldn't say, and I still don't know if it was true."

"You could have asked Mrs. Thrift if it happened," Jacob said.

"No, she couldn't," Cassie said. "Just mentioning poor Annie would make the rabbit lady sad all over again. It could give her a heart attack."

"That was the most infuriating thing," Alma said. "The truth was within my grasp, but only if I caused Mrs. Thrift pain. I realized that some truths aren't worth the cost of finding them. Maybe that was the lesson my grandfather was trying to teach me."

"Your grandfather sounds wise," Merriam said. "Is he still with us?"

"He lives in Colorado, now."

"Please invite him to dinner if he's ever in the area," Abel said.

"I've . . . lost touch with him," Alma said.

"Because you're a whore?" Jacob asked.

"Jacob!" Abel said.

"I was just asking," Jacob said with a pout.

"Shame on you for telling your brother such a thing," Merriam said to Cassie.

"But it's true, isn't it?" Cassie asked defiantly.

"It's true," Alma said, before Merriam could scold the girl.

Everyone finished their meals in silence after that.

During the next few days, Alma pitched in with the daily chores. She lacked the strength to work in the greenhouse, so spent the mornings assisting Merriam with home-schooling the children. Math and science had been her favorite subject, so she helped Cassie with her algebra.

Her withdrawal symptoms gradually subsided, but the demons remained. Though they didn't cast shadows or seem capable of affecting physical objects, they sometimes tried goading her into conversation. She ignored them as much as possible.

Occasionally, they lunged at her, then cackled with laughter when she jumped. Mostly, they lazed about and watched.

David spent most of his time outside with his father, tending to the cows, chickens, and cutting firewood. Whenever he came in, she retreated to the loft, where a few quilts served as her semi-private sleeping area.

During one home-school lesson, Merriam explained how God created the universe, animals, and humans six thousand years ago.

"That's forever!" Jacob said in awe at such a large number.

Alma's stomach tensed, but she swallowed her words.

"What's the matter, Alma?" Merriam asked.

"I shouldn't say. I don't want to offend you."

"You cannot offend me with any honest question or opinion."

Alma glanced at the children.

Don't I owe them the truth, even if they reject it?

With a sigh, she said, "The idea that the Earth is so young and that humans were created in their present form a few thousand years ago—Noah's Ark and all the rest. There's so much scientific evidence proving such stories are impossible."

"That's blasphemy!" Cassie shouted, but Merriam hushed her daughter and nodded for Alma to continue.

"The theory of evolution is supported by the entire fossil record, comparative DNA analysis, and the distribution of species across the planet. There's a mountain of evidence from multiple scientific disciplines proving it."

"Those are excellent points," Merriam said without the slightest hint of anger. "I admit I can't explain such things, but no evidence from science will ever shake my faith in the Bible."

"But isn't it irrational to ignore facts?"

Cassie's face twisted with contempt. "Believing we came from monkeys is stupid."

Merriam placed a hand on her daughter's arm. "Name-calling is not an argument, dear."

Cassie folded her arms and glared at Alma as Merriam continued.

"Imagine someone is murdered in Los Angeles at this exact moment, and tomorrow, the police arrest you for the murder. What would you say?"

"I'd explain I was here with all of you when it happened, so I couldn't have done it."

"Suppose they produced fingerprints, your DNA, and *a mountain of evidence* proving your guilt?"

"I can't be in two places at once."

"You'd dismiss their evidence, even though you couldn't explain its existence?"

"I see your point," Alma said, "but that only applies if you know the truth from first-hand experience backed by other eyewitnesses as well."

"Exactly," Merriam said.

Words from her death-dream echoed in her mind, and she spoke them aloud. "I will lead you to the Truth if you choose to follow."

Merriam nodded. "The Bible says to trust in the Lord with all your heart, and not to lean on your own understanding."

"So you're saying that evidence is not limited to our physical perceptions?"

"I'm saying that God has provided you with all the proof you need if you open yourself to it."

The familiar waking dream flashed before her eyes. Knives plunging into Mom and Gran, then slitting their throats—the faces of her uncles branded into her brain.

An illusion created by my own brain. Had her dream of God been the same?

Fatima claimed it had been three masked men who killed Mom and Gran. Could all that evidence proving they'd been in Dubai be wrong?

Her chest tightened as a third possibility forced itself from the depths of her subconscious. What if Fatima did make up the story of the masked men, not to protect her sons, but to protect her?

What if I killed them? Is my brain protecting me from the truth like Grandpa did for Mrs. Thrift?

"Are you okay, Alma?" Merriam asked.

She looked up. "So you think all the fossils, the genetic clues, and even stars that appear millions of light-years away were created to mislead us?"

"It could be Satan, or God testing our faith, or something else we can't understand."

"Doesn't it bother you?" Alma asked. "Not knowing where all this misleading evidence came from?"

"If you know two plus two equals four, do you bother with people claiming the answer is five?"

"If the police showed me so much evidence that I'd killed someone, even though I remembered something else, I might question my sanity."

"Open yourself to God, and he will show you the truth in here." Merriam placed a hand over Alma's heart.

What if I can't trust what's in my heart?

On Sunday, Merriam invited her to join their family at church. She'd never attended a religious service of any kind in her life, but how could she say no after all they'd done for her?

The church consisted of a single room with a few oil lanterns hanging from rough-hewn rafters, a wooden crucifix nailed to the far wall, a cast iron stove for heat, and a lectern with a leather-bound Bible resting on top. The small congregation resembled an extended family coming together for a reunion.

The minister wore the same clothes as the men—dark shoes, pants, and a tie over a buttoned white shirt.

They sang hymns to start the service. Awkward at first, Alma soon found her voice and accompanied the congregation.

When the last song ended, everyone sat.

The minister set aside his hymnal and placed a hand on the Bible. "Our church is not a part of any larger organization." He lifted the large book with both hands. "This is all we need. God's instruction manual."

"Amen," said the congregation.

The minister set the Bible on the podium and gazed at the seated families. "Many of you don't own televisions, or bother reading newspapers. For many of us, our sole contact with the rest of society is our mission work."

He paused, seeming to collect his thoughts before continuing. "But today, I must warn you of something that none of us can ignore. It is no less than Satan tempting mankind into a second Fall."

A low murmur spread through the room as people glanced fearfully at one another.

The minister took a newspaper from under the lectern and held it up. The headline read: Amidst Protests, Congress Accepts Theon's Terms.

"For those of you who haven't heard, our elected officials agreed to put God on trial. Should Reverend Doberson lose his case, Congress is legally bound to remove all mention of God from government buildings and currency, and to completely strip churches of their tax exempt status."

Merriam took hold of Abel's hand and gave him a frightened look.

Has the world gone mad in the past week?

"Satan is the great temptress, and what greater temptation than eternal youth? Revelation tells us the forces of evil will coalesce behind this deceiver."

The minister swept the small gathering with his gaze. "It's clear that the Antichrist foretold by prophecy is the atheist scientist going by the name Theon Torano!"

Alma's heart jolted. A rumbling voice whispered in her ear. *"Are you going to tell them or should I?"*

Alma twisted around. The blood-red eyes of the biggest demon yet stared at her. His two horns curved outward like a ram's—ending in two points level with his glowing orbs. Massive jaws jutted forward, and a pair of tusks protruded in front of his lower lips. The smell of sulfur and burning flesh caused her to gag.

"What's wrong, Alma?" Merriam asked.

She composed herself for a reply, but dozens of new demons appeared. In a matter of seconds, they filled the room, each pointing at her and shrieking their laughter.

Instead of looking at the demonic mob, the human congregation stared at her as well.

Why is everyone looking at me?

Abel shook her, and she realized she was screaming.

The demons cackled.

Alma closed her mouth and stood. Merriam grabbed for her arm, but she yanked free and sprinted out of the church. She dashed across the street and into the woods. Branches flailed at her. A few thorns caught on her dress and tore ragged holes in it, but she scrambled onward up the mountain.

All the while, the demons followed—running, slithering, and flying. They shrieked in glee at her terror.

"Leave me alone!" she shouted, but they only laughed harder.

Eventually, her body gave out, and she collapsed.

If I lay here long enough, I can freeze to death.

When she looked up, David stood there, his eyes filled with concern.

"Can't you see I'm not worth saving?" she asked.

David sat beside her and remained silent.

A veil of white covered the meadow. Above the tree line, a series of mountains rose like ancient cathedrals erected by a race of giants. The air was crisp and scented with pine. A stream gurgled at the edge of hearing.

The demons stilled, watching, waiting.

"When I was a kid, I climbed that mountain," David said. "By the time I reached the top, night was falling. I crawled into a hollow and fell asleep." His gaze drifted to the snow-covered peak and his eyebrows compressed. "I dreamed of all the sinners burning in Hell for eternity."

Had he seen me there? Crying among the damned?

"When I woke, I realized God led me there as a reminder that being saved wasn't enough. In Ezekiel, God tells those who fail to warn others that they are as guilty as the worst sinner."

I must warn him.

After three long heartbeats, Alma said, "Your minister claims Theon Torano is the Antichrist."

"What does that have to do with you?"

"I'm his granddaughter."

He frowned. "That's why you ran?"

She inhaled a deep breath and let it out. "That and the demons."

"What demons?"

The story tumbled out in a breathless rush. Her drug addiction and prostitution, her death-visions of God, the demons surrounding them, the mystery of her mother and grandmother's murders, and her suspicion that she'd been the one who killed them.

Through it all, David held her hand. It was his strength that drew the poison out.

When she finished, David guided her chin upward. "There is no sin so great the Lord cannot forgive it—if you're willing to ask."

If only it were true.

David placed the palm of his hand against her cheek. Warmth spread through every vein of her body, into every muscle, every nerve. A sensation absent since before her mother died.

"Alma, I—"

"You're a Jezebel! A dirty whore! I won't let you take my brother away, I won't!" Cassie ran toward them, shouting at the top of her lungs. She grabbed a rock and lunged for Alma with it held high.

Alma made no move to stop her. Wasn't stoning the proper punishment for murder?

David stood and grabbed the rock from his sister. "Cassie, what's wrong with you?"

The demons hooted at the mayhem.

"The Devil is using her to tempt you!" Cassie shouted at David. "Can't you see the evil in her?" The girl pulled free of her big brother and ran toward home, the echo of her sobs swallowed by the forest.

Alma stood and faced David. "She's right, my soul is more filthy than you know. Demons surround me. I'm either insane, or a demon myself."

David enfolded her in his arms and kissed her. A miracle more astonishing than surviving death. She melted against him and became whole.

"I loved you from the first moment I saw you," he said.

She looked around the meadow—the demons were there, but silent. The mountains stood as they had since the beginning of time. Watching, waiting—but for what?

I have to tell him everything, even if it means losing him.

"I'm pregnant," she said.

David went still. "The father?"

"I don't know who he is, and I'm sure he doesn't want to know. I won't blame you if—"

"Do you love me?" he asked.

"Yes, I love you," she said.

"Will you marry me?"

Alma looked away from him. "I can't do that to you. My sins are too great."

David gently placed a hand on her cheek and guided her face back to his. "There is a way that all your sins can be forgiven."

Her heart pounded as she looked into his pale blue eyes. "Tell me."

Chapter 9

As their limousine crossed the Potomac, Theon glanced at his reflection in the partition separating them from their driver.

"How old do you think I look?" he asked.

Helena remained glued to her smartphone. "You sound like a teenage girl."

"I'd estimate the low sixties."

"You wish."

He turned to her. "You've been avoiding me."

"You noticed—I'm flattered." Her fingers flew across her phone's screen.

The towering spike of the Washington Monument came into view.

"I can't stop thinking about your answer to the president's question—"

"I don't want to discuss it," she said.

Why won't she look at me?

"Helena, please."

She turned to him. "I'm begging you to abandon this misguided crusade."

Bits of yellow ochre flecked her green eyes. Why hadn't he noticed that before?

"You know I can't."

"Then there's nothing to discuss," she said, and returned to her phone.

Traffic slowed near the Lincoln Memorial and worsened as they eased onto Constitution Avenue.

"Why can't you see that religion poses a grave threat to—"

"Listen to yourself," Helena said. "You're a caricature of a bitter atheist."

"With good reason!"

"Taslima's death is no excuse for declaring your own Jihad."

"You're the only one involved in this project that's expressed doubts."

"Because your employees worship you as a god. They've drunk the Kool-Aid and would give their lives for their charismatic leader with equal zeal to any Islamic suicide bomber or Christian Crusader."

At the base of the Washington Monument, a sea of protesters flooded the length of the National Mall and overflowed into Constitution Avenue.

The opposed groups taunted each other with signs, shouts, and the occasional thrown rock or bottle. The police wore full riot gear.

With the threat of losing their funding and tax breaks, every church, mosque, and temple were fighting for survival. Busloads of the faithful arrived from congregations across the country.

With the hotels filled, tent cities sprouted on public ground, reminiscent of the Depression Era protests by desperate WWI veterans seeking early payment of their promised bonus checks.

Acting on orders from President Hoover, General MacArthur drove the so-called "Bonus Army" out of Washington with infantry and cavalry regiments.

As their limo neared the Capitol Building, the crowds thickened. Despite their police escort, the limousine slowed to a crawl.

Banners proclaimed Theon the Antichrist, or demanded religious freedom, or warned that Hell awaited any who abandoned God.

"This is nothing but the last gasps of a dying system," Theon said.

Helena's fingers whitened on her cell phone as her eyes darted right and left. Now and then a bang against the car made her jump.

"We're almost there," he said, pointing to the dome of the Supreme Court.

From outside the car, a bearded man peered in at them. He wore a motorcycle jacket emblazoned with Christian symbols. "It's him!" the man shouted. "It's Theon Torano and that lying woman!"

Christian protesters surrounded the car.

Their driver leaned on the horn, and a knot of police in riot gear fought through the crowd toward them.

"Witch!" a Catholic nun shouted.

A brick banged into the side window, chipping the bulletproof glass. A group of men wearing T-shirts reading *Warriors for Christ* rocked the car as if trying to flip it like a giant turtle.

Helena filmed the attackers with her phone—no doubt uploading it to Amara's servers in real time.

The car's wheels slammed to the ground, then rocked upward. Then down and up again. The third time, the limousine didn't fall, but tilted higher and higher.

"Hold on!" Theon shouted as the right side of the car rose to forty-five degrees.

The car hovered on the brink of going over.

The crowd cheered as it inched higher.

"They're going to flip us!" Helena said.

Suddenly, the car fell back onto its wheels.

A squad of riot police cleared the attackers and surrounded the car. Other officers made arrests, while Theon's supporters cheered and waved their signs. The police used their shields like battering rams and plowed a way through the crowd to barricades encircling the Supreme Court.

Helena exhaled in relief.

Theon's racing heart slowed as the driver inched past the various security checkpoints.

Equal Justice Under Law, read an inscription atop the west facade of what was essentially a palace for nine people.

"We made it through the first skirmish," he said.

"This isn't a war."

"Tell them that." He motioned to the crowd. "Tell that to my wife and daughter."

He slumped into the seat and pressed the palms of his hands against his eyes. "I know you're only trying to help, but I'm not changing my mind."

The car halted at a side entrance.

A Supreme Court police officer opened the limo door. "Principals on-site," he said into his walkie-talkie.

Theon exited the car and straightened to his full height of six foot two inches—quite a different perspective on the world than from that damn wheelchair. Even the cane was gone now.

Helena stood and faced him. "Which way to the windmill, Don Quixote?"

Before he could answer, she kissed him flush on the lips.

"What was that?" he asked.

"For someone with such a high IQ, you sure are an idiot." She dashed toward a service entrance, then paused and looked back. "Too much sanity may be madness!"

Theon laughed. *La Mancha* was his favorite play. "But maddest of all is to see life as it is and not as it should be."

She vanished into the building.

What a strange, infuriating, marvelous girl.

"Thank Zeus you made it!" Kyoko shouted and rushed over with Lamarr limping behind. His white beard and clothes were wildly unkempt, as usual, in contrast to her meticulous hair and business suit.

"CNN broadcast your close call," Lamarr said. "I knew I should have come with you."

"It was a grand entrance, don't you think?"

"At the expense of giving me a heart attack!" Kyoko said.

Lamarr rolled his eyes at her melodrama.

"I saw that!" Kyoko said.

Lamarr wilted under her glare. "It was the pollen . . ."

"In January?"

"Don't tell me you two are getting divorced?" Theon asked.

"We're not married," Kyoko said. "You think I'd marry an old man like him?"

Lamarr rolled his eyes again. "Can't you tell he's joking?"

Kyoko wagged her finger at them. "You two are children. Always making joking."

It was amazing how far she'd come since walking through the doors of their startup office in Chicago. In her early forties at the time, she'd never been to college or held a job. Her shoes had been worn to the point of falling apart.

Taslima had hired her on the spot, and the two women became lifetime friends almost immediately.

Kyoko had been born in the industrial city of Hiroshima just before the start of World War II.

Truman credited God with giving the atomic bomb to America and went on to say that the Japanese could *"expect a rain of ruin from the air, the like of which has never been seen on this Earth."*

Kyoko was seven when Truman made good on his promise.

Her mother had placed her in the root cellar while going to find rice. The missionaries at the Christian orphanage said God saved her. She asked why God hadn't saved her mother as well. They told her not to question the Lord's plan.

She kept her mouth shut and pretended to believe. This got her through the mission school with high marks, and then to the notice of a visiting businessman from Atlanta. At seventeen, she was thirty-five years younger than him when he proposed. The minister called it a match made in Heaven.

She'd submitted to the role of docile Japanese doll, housekeeper, and sex toy. He displayed her to his friends, along with the other artifacts collected on his travels.

The husbands gazed with sly smiles every Sunday at Atlanta's First Baptist Church. Their wives glared in open contempt.

Her son inherited his father's religion, along with his imperious manner toward her. Kyoko thought she loved them. Only after her husband hanged himself in the garage did she learn of the numerous adulterous affairs that had bankrupted him.

The boy came home from Harvard Business School to salvage something from the financial ruin. Instead of offering comfort, he demanded food. "Real food," he said with a contemptuous sneer. "Not that rice crap you push on me."

Those words snatched the blindfold from her eyes. How long had she ignored the truth of what she was to all of them? She threw a bottle of olives on the fancy tiles at her son's feet. It shattered, ruining his Ivy League loafers.

Ignoring his shouts, she walked out the door and bought a train ticket to Chicago with the remains of her grocery allowance. She reached the rundown offices of the struggling biotech startup without a penny to her name.

Decades later, when her five-percent stake in the company made her a billionaire, her son visited. She kissed her American grandchildren and promised to pay for their education. Beyond that, her obligations ended. She explained that her money would go to charity when she died, and they never visited again.

She might be the one person who wanted revenge for Taslima's death even more than him.

"Is everything ready?" Theon asked.

Kyoko nodded. "Helena and Anna are coordinating last-minute details."

Lamarr and Kyoko had worked together from the start of his company, maintaining a steady stream of bickering for the past fifty years.

They led him through security, and then left to make final preparations.

The chief justice greeted him on the other side of the metal detector with his hand extended. "Doctor Torano."

Theon shook his hand. "A pleasure to meet you, Judge Dunn."

The judge's receding white hair exposed a generous bald cap on the top of his head. Combined with his unadorned black robes and wire-rimmed spectacles, he resembled a monk from the Middle Ages. His one extravagance was the tips of two snake-skin cowboy boots peeking from beneath his robes.

"What assurance do I have that you'll honor my decision?" Justice Dunn asked.

"I could swear it on Newton's *Principia* if you'd like."

The judge frowned. "I suppose we'd better get started."

A few moments later, Theon took his seat in the great hall of American justice. The edges of the mahogany desk had been softened by decades of lawyers sitting in this spot. Modeled on a classical Greco-Roman temple, the sixty-four-foot square chamber seemed oddly top-heavy.

Two American flags hung limp on poles flanking the raised dais, where the nine empty seats of the justices faced the courtroom. Immense burgundy curtains backed four Doric columns made of imported sienna marble. A plain circular clock hung between the center columns, challenging the impression that the tableau dated from the first century rather than the twenty-first.

Theon gazed upward at the procession of the great lawgivers of history carved into the south end of the marble frieze. His grandfather would approve of the craftsmanship.

The first figure was the unifier of Egypt over five thousand years ago. Considered a god, the Pharaoh Menes held the Egyptian symbol of eternal life—certainly appropriate for the current trial.

Next in line stood King Hammurabi, who received the law from the Babylonian Sun God himself.

Then came Moses, also an intermediary of divine law.

King Solomon, Lycurgus, Solon, Draco, Confucius, and the first Roman Emperor, Octavian, finished off the South Frieze.

The procession continued on the north wall with the Byzantine Emperor Justinian holding a sword in one hand and his *Justinian Code* in the other.

The Prophet Muhammad stood beside him—also pairing a sword with his deity-dictated Qur'an.

What good are laws without enforcement?

To mollify Muslim outrage at the depiction of their prophet, the Court had published a statement explaining that the statue is meant "*to honor Muhammad and bears no resemblance to Muhammad.*" How one could know a sculpture doesn't resemble someone who forbade any depiction of himself, was not clear.

Charlemagne was followed by King John of England holding a scroll of the Magna Carta. The fact that John only signed the document under threat of revolt by his Barons would seem to disqualify him from being a "lawgiver," but history is never easy to categorize.

Louis IX of France, Hugo Grotius, Sir William Blackstone, John Marshall, and Napoleon Bonaparte completed the elevated onlookers.

Cyril sat at the other end of the same wooden desk as his. The evangelist's attention was fixed on the cardboard box placed between them.

No doubt television commentators were obsessing over its contents—interviewing legal experts, box experts, or even psychics to divine what lurked inside. In the absence of facts, the news media degenerated into the wildest conspiracy theorists on the planet.

Bailiff Harlan stood to one side of the court bench. His 9mm pistol was the sole weapon allowed within the hallowed hall. The buzz-cut officer had introduced himself to Cyril with an expression of hero worship, but said nothing to him.

The chairs behind them held the other eight Supreme Court Justices and selected dignitaries. Reporters crammed the customary benches to the left, while the right side of the room housed the court functionaries necessary for greasing the wheels of justice.

For the first time in the history of the Supreme Court, half a dozen remote-controlled cameras were mounted at strategic points in the chamber. They would transmit live audio and video in what would likely be the largest worldwide audience of a single event, ever.

Bailiff Harlan projected his voice through the room as if reciting the opening monologue of a Shakespearean drama. "All rise for presiding Chief Justice James R. Dunn!"

Theon's chair added to the rumble as everyone stood in deference to the black-robed figure emerging from behind the towering curtain.

The chief justice settled into his high-backed leather chair at the central point of the three-sided dais. Despite his four Ivy League degrees, the eighty-two-year-old judge was a Texan through and through. The eight empty chairs radiating outward made him seem a lonely beetle sitting in an ancient ruin.

"Be seated," the bailiff commanded, and four hundred people complied as reverently as any church congregation.

The chief justice cleared his throat and addressed the audience. "When I attended my first university outside of Texas, a professor mentioned *barbed wire* in a lecture. When I admitted that I didn't know what barbed wire was, he showed me a picture of it. I exclaimed in my native Texan accent, 'Oh, you mean bobwar!' "

The courtroom roared with laughter.

Judge Dunn smiled and then clapped his gavel to restore silence.

"Every one of you in this room got my joke in an instant," the judge said. "Those of you watching in other countries are probably scratching your heads at its meaning."

The judge looked at one of the cameras. "Since my ruling has global implications, I will do my best to keep everything as clear as possible to avoid such confusion, but the lens of culture and language may distort some of it. For this, I apologize in advance."

With that, the chief justice opened a notebook and placed a pen beside it. "Doctor Torano, you agreed to present your evidence first, with the understanding that these proceedings will go no further should you fail to prove your case to my satisfaction."

Theon nodded and stepped to the elaborately carved lectern stationed between him and Cyril. His heart pounded from the adrenaline coursing through his veins.

It's actually happening.

"Mr. Chief Justice," he said, "may it please the court if I proceed with my case?" It was the traditional start to all Supreme Court cases, at least according to Wikipedia.

"You may proceed."

Theon straightened. "Religion and science both make claims about the universe. How does one evaluate which assertions are true? I am here to offer the evidence supporting my claim."

He opened the cardboard box and removed a clear Plexiglas cube, then set it on the lectern.

The audience shifted in their seats, and Theon stepped aside to give the cameras an unobstructed view. Inside the transparent container sat a slice of decaying apple with a swarm of tiny black specks hovering around it.

"Your Honor, I present one hundred and fifty Drosophila Melanogaster, also known as the common fruit fly."

The judge leaned forward and squinted at the imprisoned bugs.

"The normal lifespan of a fruit fly is, on average, thirty-five days. In the year 2000, scientists at Brown University doubled the fruit fly's life to seventy days, a truly monumental achievement."

Theon's voice deepened. "Each fruit fly in this container is . . . three years old."

With a triumphant smile, he returned to his seat.

"That's it?" Cyril asked. "That's your evidence?"

"Pretty conclusive, don't you think?"

A low murmur rolled through the crowd.

"Is this a joke?" Cyril turned to the judge. "Your Honor, how can anyone know these fruit flies are three years old?"

"A valid question," the judge said.

Theon removed a sheaf of papers from underneath the box and held them up. "Here are twelve signed and notarized testimonies of the members of my team, each of whom witnessed every step of this process for three years."

Cyril pointed at the pages. "You could have written those yourself, or someone in your lab might have substituted new fruit flies every few weeks to fool the witnesses."

Theon rubbed his chin. "I suppose that's possible."

The reporters exchanged knowing smirks.

"Twelve witnesses over a three-year period?" The judge frowned. "Doctor Torano, if I thought for one minute you were mocking these proceedings . . ."

"I assure you that all my evidence is crucial to my case, Your Honor."

Judge Dunn tapped his pen on the table and stared hard at him. "I'm afraid this evidence does not meet the legal standards required in a matter of such importance as this."

"I see," Theon said. With care, he removed the Plexiglas cage from the podium and eased it into the cardboard box.

"Do you have anything other than bugs?" the chief justice asked.

"My lab has tested one other animal."

Cyril stood. "Your Honor, how many mice, cats, or monkeys will we be subjected to, with only his word they are as old as he says?"

"If this next exhibit is not more substantive," the judge said, "I *will* hold you in contempt."

Theon inclined his head. "This test subject hails from the family Hominidae—taxonomically known as Homo Sapiens, or, to translate the Latin, *wise human*."

On cue, a man in the prime of life strolled down the aisle. A professorial tweed jacket draped his slight frame, while thick brown hair fell across his forehead and brushed the top of his eyebrows. His boyish blue eyes surveyed the courtroom with a grave, almost analytical, slowness.

Theon motioned him to the witness chair.

The young man settled in and flashed a broad smile as the bailiff retrieved the court Bible. "I don't believe in any supernatural being controlling the destiny of the universe," the witness said.

Harlan frowned and looked toward the judge.

"Administer the secular oath instead."

Harlan withdrew the Bible. "Do you solemnly affirm that you will tell the truth, the whole truth, and nothing but the truth, under pains and penalties of perjury?"

"I do."

Harlan placed the Bible back on its stand and returned to his post.

"Please state your name, age, occupation, and place of residence for the record," the chief justice said.

"I am the Lucasian Doctor of Mathematics at Cambridge University. I was born in 1942, and my name is Stephen William Hawking."

Gasps raced the length of the room, followed by murmurs.

"Order!" the judge commanded. "I will not hesitate to clear this court if those in attendance cannot control themselves." Silence returned. "Doctor Torano, you may proceed with questioning your witness."

Theon walked around the desk and stood before the young man. "It's been a couple of weeks since I saw you last, Professor Hawking. I must say you're looking well."

The young man wiped a tear from his eye. "I do not thank any god for this miracle, since it is you, Doctor Torano, and science, that have saved my life."

"It was my pleasure," Theon said. "Professor Hawking, would you mind telling the court the details of your experience?"

The young man nodded and looked toward the cameras. "At the age of twenty-one, I was diagnosed with amyotrophic lateral sclerosis— commonly known as ALS, or Lou Gehrig's disease. Doctors gave me two years to live. I have beaten those odds for the past half century, thanks in equal measure to luck and advances in science.

"By the time Doctor Torano contacted me last year, I'd reached the end, both in terms of my disease and advanced age. When Theon presented his Immortality Contract, I agreed to the conditions instantly. As an atheist, what did I have to lose?"

The young man's eyes drifted to the emptiness above the audience. "As the pill restored the telomeres in every cell in my body, new division commenced at an exponential rate.

"Within two days, I breathed independent of the mechanical ventilator. On the fourth day, the muscles in my cheeks twitched in response to my mental commands. Each day brought more nerves online. At first my vocal cords produced nothing but guttural moans, but after three weeks of near continuous practice, I spoke my first words in thirty years."

The judge seemed transfixed along with the audience. Only Cyril wore a frown.

"As I grew younger, my disease retreated—somehow tied to my body's biological clock. My teeth fell out, and then regrew from scratch. It took a grueling regiment of physical therapy and exercise to rebuild bone density, muscle mass, and balance. My brain gradually reconstructed the neural pathways we all take for granted when doing the simplest of tasks."

The witness stood and gazed at his legs. "Four months into my recovery, I walked unaided for the first time in decades. When I reached the biological equivalent of thirty, my disease regressed to a mild clumsiness.

"Now, six months into Doctor Theon's treatment, I've been restored to my physical and mental peak. I will not win any Olympic competitions, since my genes are still as nature designed me, but I can continue my research as long as I take this pill every month. Should life lose its appeal, the choice of when and how to exit will be mine alone."

Cyril rose. "Your Honor, how do we know this isn't an actor playing a part?"

"As a scientist myself," the witness said, "I helped document every step of my cure—from DNA samples, physical examinations, and filming a daily video diary. The raw data is being made available on Amara Pharmaceutical's website as I speak."

"None of this *evidence* comes from an independent third party," Cyril said. "Any special effects studio could create convincing video footage of a turtle turning into a dragon."

"Reverend Cyril raises a valid point," Theon said. "I guess there are numerous ways one might even fake a resurrection."

Cyril glared. "You're not comparing—"

"Certainly not! Raising someone from the dead would be an extra-extra-extraordinary claim. Such an assertion requires magnitudes more proof than merely making someone young again. Wouldn't you agree, Reverend?"

Cyril ground his teeth. "I don't see that I will get a chance to present my evidence, since this man is clearly a fraud—no different than that actor you passed off as Helena Mueller at your press conference!"

The chief justice sighed. "As noted by Reverend Doberson, advances in computer technologies place all video documentation in question. With no verifiable chain of custody, I must rule this evidence inadmissible."

Theon's shoulders slumped. "Chain of custody. Why didn't I think of that? It certainly rules out my video diary, and even the day-by-day notes of people in my lab tracking the experiment's progress."

Cyril's chin rose triumphantly—a modern-day Saint George having slain the evil dragon. "You're Honor, I move that this case be dismissed."

"You may step down from the witness stand," the judge said, and the young man took a seat in a row of chairs behind Theon and Cyril.

"Doctor Torano, if you have nothing more solid to present, I must rule against you."

A smile twitched at the corners of Theon's mouth, but he masked it with an exaggerated sigh. "I did bring one final witness, Your Honor. It is another person who has taken my drug for the past six months."

Cyril didn't bother standing. "What is it this time? A Fred Astaire impersonator? This is nothing but smoke and mirrors."

"I'm inclined to agree," the judge said. "Does this witness provide more proof than the last?"

"I think so, Your Honor, but I'll leave it to your judgment."

The judge fixed him with a stern gaze. "I'll allow one more witness, but this is your final chance."

Theon nodded.

Helena escorted a young woman down the aisle. Her almond hair matched her eyes, and she wore a subdued navy-blue dress. She was not a celebrity. Most would describe her as plain.

Every gaze followed the trembling girl's progress as Helena guided her to the witness stand.

"Your Honor, I must object to yet another . . ." The reverend's voice trailed off as he turned toward the judge.

Chief Justice James Dunn stood, eyes wide and mouth agape.

The witness stopped below him, tears dripping from her chin. "Jimmy, I . . . I'm so happy to see you."

The judge stumbled to the end of the platform and descended the stairs. Helena relinquished the sobbing girl into his arms.

"Ruth, is it really you?" he asked.

"Don't you know me?" The girl caressed his cheek. "Remember, on our honeymoon, when you—" She glanced at the rapt faces of the audience, and then at the cameras. She cupped a hand around his ear and whispered something.

The judge burst into laughter and sobs at the same time. Forgotten were the sober surroundings, or his role as dispassionate arbiter. The eighty-two-year-old man wrapped the waif of a girl in his arms and kissed her over and over.

She kissed him back with equal abandon.

The heartbreaking story of his wife's descent into Alzheimer's was common knowledge after *60 Minutes* profiled the chief justice several years before.

Theon wiped tears from his face. If only such a reunion with Taslima were possible.

At least I've made two people happy.

Despite the warning against emotive outbursts, the audience applauded, while the reporters scribbled furiously. Judith, the *Time* magazine correspondent, ignored her notepad and exchanged a look with Helena. The reporter inclined her head as if saying, *Now I believe you.*

Helena smiled and nodded back.

Cyril slumped into his chair as the crowd rose to their feet and applauded louder. The noise drowned out the reverend's mumbled words, but his lips clearly said, "My God, it's true."

Theon beamed, wiped his own tears, and took his seat. Helena settled in the chair beside him and held his hand.

After a final extended kiss, the octogenarian chief justice disentangled himself from the young girl. Red lipstick covered his mouth, cheeks, and earlobes. The audience laughed when Ruth used a handkerchief to restore a measure of solemnity to his wrinkled visage. Once this housekeeping was complete, she took a seat next to Stephen Hawking.

The bailiff held the judge's arm as he ascended to his lonely perch.

When the courtroom settled, the judge turned his eyes on Theon. "Doctor Torano, what can I say? For the past ten years I've watched my wife of fifty-six years vanish before my eyes. When my daughter took her to live in Minnesota these past months, I never suspected . . ." His eyes drifted past Theon to Ruth.

"I'm sorry for the deception, Your Honor," Theon said.

The judge waved his hand. "You have nothing to apologize for, nothing at all." The judge wiped new tears from his eyes. "I must admit, that before this moment, I assumed this was a publicity stunt in bad taste."

Theon inclined his head. "I could think of no other way of surmounting the high bar my extraordinary claim entailed."

"And you've done so, within my mind at least," the judge said. "My relationship to this witness may cause the appearance of a conflict of interest. In the service of judicial fairness, I submit my offer of recusing myself from this case if Reverend Doberson no longer considers me an impartial arbiter."

Cyril jerked at the sound of his name. "That won't be necessary, Your Honor. I admit that Doctor Torano has proved his pill works as he claims."

The evangelist's gaze drifted to an empty spot on the floor. His left hand trembled.

"In that case, I assume you do not wish to call any rebuttal witnesses?"

"Um . . . no," Cyril said.

"Then I officially rule in favor of Doctor Theon Torano on phase one of this trial." He brought his gavel down with a clap. "I think this has been enough for one day. Why don't we wait until tomorrow morning to begin phase two of this process?"

Cyril looked up with an expression verging on panic. "Your Honor, might I request two days to . . . um . . . get everything ready?"

Theon smiled.

He never expected to have his turn and hasn't prepared a damn thing.

"Very well," the judge said with an annoyed shake of his head. "We will resume on Saturday at 9:00 sharp, at which time Reverend Doberson will present his evidence for the existence of God. Court is adjourned!"

The gavel sounded a final time, and Cyril wiped his brow.

A crowd of reporters headed for Theon, but Helena steered him out a side exit to the basement, where an unmarked police car waited.

Chapter 10

The snow-topped peaks of Mount Ararat poked above the northern horizon, and Ahmad's hands tightened on the steering wheel of Grandpa's beat-up 1970 Paykan.

We're close.

He'd been twelve years old—and his brother, Reza, eight—when his father took them to Turkey for a medical conference he was speaking at. They had crossed the border at this same remote outpost at Bazargan—and in the same car. Those days of family unity seemed an illusion now.

"Mount Ararat is where some believe Noah's Ark landed," Father had told them.

Reza had stared in wonder at the legendary mountain. "Imam Qajar says water swallowed the entire world as Allah's punishment."

"Those are poetic myths, Reza," his mother had said. "Don't take them literally."

"They're not myths!" his brother had shouted, surprising them with his vehemence.

Papa and Mamma tried moderating Reza's religious fervor for years, since theirs was a family of education and learning, but swimming against the tide of indoctrination had been difficult.

Now, decades later, his brother was lost to him.

The setting sun stained the legendary mountain with its final rays. The convoy had dwindled to a few hundred. Fuel stations along the northern stretch of the Basij Expressway were closed by decree of the Ayatollah. Only those who'd brought extra petrol remained.

In the backseat of the car, Grandpa held his wife's hand. The blue headscarf was a parting gift from Mom. She'd given them all something and cried when they drove away.

"Your grandfather served under Mosaddegh in '52," Grandma said, motioning to the laminated photograph dangling from the rearview mirror.

"He knows," Grandpa said, patting his bride's hand. It was for her sake more than himself that they attempted this trip. At ninety-two, her health was declining at a distressing pace. This seemed the only way to save her.

"If only the Americans had given us our chance at freedom," Grandma said. "Mohammed Mosaddegh was democratically elected! He'd studied law in Paris and received his doctorate in Switzerland and dreamed of an Iran governed on the same secular principles of Western democracies. You'd think they would have welcomed him."

Grandpa shook his head. "Why dwell on things we can't—"

"It was all about oil and greed," Grandma said. "Saudi Arabia received fifty percent of the profits on its oil, but the British paid Iran a mere seventeen percent. Maybe even less, since they refused to open their books to us."

"I didn't realize it was that lopsided," Ahmad said. "How did the British justify that?"

"They'd struck a long-term deal with unelected warlords at the turn of the century," Grandpa said. "I think they feared the precedent renegotiating would set with other Third World countries they were exploiting."

"None of Mosaddegh's progressive reforms were possible without money from the oil fields," Grandma said. "He had no choice but to nationalize the wells."

Grandpa nodded. "I was one of the team that drafted a policy promising twenty-five percent of future oil revenues to British Petroleum to compensate them for the infrastructure they'd built."

"They didn't deserve anything!" Grandma said.

"Mosaddegh felt maintaining good relations with the West was worth it, but even that wasn't enough to satisfy their greed."

Grandma caressed her husband's cheek. "Your grandpa spent a year in prison after the CIA overthrew Mosaddegh and put their puppet back in power. In thanks, the British gave America a slice of the oil pie."

Grandpa kissed her on the forehead. "Your grandmother's teaching position in the philosophy department saved us."

"Saved us for what?" she said. "For the Ayatollah? Those theocrats would never have taken over if the Americans hadn't—"

"Now, now," Grandpa said. "The past is the past. Let's focus on the future."

She smiled at him. "I can't wait for our second youth together."

"Me too, my dear Oriana."

As the sun touched the western horizon, Ahmad switched on the headlights. Now and then, a cargo truck sped past, headed toward Iran's most important land trade-link. Sometimes the drivers waved, but mostly they cursed and made obscene gestures.

Beyond the crossing, the Turkish village of Gurbulak marked the start of Route 80. The Trans-European Motorway stretched four thousand miles across ten countries and ended at the Atlantic Ocean in Portugal. What wonders of freedom that road must witness.

Ahmad's heart ached with the nearness of liberation.

Will they let us leave?

The answer came as they topped a hill. The rays of the dying sun glinted off tanks squatting before the road's terminus.

Behind them stood tight formations of the Revolutionary Guard's elite Quds Force—controlled by Iran's supreme religious leader, Ali Khamenei.

"Do you think Reza is among them?" Grandma asked.

Ahmad said nothing.

Every male between eighteen and thirty-five was required to serve twenty-one months in the Iranian army, but many avoided it. Father took the proactive step of having their family doctor diagnose both sons with epilepsy as children. Despite this immunization, Reza enlisted the day after graduating university. He saw it as his Islamic duty.

Family gatherings soured after that. The first shouting match erupted when Reza claimed that the CIA destroyed the Word Trade Center as a pretense for attacking Muslims. Every time he visited, there was another anti-American conspiracy theory. After a while, Papa stopped talking to him altogether.

Reza never gave up trying to save his family from eternal torture in the fires of Jahannam. He would entice them with descriptions of the paradise awaiting those that submitted. Even though well-meaning, Reza's view of the afterlife seemed like something a horny teenage boy might imagine. Seventy-two virgins, indeed.

And yet, hundreds of millions of Muslims believed in this mythical realm of pleasure and plenty—even to the point of blowing themselves up as a shortcut.

Ahmad never met Reza's two children. His brother considered him an unholy influence on such impressionable young minds.

Grandma laughed, suddenly. "I was just thinking about how Theon took that Christian minister to task!"

The Iranian press had blocked the American scientist's announcement, but they'd been able to find a friend with a black-market satellite dish. Once Theon proved his pill worked, news raced through Internet back channels, text messages, and word of mouth.

"Please, Allah, let us make it through," Gran said to the tattered roof of the old car. Though not a fundamentalist, she still believed in God, though Grandpa had told him long ago that he was an atheist.

And what do I believe? Maybe I'll find out when I'm free.

But wasn't Theon's contract simply another form of censorship?

The lead car halted before the concrete barriers a hundred yards from the armored blockade. Ahmad pulled onto the dirt shoulder, as did the rest of the convoy. They sat atop a slight hill overlooking the long line of cars.

A stentorian voice boomed from loudspeakers. "By decree of the supreme leader, you are ordered back to your homes. Those who refuse are enemies of the Revolution!"

A few turned back, but the majority sat motionless, defying the overwhelming display of military might.

All along the thwarted convoy, people got out of their vehicles, leaning on canes, walkers, and helping the lame into wheelchairs.

"You must take the car and leave," Grandpa said.

"Not without you."

"You're a good boy," Grandma said, her voice brittle from the days of travel. "But there's no point in you staying."

Tears stung Ahmad's eyes at the sight of her life-worn face. When the Islamists imprisoned his parents for two years during grade school, his grandparents cared for him and his brother.

"We have only a few years left," Grandpa said, "while your entire lifetime lies ahead."

"I won't leave you."

Grandpa placed a hand on his shoulder. "Please, go."

Ahmad stared into Grandpa's cloudy eyes and gently held his gnarled fingers. "Reza says the willingness to die for one's beliefs is the test of its truth. I've kept my beliefs hidden my whole life—maybe even from myself. No more. It's time I made a stand."

"He sounds like you during Mosaddegh's rule," Grandma said.

The old man looked at her, then back at him. He sighed. "I suppose if we're not willing to make a stand now, then when would we?"

*   *   *

Colonel Reza Fatemi gazed through his binoculars at the mob hobbling forward despite his warning. A few younger ones pushed wheelchairs or carried stretchers, but most were elderly.

Apostates. Do they not fear the eternal torment of Jahannam?

Twelve Zulfiqar MBT tanks blocked the road. Five T-72Zs, and two of the newest Sabalans with the latest laser range finders and communication systems sat behind on higher ground.

SPG-9 Kopye rifles continued outward in a crescent to both sides of the tanks, their splayed legs insect-like. Their rocket-assisted 73-mm projectiles could pierce the thickest armor.

The main force of five hundred men came next. A few manned Akhgar rotary machine guns, but most carried the standard issue G3A6 service rifle, plus a PC-9 ZOAF 9 mm pistol.

Some might call it overkill, but it would send a clear message that should require no repeat. In the long run, his actions would save lives—and souls.

The pathetic rabble descended the gradual slope of the highway into the no-man's-land. Did they believe he'd let them insult Islam and their homeland in such a disgraceful manner?

How could so many fall prey to the American Shaytan and his lies?

The Qur'an left no room for debate when it came to dealing with such traitors to Allah. *"Strive against the disbelievers and the hypocrites! Be harsh with them. Their ultimate abode is Hell, a hapless journey's end."*

When the edge of the refugees came to within a few yards of the first tank, Reza spoke into his walkie-talkie. "Commence firing."

The Army of the Guardians of the Islamic Revolution unleashed their machines of death in a deafening barrage.

The crossfire sliced through the crowd like a scythe. Those in the open fell, while the rest dived for shelter behind the line of cars. Screams of agony rose in counterpoint to the explosions.

A soothing warmth spread through his body.

God is great.

Tanks, mortars, rocket-propelled grenades, and the devastating Kopyes blasted the civilian vehicles apart like tin cans at a firing range.

A Toufan II helicopter lifted into the air from the checkpoint's parking lot. It flew low along the mile-long line, its machine guns tearing through them with ease.

Some fled into the fields surrounding the road. Snipers picked them off as easily as pop-up targets at a carnival shooting gallery.

A college-aged girl desperately pushed an old woman in a wheelchair. The chair bucked and bounced, yanking the girl left and right as she ran, creating a challenging target. A bullet tore her headscarf off, freeing her long black hair. Another shot grazed her shoulder, and she fell. She struggled to her feet and continued pushing the ridiculous wheelchair.

Does she believe there's a chance?

Finally, the top of the girl's skull erupted in a crimson volcano. As she fell, another bullet tore through her neck. Her body crumpled, head askew at a ninety-degree angle.

The old woman tumbled from the wheelchair and crawled toward the girl. A thunderous barrage swallowed her wails of torment. Then she too went still, her white robe dyed red.

After five minutes, Reza signaled a cease-fire. The helicopter gunship rose into the darkening sky and headed back to base.

A haze of smoke drifted across the battlefield in an eerie mist.

The Americans would label it a crime against humanity—as if they were not the ones spreading war and death. No doubt the Immortality Contract was another plot by the CIA to strike at Islam.

When the disk of the sun vanished, Reza motioned to the company's muezzin.

The bearded holy man walked to the communications van and chanted the Adhan into a microphone. "Allah is the greatest. I acknowledge there is no god but Allah. I acknowledge that Muhammad is the Messenger of Allah. Hasten to prayer. Hasten to success. Prayer is better than sleep."

The amplified words subsumed the cries of the dead and dying.

Reza closed his eyes, letting the sacred words wash through him with their resonance. The five daily prayers prescribed by Allah marked the highlights of his day.

There is no strength or power except from Allah.

When the muezzin called out the Iqama, Reza and each of his soldiers set aside their weapons, climbed out of their tanks, and performed their ablutions in preparation for prayer.

Reza used water from his canteen to rinse his hands, face, and hair.

Once clean, Reza removed his prayer rug from his jeep and faced it toward the holy city of Mecca.

He performed the movements of the rakat alongside his men—bowing, prostrating, and chanting in total submission to Allah.

Love spread through Reza's every vein, muscle, and nerve. A total communion with Allah and his brother soldiers.

There was peace in serving a purpose greater than one's self—in following the commands of Allah without question. Shades of gray no longer plagued him.

When the final prayer ended, Reza rose and stored his mat.

Physically and spiritually refreshed, he lifted his rifle and resumed the holy duty before him. Just as he'd cleansed himself, so must he cleanse creation. It was the will of Allah.

The screams had subsided.

He led his soldiers on foot into the moonlit valley of the shadow of death without a word. The smell of burning tires, fuel, cordite, and cooked flesh held a cascade of memories.

Into each skull went a bullet. No exceptions.

On the Haj to Mecca, he'd circled the Ka'aba seven times and drank holy water from the Zamzam Well. He'd thrown the customary stones at the pillars representing the Shaytan telling Abraham not to sacrifice his son Isaac on Allah's orders. It was a reminder never to disobey Allah, no matter how difficult the command.

The task was tedious, but necessary. Some of the apostates begged for their lives.

What true Muslim fears death?

Reza's walkie-talkie crackled with the general's voice, requesting a status report.

While his soldiers passed, he gave his report—estimating the number of enemies killed, his own lack of casualties, and the resources needed to dig the mass graves. If all proceeded according to schedule, he'd open the border by first light.

"Well done, Colonel. Continue with cleanup."

Reza started toward the distant line of his soldiers. Then he froze at a slight movement from a 1970 Paykan, its windows shattered, and the sides pockmarked with holes.

The same car as Grandpa's.

The inside was empty, and the trunk open.

His eyes settled on a rectangle dangling from the rearview mirror. It swayed in the slight wind, revealing a faded photo of Mohammed Mosaddegh.

He tensed, but remained motionless.

The intermittent shot of his brothers-in-arms diminished until they resembled a child's pop gun.

Reza pointed his rifle under the car and slid his finger onto the trigger. Nothing moved. He took four silent steps backward. He eased into a crouch, the muzzle steady.

There was nothing but sandy dirt beneath the car. He couldn't blame his soldiers. It was an expert job of camouflage.

"You can't hide from me," he said.

Silence.

"In two seconds, I will shoot."

"Is that you, Reza?" came a muffled voice.

"It's me, . . . Brother."

The whites of two eyes appeared within the slight mound. Then his brother rose out of the shallow depression beneath the car, loose dirt sliding off him like waves breaking over rocks.

Ahmad crawled into the open and pulled himself to his feet, still gripping a garden spade in his hand. His left leg seemed incapable of supporting any weight, and a bloody rag was bound around his thigh.

A look of hatred twisted Ahmad's dirt-smeared face as he leaned against Grandpa's shattered car to keep upright. "They're dead, both of them. You killed your own grandparents."

Guilt spasmed Reza's chest. He could see Grandma's face as she comforted him after his parents' arrest. They'd loved and sheltered him when he needed them most. Grandpa had taught him to shoot and hunt in the marshes. They'd wander sometimes for days, sleeping in the canoe under the stars, Grandpa telling him stories of the old days and teaching him the names of the constellations.

My happiest childhood memories.

"They're here?" Reza asked.

Ahmad motioned to the line of the cars. "A mortar blew their bodies to pieces."

Reza swallowed the lump in his throat and blinked back tears. "They betrayed Allah."

"Stop hiding behind your damn god. You slaughtered unarmed civilians who only wanted a chance to live!"

Reza's hands trembled as he placed his rifle against his shoulder. Grandpa's words echoed in his mind. *"Keep the sights aligned on your target, then take a breath and hold it."*

Tears blurred his vision. *Was this what Abraham felt when Allah ordered him to kill his own son?*

Ahmad's eyes bore into him, unblinking. "What are you waiting for, Brother? I tried to save our grandparents' lives. For that I'm a criminal."

In a trembling voice, Reza recited words from the Qur'an. *"If they turn away, Allah will afflict them with a painful doom in the world and the hereafter, and they have no protecting friend nor helper in the earth."*

Searing pain sliced into Reza's back. As he fell, he fired. The bullet tore into his brother's stomach.

Ahmad cried out and fell.

Reza hit the ground and rolled. He pointed the rifle and squeezed the trigger a second time.

Grandpa jerked to a stop, the bloody knife still gripped in his fist. A crimson circle expanded in the center of his dirt-caked shirt.

They used the call to prayer to bury themselves like serpents.

Behind the old man stood Grandma, tears streaking her muddy face. She stumbled toward her husband and eased him to the ground.

The rifle gained in weight until gravity tore it from Reza's hands.

Ahmad inched toward the fallen gun, leaving a trail of red in his wake. With a groan, he reached for the rifle.

Reza drew his pistol and pointed it at Ahmad.

Grandma's voice was a distant whisper above the ringing in his ears. "Don't do it, Reza. Don't kill your own brother."

Ahmad gazed at him with eyes filled with contempt.

How many times had his big brother protected him from bullies when their parents sat in jail? Without Ahmad's help with homework, he might never have graduated and become eligible for officer training.

Forgive me, Brother.

"Reza, no!" Grandma shouted.

Reza pulled the trigger and put a bullet through his brother's forehead.

Ahmad crumpled to the ground, the back of his skull blown apart.

Grandma rocked her husband's body back and forth while humming under her breath. Grandpa's head slumped to the side, eyes glazed with that distant stare he'd seen a thousand times on the battlefield.

Grandma looked at him with pity. "What's happened to you, my little strawberry?" It was the nickname she'd given him as a child because he loved her strawberry pie so much.

Here it is—Allah's final test.

He raised the 9 mm ZOAF.

An overwhelming lethargy spread through him as he pointed the instrument of judgment at the apostate. His vision narrowed to a tunnel.

Soon I'll be in paradise.

In a gurgling whisper, he recited the famed words of Amir ul Mu'mineen Ali. *"He who sells his next life for his present life, loses both."*

He squeezed the trigger, and the recoil tore the gun out of his weakened hand. The old woman slumped atop the body of her mate and lay still.

Reza's head slumped to the dirt. Blood foamed out of his mouth with each breath.

A smile anointed his lips. "Truly, to Allah we belong, and truly to him we shall return."

Chapter 11

The congregation escorted Alma through the woods in solemn procession. It was crisp and overcast, with the scent of coming snow.

The demons followed, as always, unseen by any but her. Some flew, some scurried, and some leaped from branch to branch. A few shouted obscenities.

Will I never be free of them?

Only David's hand in hers kept the fear manageable. The rest of his family walked beside them, a psychological shield from the monsters.

Only Cassie was absent. She trailed at the back of the group, her twelve-year-old face bottled with resentment.

Her every attempt to befriend the girl had failed.

Maybe she's right not to trust me.

As they neared the river, Minister Gerhartz led them in song.

"Amazing grace. How sweet the sound that saved a wretch like me! I once was lost, but now am found; was blind, but now I see."

A former slave trader wrote the hymn over two hundred years ago.

Blind, lost, wretched. It's as if the words were written for me.

Their voices filled the forest with God's promise of protection through all of life's trials and temptations. But the most comforting promise came toward the end of the song.

"Yea, when this flesh and heart shall fail, and mortal life shall cease, I shall possess, within the veil, a life of joy and peace."

They reached the river. A thin layer of ice cloaked the edges, but the main channel flowed free, even in the depths of winter.

"When we've been there ten thousand years, bright shining as the sun, we've no less days to sing God's praise than when we first begun."

The song ended, and everyone stood silent as the river continued singing.

The men cleared the ice along the bank with axes.

Merriam helped her remove her hat, coat, and gloves.

The demons hooted and shrieked.

"Best keep your wool socks and shoes on," David's father said. "You don't want to cut yourself on the rocks."

Standing in the white baptismal dress, Alma began to shiver.

David and the minister removed their coats, and each grasped one of her hands.

"Ready?" David asked.

She nodded, despite the fear churning inside her.

What if God rejects me?

Alma waded into the river with David holding her left hand and the minister holding her right.

The cold shocked the air out of her lungs in short gasps.

When they were waist-deep, David and the minister each placed a hand against her back.

The demons continued their shrieks and rude gestures from the shore, seemingly afraid of the river.

Minister Gerhartz spoke. "Jesus said, 'I say unto thee, except a man be born of water and of the Spirit, he cannot enter into the kingdom of God. That which is born of the flesh is flesh; and that which is born of the Spirit is spirit. Marvel not that I said unto thee, Ye must be born again.' "

Alma's body trembled as the icy water leeched the warmth from her legs.

"Alma, Jesus gave his life to cleanse the sins of the human race. Are you ready to accept Christ as your personal savior and be born again in the Spirit?"

Through chattering teeth, she said, "Yes, I accept Jesus as my personal Lord and Savior." She closed her eyes and spread her arms wide in honor of Jesus dying on the cross—just as Merriam had instructed.

"Lord, bathe this sinner in your Grace!"

David and the minister lowered her backward into the freezing river.

The water engulfed her, and her heart jolted at the shock.

For the second time, her heart stopped and she died.

I've returned to the womb of creation.

An inner heat flared inside every fiber and drove out the cold.

"*I am here,*" God said.

I feel you, Lord.

Truth flowed through her like blood.

Without a Creator, life was nothing but atoms without purpose.

That's what I've missed my entire life—a purpose to live.

God emerged from within her. His voice was as deep as the roots of the universe. He spoke for what seemed ages, answering every mystery she'd ever puzzled over, and some she hadn't considered.

Finally, he said, "*I am sending a messenger to lead you to your purpose.*"

Hands drew her toward the surface of the river.

Let me stay with you, my Lord.

"*I will call you to my side when your time has come.*"

She emerged from the water and drew life into her lungs.

Steam rose from her body.

"You are born again in Christ," the minister said. "Your sins have been washed away."

I'm not cold anymore.

David helped her out of the stream. Merriam and Abel wrapped blankets around them both.

The first flakes of snow drifted to the earth.

Minster Gerhartz looked to the sky and recited words from the Gospel of Mark. "*And coming up out of the water, he saw the heavens opened, and the Spirit like a dove descending upon him.*"

The snow increased like a million doves descending.

Each member of the congregation hugged her and said, "Welcome, Sister."

Only Cassie hung back, her eyes bitter.

The world sparkled as if brand-new. It all made sense. Each thing played its part in God's plan.

Her eyes darted left and right. Then to the tree branches against the winter sky.

The demons are gone.

When the last of the congregants welcomed her back, David got down on one knee and took her hands.

"Alma, will you marry me?" he asked.

"Yes," she said without hesitation.

Cassie let out a primal scream and took off running.

Merriam started after her, but Abel placed a hand on her arm. "Talk to her later."

When they returned, Alma entered Cassie's room alone. Her hair was wet, and the blanket still wrapped around her.

Cassie lay on her bed, facing the wall.

"I won't let you take him away from me," the girl said.

So that's what she's afraid of.

Alma sat on the edge of the bed. "We've decided to build a cabin here on your farm."

Silence.

"David's not leaving?"

"Neither of us could bear to leave any of you."

After several moments, Cassie asked, "What happened to you under the water?"

"God spoke to me."

Cassie sat up and faced her. Tears glistened on her cheeks, but her eyes were wide. "What did he say?"

"He said he was sending me a guide."

"What does that mean?"

"I don't know."

Cassie jumped across the bed and hugged her. "I'm sorry for hating you. I thought you were stealing David. I thought you'd turn him into a drug dealer or an atheist."

Alma smoothed her hair. "It's David who has changed me."

Cassie sat back and wiped away her tears. "You look different."

Alma smiled. "I always wanted a sister."

Cassie hesitated. "Do you still doubt the Bible?"

"I accept the word of the Lord completely," she said. "If the Bible said God put all the animals in the world in a cracker box, I'd believe it because there's nothing God can't do."

Cassie smiled, her relief evident. "Can I be your maid of honor?"

"I'd love that."

"I can help Mamma make the dresses and—"

There was a knock at the door, and Merriam half-opened it.

"I'm going to be Alma's maid of honor!" Cassie said.

"That's wonderful, dear." Merriam turned to Alma. "There's someone here to see you."

"To see me?"

"He says he was sent by God."

Chapter 12

Reza opened his eyes, and a world of splendor greeted him. Trees loaded with almonds, figs, pomegranates, oranges, and every variety of fragrant fruit surrounded him. Waterfalls sent plumes of mist into the heavens, and clouds drifted through rainbows against a purple sky.

He wore the olive-green shirt and trousers of his cadet days. His pants were tucked into polished black leather boots. This first uniform was his favorite. It marked the moment he found his life's purpose.

A voice filled with sunshine whispered in his ear. "This is Jannah, known as the gardens of perpetual bliss."

Reza turned and froze. Could one call such a being a woman? Her eyes sparkled with a light no earthly jewel could rival, with irises as black as midnight. The girl's perfectly formed nose seemed sculpted from alabaster. And her lips. Their sensuous curves would take years to fully appreciate.

"Do I please you, master?" she asked and displayed her body for his inspection.

A sheer veil of white silk hid nothing from his gaze. Her breasts seemed suspended in water—large but not awkwardly so—with nipples begging for his kiss.

His eyes descended the curve of her waist to where a belly button would have been if she were mortal.

"You are a Houri?" he asked.

"I am *your* Houri. My name is Qabilah."

If only I could kiss those lips once.

She leaned forward and kissed him with delicious slowness.

"Fulfilling your every desire is what I was created for."

"You have no will of your own?"

"Allah fashioned me to serve you. I have no soul, and my desires are a reflection of yours."

"And my earthly wife?" Reza asked.

"If Allah finds her worthy when she dies, she will join me in serving you. There is no jealousy, no hunger, and no pain in Jannah."

A crystal glass filled with wine appeared in her hand. She offered it to him and he took it. The fragrance filled his nostrils with their nectar. He put the glass to his lips and took the first sip of wine he'd ever tasted.

"It will not intoxicate you like earthly wine," Qabilah said.

He drained the glass and his mind cleared.

I'm actually here.

"Come to your palace." She took his hand and led him across a meadow of poppies. When they topped the hill, a golden building with pearl-encrusted towers came into view. The stable held white horses and camels.

"It's just as I imagined."

"Of course it is," she replied, leading him along a path toward his eternal home. "Allah knows your every dream and desire. He created me, this palace, and the landscape based on your own dreams."

They approached a towering archway constructed from every type of machine gun ever produced. The scent of oil and gunpowder filled the air with pleasant memories of his past life.

He removed a Ceska Zbrojovka Scorpion EV03 from the archway and ran his hands over its surface.

Truly, this is paradise.

Inside the courtyard, at the center of the garden, sat a Zulfiqar MBT tank—also his favorite. Its surface gleamed liquid in the sun.

He followed Qabilah through the main entryway of the palace. The lithe muscles of her back swayed, while her naked buttocks tensed and relaxed in time with her steps.

The only naked woman he'd seen before this was his wife, and only in the darkness of their bedroom. A twinge of shame interrupted his lustful thoughts.

Qabilah stopped and turned. "There's no need to hide your natural urges here," she said. "I realize it's difficult abandoning a lifetime of discipline, but those rules applied only to the physical world. Now that you have proven yourself worthy, I am your reward."

She pressed her body against his and kissed him. His penis hardened, and he pulled away in embarrassment, but she turned and rubbed her buttocks against him. His muscles tensed in response, and a deep moan escaped his chest.

Qabilah guided him through the entryway and into a dazzling room the size of a gymnasium. A circular pool served as the focal point, with dozens of naked women swimming or lounging along the edge. Sunlight filtered through a glass dome crisscrossed by a trellis of grape vines. Each Houri was as stunning in her own unique way as Qabilah, and every one of them greeted him with a shy glance from their gazelle-like dark eyes.

"These are your personal Houris. We are seventy-two in all. Unlike a mortal woman, you cannot offend us with any fantasy. Your desire is our desire."

His heart pounding in his ears seemed oddly physical for such a place, but how could one feel pleasure without a body?

Qabilah led him toward an enormous bed beneath a translucent dome of glowing quartz, and the other Houris joined them. They removed every bit of his clothing. Those nearest stroked his manhood with silken fingers.

Qabilah slithered onto the silken sheets and opened her veil. Then she pulled him on top of her. She whispered into his ear, "Anything you desire, my love."

She did things he'd hardly realized he wanted—using lips, tongue, and breasts to please him in ways both exotic and pure.

After reaching climax, he rolled onto his back, his body tingling.

The next Houri mounted him.

How is it possible?

And so it continued with each until the day became night. When he'd enjoyed the final girl, he swam in the pool alongside them. They washed his body, his hair, and fed him fruits from the garden. He vibrated with a strange energy.

If only the unbelievers knew the truth.

After the bath and meal, Qabilah helped him dress in a robe embroidered in golden thread, silk slippers, and an ivory turban.

Then she brought him to the garden.

An elderly man with a pale beard and black clothing sat cross-legged at the edge of a pond. Next to him stood a young boy. He wore a simple blue robe and a turban of red, gold, and white, with wildflowers tucked into the right side. The boy's head was bowed, obscuring his face.

Qabilah turned and left.

"Not many would kill their brother and grandparents," the old man said.

Reza tensed. "The Prophet Muhammad said, 'If a Muslim discards his religion, kill him.' "

The old man gazed at him with intelligent dark eyes. "That is correct, I spoke those words."

Reza fell to his knees and bowed before him. "My prophet."

"Bow to none but Allah," Muhammad said, and gestured toward the youth beside him.

The boy raised his head, eyes shimmering with the brilliance of a thousand suns.

Reza prostrated before Allah. "My Lord, guide me on the path of righteousness."

Allah rose and led them to the battlements. Below, a river wound its way through the valley between the two mountains. The boy waved a hand, and the valley floor split into a chasm. Plumes of smoke poured from within. A vast horde of tormented souls cried out as the flames consumed them.

Allah spoke. "Those who reject faith, and die rejecting—on them is my curse, and the curse of angels, and of all mankind. They will abide therein. Their penalty will not be lightened, nor will they receive respite."

Was this the fate of Ahmad and his grandparents?

"Blame not yourself," Muhammad said. "None can force enlightenment on those who refuse Allah's gifts."

The chasm closed, and the wails of the damned were replaced by the songbirds in the garden.

Allah set both hands on Reza's shoulders and gazed into his eyes.

"It is time you learned who you are."

*   *   *

Reza jerked upright, opened his eyes, and gasped for breath.

The squad's medic shouted, "By Allah, the colonel lives!"

The squad rushed to his side.

Eventually, his breathing slowed. With the help of the nearest soldier, he got to his feet. Under the bandages, the knife wound burned. The bodies of his brother and grandparents lay on the ground next to their mutilated car.

The medic placed a stethoscope against his chest and listened. Then he flashed a penlight into each eye. "Colonel, can you tell me your name?"

Reza looked at the medic, then at the worried faces of his soldiers.

"My name is . . . Mahdi," he said. "I've returned from Jannah to tell you that the Day of Judgment is close upon us."

The soldiers stood in stunned silence. Then one of them raised his rifle into the air and shouted. "The Mahdi has risen!"

One by one, the rest of the soldiers raised their guns and proclaimed his name.

"Mahdi, Mahdi, Mahdi!"

Chapter 13

Theon sat slumped at a table in the Supreme Court's towering cathedral to knowledge—its law library.

He gazed at the front page of the *New York Times* without moving a muscle. The headline read: "Massacre at Iranian Border." A photograph showed a gruesome field of wrecked cars and dead bodies—mostly elderly. Iran's government had released the image to the AP themselves—a message to the world and their own people.

Upon hearing the news, he had stumbled to the bathroom and thrown up.

I must rescue humanity from this beast.

A hundred of the most influential Imams across the globe had issued a joint fatwa calling for his death. A million-dollar bounty had been placed on his head. With their usual twisted logic, they blamed him for the slaughter and promised more if the Immortality Contract was not withdrawn.

It was the age-old tactic—a game of chicken the theocrats usually won.

Not this time.

The door banged, and Helena marched into the room. She dumped an armful of newspapers on the table and glared.

"Riots in Indonesia, violence in the streets of Rome, Buddhist monks setting themselves on fire in protest, and hundreds of attacks against university science departments."

"We might as well confront this now as later," he said. "It only takes one zealot to ignite Armageddon, and the opportunities will only increase as technology advances."

"The president was right about one thing," Helena replied. "You've created chaos."

He stood and rounded the table. "You're wrong. It may be messy at the start, but I'm going to set the world free."

"Who's deluding themselves now?"

He remained silent. They'd already had this argument. What more was there to say?

"Do you remember when we first met?" she asked.

"It was in Professor Kilnear's molecular genetics class, wasn't it? What a piece of work he was."

She nodded. "Kilnear enjoyed torturing me because I was so shy—and a woman."

"By the end of those four years you were one of the toughest, most self-confident people I've ever met."

"I have you to thank for that," she said.

"What do you mean?"

"Don't you remember that day halfway through the semester, when Kilnear singled me out for ridicule?"

"He did that to lots of people, but I don't recall it happening to you."

"I confused metaphase and anaphase in the order of mitosis, and he made a point of reading my answer out loud to the class." She paused and raised an eyebrow. "Everyone laughed, except you."

"That guy was a real ass."

"I felt more alone than I ever had in my entire life. Out of my depth, humiliated, defeated." She lowered her gaze, as if reliving the emotions. "I waited for class to end so I could catch the first train home."

"You were going to quit MIT because of a rude professor?"

"Sitting there, I planned everything. I'd pack my suitcase, go straight to the train station, and go home. I'd take a job as a grade-school teacher, marry, have kids, et cetera. I literally set a course for the rest of my life in that chair." Her eyes rose to his. "But when class ended, you passed me on your way out and said, 'Don't worry, you'll be a great scientist someday, but he'll always be a bald dwarf asshole.' "

"No shit?" He scratched his head. "I admit it sounds like me."

Helena's mouth fell open. "How can you not remember? You changed my life with those words. I replayed them in my mind every time someone insinuated a woman couldn't handle a career beyond teaching."

"I'm sorry, I just don't recall."

"That was the moment I fell in love with you!"

Theon placed a hand on the table to steady himself.

This can't be.

When they met, her beauty had intimidated him. She'd graduated near the top of her class at Bryn Mawr and made it to MIT on a full scholarship. He'd considered asking her out, but rejected it as ridiculous. She was clearly out of his league.

"Why didn't you tell me?"

"Each time I tried, I lost my nerve. Then Taslima transferred to the school, and you started dating her. I realized I'd missed my chance and settled for friendship. When people ask me why I didn't marry, I say I never met the right person, but that's a lie."

Have I known all along? Is that why I chose her to save first?

Helena rose onto her toes and kissed him for the second time. Her lips released a flood of forgotten emotions. His arms enfolded her, and she responded in kind.

After a luxuriant moment, she whispered, "Let's walk away from this mess and start our lives over."

He jerked back from her. "I owe this to Taslima."

"I knew her for as long as you—she was my best friend—and I'm certain she wouldn't have wanted this."

The words pierced his heart.

He flung a newspaper across the room. "Should I let this scourge rule humanity?"

"It's not your decision. You can't force people to think!"

"It's their own choice to sign my contract!"

Helena said nothing for a long moment. Then she turned and walked to the door.

"Where are you going?"

She grasped the handle and stopped. "You won't see me again until you abandon this madness."

She opened the oak door, walked through, and slammed it shut.

Not everyone has the stomach for revolution.

* * *

Theon entered the courtroom from the side door.

The looks of admiration had transformed to disapproval.

How can they blame me for the actions of madmen?

Theon took his seat, his jaw clamped tight.

Cyril strolled through the main entrance with the bounce back in his step. A few in the audience applauded. The preacher waved, a jovial smile parting his generous jowls.

When the celebrated evangelist neared his seat, the court bailiff deserted his post and shook Cyril's hand. "My wife and I watch your show every Sunday. We tithe the full ten percent and use your holy anointed oil before bed."

"Thank you, Officer . . ." Cyril frowned. "I'm sorry, but I've forgotten your name."

"Harlan Kerns, sir."

Cyril placed his right hand on Harlan's forehead. The bailiff entwined his hands before his chest.

"Jesus, bless this poor sinner and welcome him into your eternal kingdom."

When Cyril removed his magic hand, Harlan's face glowed joyously. "God bless you, Reverend, for standing up to this evil." Harlan's eyes narrowed as he glanced at Theon.

He doesn't realize he's being played for a fool.

Was the reverend himself aware of it?

One way or the other, I'm going to find out.

Cyril smiled at Harlan. "With God on our side, how can we fail?"

The chief justice walked through the gap in the curtain alongside his wife, Ruth. They held hands as the judge escorted her to an empty seat at the front of the audience. Dark circles ringed the judge's eyes.

Ruth took her seat. The judge kissed her hand and climbed to his perch.

After the customary standing and sitting ritual, the judge turned to him. "Doctor Torano, have recent world events changed your mind on pursuing this?"

"If anything, this display of murderous coercion on behalf of religion strengthens my resolve."

The judge frowned. "Even knowing your Immortality Contract will likely cause more people to die?"

Theon's hands gripped the edge of the desk until his knuckles ached. "When Ayatollah Khomeini declared a fatwa calling for Salmon Rushdie's assassination, John le Carré blamed Rushdie for writing *The Satanic Verses* and bringing it on himself. It seemed that freedom of speech and artistic expression ends at the sacred shores of superstition."

"Just because it's legal, doesn't make it right," the judge said.

"If people threatened to riot and kill over a book claiming unicorns don't exist, should unicorn-doubting books be banned?" Theon asked. "Or someone who said he'd shoot anyone who claimed the Earth was round instead of flat? Why give killers the power of deciding what the rest of us can or cannot say simply because they label it religion?"

"We're talking about people's lives," the judge said sharply.

"Yes, we are," Theon said. "Those people in Iran were only the latest victims of the religious delusions that killed my wife and daughter. This is exactly why my Immortality Contract is necessary!"

The judge's face had turned an angry shade of red. "You can't lump every religion in the same—"

The judge stopped in mid-sentence, closed his eyes, and took several breaths. After a moment, he opened them and resumed his even tone. "It's not my place to debate you, Professor Torano. My job is to arbitrate the agreement struck between you and the other two branches of our government."

The judge faced Cyril. "Are you ready to present your case, Reverend?"

"I am, Your Honor." Cyril rose and walked to the podium. He placed a sheaf of typed pages on the angled top, and then smoothed his ivory jacket.

Theon's hands trembled with the fury.

Calm down. Don't let them get to you.

Cyril cleared his throat. "Your Honor, members of the audience, and those of you watching on television across this magnificent planet the Lord has blessed us with—I am not here to argue against Doctor Torano's monumental achievement. This is undeniably one of the great moments in human history, and I congratulate him."

Breathe, relax. This will be easy if I control my emotions.

"But can any scientific discovery compete with God's creation? Does it equal the clouds, the oceans, or the miracle of life itself?"

Cyril spread his arms wide. "Theon asks for proof. It doesn't take scientific instruments to sense the love of the Creator within your heart. I remember the first time I experienced God's presence—"

"Reverend," the judge interrupted, "this is not a sermon, and a feeling in your heart is not admissible evidence in a courtroom."

A few chuckles sounded from the audience.

Cyril shuffled his notes. "Yes, of course, Your Honor. Er . . . um . . ." He stopped on one page and looked up. "As my first witness, I call the eminent historian and Doctor of Theology, Professor Philip Clayborn."

A diminutive man in his early fifties rose from the chairs behind Cyril and scampered to the witness stand. His close-set eyes resembled a possum, and his coke-bottle glasses only accentuated this.

Bailiff Harlan approached with the official court Bible, and the professor placed his hand on it.

"Do you solemnly swear—"

"Your Honor, I object to using a Bible to swear in witnesses," Theon said. "The phrase 'so help me God,' is an assumption that such a being is an established fact, which is exactly what's in question here."

Harlan's eyes bored into him with undisguised hatred.

"As much as I hate to admit it, you do have a point," the chief justice said.

Cyril spluttered indignantly. "The use of a Bible in court is—"

"Nothing but tradition," the judge said.

"Having a witness swear on a book they hold sacred makes it far more likely they will tell the truth."

The chief justice sighed. "Reverend, are you saying you don't trust your own witness without an oath sworn on the Bible?"

"Well, no, I'm not saying that."

"Then, let's proceed, shall we?"

Cyril took a deep breath and resumed his air of confident command. "Professor Clayborn, as an eminent biblical scholar, could you give us your expert opinion of the Bible?"

"My conclusion after a lifetime of study is that the Bible is unparalleled in its historical accuracy. What truly sets it apart from other historical records, however, are its uncanny predictions of the future, the most famous of which is the birth and resurrection of Jesus Christ. Such precognition would be impossible for a human author."

I guess he hasn't read the horoscope page lately.

"So your conclusion is that the Bible itself is evidence of God?"

"That is correct."

"How do you know the Bible's account of Jesus is accurate?" Cyril asked.

"First, we have not one, but four witnesses. One person might fabricate or hallucinate an event, but four is statistically improbable."

"And how consistent are these testimonies?" Cyril asked.

"The accounts agree on the major points, with slight variations of details, which is what we see in eyewitness accounts even today."

"Is it possible that four people might concoct such a tale together?"

The professor leaned forward, his eyes sparkling. "That's where the manner of death of these witnesses comes into play. All twelve of the apostles chose a painful death rather than recanting their witness of the resurrection. Would anyone die for something they knew was a lie?"

Cyril approached the witness. "In your expert opinion, does God exist?"

"Absolutely," the professor said. "God not only exists, but is thoroughly documented in extraordinary detail in that book sitting right there." The professor pointed to the court Bible. "There is more evidence for the existence of God than for any human historical figure before the modern age."

Reverend Doberson turned to the cameras with a theatrical flourish. "I would never dispute a point of mathematics with Doctor Torano. I ask him to show the same humility and admit Professor Clayborn's knowledge of this subject far surpasses his own."

Ah, yes, the argument from false authority. So often the refuge of those lacking evidence.

Cyril took his seat.

"Doctor Torano, do you wish to cross-examine the witness?" the chief justice asked.

"I will try, despite my paucity of knowledge in comparison to this acknowledged expert." He stood and approached the witness. "Professor Clayborn, in your expert opinion, is Zeus real?"

"He is not," the professor said.

"How about Shiva, Ganesh, Vishnu, or the million other Hindu gods that a billion people on the planet believe exist?"

"Respectfully, I must say they are all man-made myths."

"And the gods predating Christianity that performed similar miracles to Jesus, including turning water into wine, rising from the dead, healing the sick, and so on. Are any of these gods real?"

"In my expert opinion, they are not."

"I see. And in your *expert opinion*, are there any gods, other than the Christian god, that are real?"

Professor Clayborn glanced at the television cameras. Telling two-thirds of the planet that their gods were imaginary was rude, but the little man leaned toward the microphone and bravely delivered the bad news. "Respectfully, I must say there is only one true God, and that is the Christian one."

"What a relief!" Theon exclaimed. "Here I thought I was up against thousands of gods, and this one expert has disproved 99.99 percent of them in less than a minute. At this pace, I should have this last holdout taken care of in no time at all."

Justice Dunn chuckled, then covered his mouth and coughed.

Theon turned to the witness. "Since we agree that humans have a boundless propensity for conjuring gods by the thousands, let's examine this proposed lone exception. Since you presented the New Testament as your primary proof of God, I'll set aside talking snakes, global floods, people being swallowed by whales, six-hundred-year-old men, the sun stopping in the sky, ripped-out ribs turning into people, and all the rest from the Old Testament. Let's concentrate instead on the most central fact of Christian belief you cite as your evidence—the resurrection of Jesus."

Professor Clayborn nodded stiffly.

"You claim the apostles chose death rather than recanting the story of Christ's resurrection?"

"That's right."

"I assume your information comes from Roman records of the trials of these men?"

"There's no written account," the professor admitted, "but oral histories can be quite accurate."

"Like the Iliad and the Odyssey?"

"Aspects of the Trojan War are no doubt historical," the professor said, "but much of that story has obviously been mythicized."

"Why *obviously*?"

"Well, . . . I mean . . . this isn't a serious question, is it? Surely you're not arguing that Poseidon, Zeus, and Aphrodite are real?"

"You do realize that many people once believed these gods were real?"

"I suppose that's true," the professor said.

"If those believers were alive today, they might point to Homer's account as evidence of their gods in the same way you're pointing to the oral traditions of the apostles."

"Not all traditions are equally reliable," the professor said.

"On what basis do you dismiss the tales of the Greek gods in the Iliad and the Odyssey, or the story of the war god Mars impregnating the vestal virgin Alba Longa with the twins Romulus and Remus, or Zeus fathering Hercules, or any of the dozens of other oral traditions involving a god planting his divine seed in a mortal woman?"

"I . . . I guess I can't prove—"

"So there's no more evidence for the deaths of the apostles than for the stories told of Hercules?"

"Not of the apostle's deaths, but the gospels themselves are eyewitness accounts."

"Ah, yes, the gospels," Theon said. "I'm assuming these four are the only first-hand accounts?"

"There are many others," the professor said with an air of authority. "The Gospel of Thomas, Marcion, Basilides, James, Mary, Philip. There might have been as many as forty or more—each with their own followers."

"And these other gospels agree on the main points with the four biblical accounts?"

"They disagree on everything from the divinity of Jesus, his childhood, his death, and even his actual existence in physical form." The professor glanced at the frowning Cyril. "But Saint Athanasius banned such false gospels in 367 AD."

Theon walked to the witness stand and crossed his arms. "And how do you know the four gospels in the Bible are the true accounts and not one of those forty others?"

"Because learned men at the Council of Nicaea determined which gospels were true and which were forgeries."

"How could they know which were true after three hundred years had passed?"

"With the Holy Spirit's guidance."

Theon shook his head at that bit of circular logic, but forged onward. "And what happened to the adherents of these other gospels?"

"The church punished them for blasphemy and destroyed their heretical texts."

"So the argument was settled by force?"

The professor shrugged. "Sometimes reason is not enough."

"On that point, we definitely agree," Theon said.

A few chuckles rippled through the gallery, but a sharp glance from the judge restored the silence.

"Professor Clayborn, what language were these four victorious gospels written in?"

"As far as we can tell, the originals were written in Greek—even quoting verbatim the Greek translation of the Old Testament, which is called the Septuagint."

"Wouldn't the apostles, many of them simple fishermen, read and write in their native tongues, if they were literate at all?"

"It's possible they dictated their accounts to someone who recorded them in Greek."

"Interesting," Theon said. "But I assume these oral testimonies were at least signed by the witness?"

"Well, no," the professor said. "The manuscripts were not signed or dated." The professor shoved his eyeglasses up the slope of his sweaty nose with a nervous gesture. "Church tradition later assigned them to Matthew, Mark, Luke, and John, but the documents themselves never state who the author is of any of them."

"So they are essentially anonymous accounts?"

"Who else but an apostle could have written them?" the professor asked.

"Who else, indeed." Theon glanced at his notes again. "Do we know which of these anonymous stories came first?"

"Mark, the shortest gospel, must have been written first for many reasons, and the others quote passages from Mark verbatim."

"Doesn't it seem odd that an eyewitness would repeat passages word-for-word from someone else's account written in a different language?"

The professor frowned but said nothing.

"Professor Clayborn, at the time of Jesus' death, the gospel of Matthew reports a three-hour darkness falling across the land, an earthquake so intense that it splits the stone entrance to the sacred temple of the Jews, and the long-dead saints rising out of their tombs and walking the streets of Jerusalem like a zombie apocalypse movie."

"It was a display of the power of God," the professor said.

Theon raised an eyebrow. "Yet, none of the chroniclers of the time period mention this miraculous event. Even Mark, Luke, and John skip this awesome display of God's power."

A flush spread up the professor's neck, but he remained silent.

"Might these later Gospel writers have plagiarized Mark's much shorter account and decided to spice things up a bit by adding the virgin birth, zombie saints wandering Jerusalem, and the encounters with Jesus after the tomb is found empty?"

"I'm certain the Gospels are independent—and accurate—accounts of all the events they portray."

"But you're equally certain the stories of Ganesh—also the son of a god, also raised from the dead, also reported to have done miracles—are not true? Or Osiris, or Attis, or any of the other dying and resurrected gods?"

"None of those represent documented historical figures."

The man is so predictable.

"A good point," Theon said. "The Gospels state that Jesus was famed far and wide, which is understandable for someone who did all those magic tricks."

"Miracles," corrected the professor.

"I suppose with someone this famous, the many writers and historians of the time mentioned Jesus, his resurrection, and so-called miracles?"

"Not during Jesus' life, but one of the most famous historians of all—Titus Flavius Josephus—writes a full paragraph confirming his miracles, resurrection, and specifically states he was the Messiah."

From his chair, Cyril crossed his arms and beamed.

He actually thinks he's won.

"Josephus was born in Jerusalem a few years after Jesus died, was he not?" Theon asked.

"That's correct," the professor said, "but he must have known people who'd seen the events first-hand."

"So you're claiming that Josephus, a messianic Jew his entire life, a man who wrote volumes about major and minor historical figures of his time, recorded only one paragraph describing the coming of the Messiah in his own hometown?"

Silence.

"Professor Clayborn, are you aware that most historians conclude that this brief paragraph is largely a forgery, since no one mentions it until two hundred and forty years after Josephus penned his history, of which we have no original?"

"My expert assessment is that the passage is genuine."

"And who was it that *discovered* this lone mention of Christ?"

"Church historian Eusebius first mentions it in 324 AD."

"And all later copies of this book trace back to the manuscript Eusebius used?"

"That is correct."

"I guess it would be awkward if the most famous Jewish historian of the time didn't mention Jesus in his comprehensive history of the Jews."

Cyril surged to his feet. "Your Honor, the witness already delivered his expert opinion on this matter."

"Objection sustained," the judge said. "Asked and answered. Move on."

Theon's shoulders slumped. "I guess I'll just have to take this expert's word for it, then."

Cyril smirked.

Theon's eyes widened, and he looked up as if he had just received his own divine revelation. "Your Honor, something just occurred to me! Even if we accept that Josephus wrote that paragraph, his account is still second-hand information, and therefore not admissible as evidence."

The judge sighed. "It only now occurred to you?"

"My mind isn't as sharp as it once was."

"I doubt that," the judge said, "but I agree that Josephus's account is inadmissible on those grounds."

Cyril's mouth fell open.

"I likewise move that the four Gospels be disqualified," Theon said.

Cyril jumped to his feet. "On what grounds?"

"On the same grounds you objected to my fruit fly evidence a few days ago. You pointed out that someone could have forged my twelve notarized affidavits, or that the miracle of their long lives might have been faked to fool the witnesses. Both objections apply even more so here."

"This is outrageous!" Cyril exclaimed. "The Bible is the most accurate record of history in the history of, well, history!"

"By your own words," the judge said, "any evidence not in accordance with modern legal standards is inadmissible."

"Scientific logic itself proves God's existence," Cyril said. "The Law of Conservation of Energy states that something can't come from nothing. Which means someone created it. That someone must be God."

"If something cannot come from nothing," Theon said, "who created the something you call God?"

"God exists outside the laws of physics without beginning or end."

"So you say," Theon said. "Now prove it."

"It seems Doctor Torano would be unsatisfied with any evidence in the Bible or anywhere else."

"That isn't true, Cyril. If the Bible predicted the number and size of the moons orbiting Saturn, or explained the composition of atoms, or listed Pi to a hundred decimal points—I'd take that as highly convincing evidence."

"Your Honor, my entire case rests on the Bible. It is considered the ultimate standard of truth by billions of people. Presidents and supreme court justices alike place their hands on the Bible when swearing their oaths of office. Isn't that proof of its reliability?"

"Reverend Doberson," the chief justice said, "I disqualified Doctor Torano's signed and notarized affidavits for the same reason I must disqualify your significantly older, unsigned testimonies that were written at a time your own witness admits forgery was commonplace. You cannot demand one standard from Doctor Torano and expect another for yourself."

"But, Your Honor, I . . ." Cyril trailed off, his face stunned.

The judge turned to the cameras. "Let me be absolutely clear. I am not ruling that the Christian god, or any other god, does not exist. I can only rule on the evidence presented. Therefore, I have no choice but to rule this testimony inadmissible."

The judge brought his gavel down with a crack.

Cyril slumped into his chair, defeated.

Triumph surged through every nerve of Theon's body.

I've done it. I've won.

"Reverend Doberson, do you have any other witnesses to call?"

"God does exist," he whispered.

"That may be," the judge said. "The question is not one of truth, but of proof by the legal standards of a court."

Cyril gazed toward the ceiling.

Is he expecting God to bail him out?

What a story it would make if a burning bush appeared on the witness stand, or Jesus beamed down and performed a few miracles with most of the world watching.

Cyril clasped his hands together, closed his eyes, and seemed to pray for a miracle.

Surprise, surprise—nothing happened. Not even a bolt of lightning or a potato chip with Jesus' face on it.

"Reverend, if you have no further evidence to present—"

"Wait!" shouted Cyril's assistant. She rushed toward the evangelist and shoved her smartphone into his hand.

Cyril eyes darted back and forth across the screen.

"I will ask one final time," the judge said. "Do you have any further evidence?"

Cyril glanced at the judge, astonishment transforming his face. Then he stood. "I call Theon Torano's granddaughter, Alma Roberts, to testify."

Chapter 14

Cyril's words hit Theon in the gut.

What possible evidence could Alma present?

A tall Jesuit monk led Alma and a young man into the courtroom.

The monk's scarred face resembled a retired boxer or soldier more than a man of the cloth. He might have been chiseled from a block of ice for all the emotion he displayed.

Alma wore a homemade white dress, with hair piled on top of her head in neatly arranged braids. Not a touch of makeup marred the harmony of her face. A simple wooden cross hung from her neck.

It's actually her.

The monk and the young man took seats at the front of the audience as Cyril ushered his witness to the stand.

Theon stood, his fists clenched. "Is this a sick joke? My granddaughter is mentally ill."

Cyril faced the judge. "I would remind Doctor Torano it was he, not I, that presented your wife as evidence in this trial."

"The reverend makes a good point," the judge said, "but I hope this witness is not mere gamesmanship."

"I'm confident this girl will provide the firsthand evidence Doctor Torano has demanded."

Cyril's assistant handed him a paper with a list of bullet points.

Alma seated herself in the witness stand, and folded her hands in her lap.

"Please state your name for the record," Cyril said.

"My name is Alma Roberts, though I will be Alma Carlson in a week, when I'm married." Alma smiled at the tall young man seated beside the monk.

"Were you raised in a religious family, Alma?" Cyril asked.

"I suppose you'd say I was a third-generation atheist."

"So you never read the stories of the Bible growing up?"

"I read a few in comparative religion class, but I viewed them as myths no different than the tales of the Greek and Roman gods."

"And now?"

"Now I know the Bible is the word of the Lord."

Theon jumped to his feet. "This is not evidence of God, only the exploitation of a troubled young girl." He pointed at Cyril. "How dare you target someone so vulnerable for your brainwashing!"

"This is the first time I've met this girl," Cyril said. "If you will let me continue, her testimony will speak for itself."

"Let's limit the outbursts to valid legal objections, shall we?" the judge said.

Theon sat, his hands trembling.

"What was your profession before a month ago?" Cyril asked in a gentle tone.

"I was a prostitute and a heroine addict," Alma said, without the slightest hesitation or shame.

"Did your grandfather try saving you from your life of sin and addiction?"

"He did his best. Treatment programs, mental institutions, and everything the doctors suggested." She faced Theon with a look of apology. "I'm sorry for the things I said to you, Grandpa. None of it was your fault."

Theon's heart ached.

I abandoned her.

"And now?" Cyril asked.

"I've been liberated from my drug addiction, and even from the nightmares of my mother and grandmother's deaths. For the first time, I'm at peace."

"Can you tell us how such a miraculous change occurred?"

Alma stared at a point far above the audience. "On the day my grandfather announced his discovery, I committed suicide by overdosing on heroine. I thought death was an empty void that would end my suffering." She fell silent, her chest rising and falling like the sporadic rhythm of a butterfly in flight. "The doctors tried saving me with their machines and drugs—but they failed."

"You died?"

"The doctors declared me dead at 2:17 in the morning."

"And what did you experience during that time?" Cyril asked.

Alma's face opened like a flower sensing the sun. "I'd never felt such warmth. It was more powerful than any drug. God appeared to me, and I absorbed His presence, His love, and His healing Grace. My mother and grandmother were there as well." Alma's eyes expanded in wonder.

Even the reporters stopped taking notes.

"I wanted to stay with them, but God returned me to this world as a beacon to those in darkness."

Tears traced their way down Theon's face. He'd experienced the evils of belief, but here was the opposite.

"Miracle is the term the doctors used," Alma said. "I thought life was nothing but a collection of atoms with no greater purpose or meaning. I though death was the end. How wrong I was."

"Did your vision continue after your near-death experience?"

Alma's arms pulled inward. "After I returned to the world of the living, I saw demons. They looked as real as everyone sitting in this courtroom. Sometimes they spoke to me, and I feared that I had suffered brain damage."

"What changed your mind?"

"My baptism. As the water claimed me, the world fractured into thousands of slivers of reality. I realized my perceptions were the illusions—constructed from my brain's infinitesimal vantage point."

My poor tortured Alma. Is it any wonder that reality became too much for you?

"In that moment, I knew God was more real than anything I'd ever seen, heard, smelled, tasted, or touched. I surrendered myself to God's love—and was born again."

Bailiff Harlan gripped the cross around his own neck, and his lips moved silently.

"When I emerged from the water," Alma said, "the demons vanished."

Alma looked at the monk sitting beside the boy. "When I lay beneath the waters, the Lord said he was sending me a guide. An hour later, Vadic found me."

The strange giant inclined his head.

"Do you still see these demons?" Cyril asked.

"Sometimes," Alma said. "But I also see angels and the souls of the dead. They come with messages for their loved ones, or to counsel me."

Theon's tears flowed openly.

How could I have let you come to this, my dear Alma?

"I'm sorry to ask such a sensitive question," Cyril said, "but with your former profession as a . . . prostitute . . . were you tested for STDs?"

Theon slammed his fist against the table. "What possible bearing could this have?"

"I tend to agree," the judge said.

"I don't mind answering," Alma said.

"The reason for this question will become obvious in a few moments," Cyril assured the judge.

The chief justice hesitated, but nodded to Alma. "Okay, you may answer."

"When I awoke in the hospital after my failed suicide, the nurse asked to test for AIDs and a variety of other things. I was in such a fog of exhaustion after my ordeal that I gave permission and forgot about it. When David asked me to marry him, I called the hospital." Alma looked at her fiancé. "They told me I have no diseases they can detect. My guess is that God cleansed my body after my death and rebirth."

Cyril consulted the paper in his hand. "You have one other medical condition, do you not?"

"Yes, I do." She turned to Theon with a soft smile. "You are to be a great-grandfather."

Sobs wracked Theon as his tortured emotions boiled over.

Alma turned her gaze on the young man sitting next to the strange monk. "That is my husband-to-be. He was willing to sacrifice his own life to save me in my darkest hour. Despite knowing I'm pregnant with an anonymous man's child, he still wants to marry me."

Only the muffled sounds of Theon crying broke the tense stillness of the room.

Undeterred, Cyril began his summation. "The fact that this miracle occurred to Theon's own granddaughter the day after his press conference can be no coincidence. The Lord did what science could not. God healed this girl's addiction, purged her body of disease, and brought her back from the dead."

Cyril pointed at Alma. "Here is your evidence of God's existence, as well as the life beyond this one that awaits us after death."

I have to get control of myself. He's giving the judge enough to save face and rule against me.

The reverend bowed to the cameras, then to the judge. "Your Honor, I rest my case."

The evangelist resumed his seat, and Judge Dunn turned to Theon. "Do you want to question the witness, Doctor Torano?"

Theon walked unsteadily to the stand, wiping his face with a handkerchief.

Alma took his hand in hers. "I'm sorry for what I put you through, Grandpa."

He embraced her. "I love you, Alma."

"I love you too, Grandpa."

Theon eased from Alma's embrace. There were tears in her eyes as well.

Was there any doubt her belief in God had saved her?

Maybe Helena is right, and I should abandon my plan.

Alma brushed a tear from his cheek. "There's something important I need to tell you."

"You can tell me anything."

"The Devil stole God's secret of immortality from the Tree of Life and placed it into Grandma's mind. In human hands, it will annihilate the world. You must destroy the formula for your pill. The Lord sent me here to tell you this."

Her words drove a spike through his mind.

My poor, innocent child. What have they done to your mind?

"Should we take a recess, Doctor Torano?" the judge asked.

Theon gazed at the silent audience. Billions more watched across the globe.

"I have only one question for the witness," he said. "Alma, would you take my drug, even if I dropped the Immortality Contract?"

She shook her head without hesitation. "No."

"Why not?"

"Because I've surrendered my life to the Lord. He alone commands life and death, and I look forward to the time I can join him in Heaven."

"Thank you for your honesty, Alma."

"You may step down from the stand," the judge said.

Alma walked across the floor and took her place beside David. He kissed her forehead and then held her hand.

Cyril rose and addressed the judge. "Since Doctor Torano has not contested the testimony of my witness, I assert that I have proven my claim and that this trial is at an end."

Theon stared at the floor.

"Doctor Torano, since you offer no rebuttal, I take it you accept the Reverend's proof of God's existence?"

Theon looked at Alma, at the judge, and finally at Cyril. His eyes narrowed to slits.

It's time someone pulled the curtain aside.

Theon squared his shoulders and faced the audience. "I could call experts to testify to the many other explanations for my granddaughter's near-death visions. Hallucinations due to brain damage, oxygen deprivation within the dying mind, and others. I might point out that Muslims, Hindus, and alien abductees have just as compelling visions. But I won't make any of these arguments."

The judge leaned forward. "Then you are conceding this case?"

He's hoping I give him a way out.

"Suppose this was a murder case and your only evidence was a witness who had just taken heroin?" Theon asked. "That may be considered evidence, if there was some corroboration by others. As we say in the scientific community: a sample of one is too small for a conclusion."

Cyril took a step forward. "Many have experienced visitations from the Lord. I myself witnessed the Divine Being in the flesh on numerous occasions."

"A second eyewitness might very well seal the matter," Theon said. "Since the reverend offers his own experience as evidence of God, I call him to testify."

Cyril hesitated, and then smiled broadly for the cameras. "I'll gladly offer witness in defense of my Savior!"

The evangelist marched to the stand and settled his generous figure into the chair.

Theon smiled. "In your case, Reverend, I'll drop my previous objection to the customary swearing in procedure."

The judge motioned to the bailiff.

Harlan carried the Bible to his hero as if presenting a precious relic to a king. Cyril placed his left hand atop its leather surface and raised his right.

"Do you solemnly swear that you will tell the truth, the whole truth, and nothing but the truth, so help you God?" Harlan asked.

"I do."

When the bailiff returned to his station, Theon approached the stand and stood with hands interlocked behind his back. "Reverend Doberson, do you believe in a life after this one?"

"I know it for an absolute fact, just as I know I'll be going to Heaven when my time comes."

"And how do you know this?"

"Because God has appeared to me in the flesh."

"So you are an eyewitness like my granddaughter?"

"I am."

"And like her, I assume you don't fear death?"

"I welcome it, which is why I would never sign your Immortality Contract." Cyril glanced at the cameras and frowned. "I might take your pill without the contract, but only if God asked me to delay my reward in Heaven to save more souls from Hell."

"Very noble of you," Theon said. "Earlier, Professor Clayborn claimed that no one would willingly sacrifice their life for a lie. Do you agree with that statement?"

"I . . . suppose so," Cyril said.

Theon smiled, the anger burning through his veins. "How about we put that theory to the test right now?"

Chapter 15

Theon removed a vial from his jacket pocket. "This is a year's supply of my pills, enough to restore you to your prime."

Cyril frowned.

Theon rattled the vial. "I've set no deadline for the world to sign my Immortality Contract. For you, the time limit is two minutes."

"I . . . I don't understand," the evangelist stammered.

"I'll make it crystal clear." Theon pressed the front of his watch and a beep sounded. "In one hundred and twenty seconds, when my watch beeps again, if you have not agreed to the conditions of my Immortality Contract—and declared before the world that you lied about seeing God in person—you will never receive a single one of my pills for as long as your time span on this Earth persists."

"But if the judge rules—"

"This case is over," Theon said. "It ended the moment you exploited my granddaughter's psychosis for your self-serving ends. Those who want my drug will have to agree to my conditions or I will withdraw it forever." He addressed the cameras. "It's time for every person on the planet to choose between science or superstition!"

Cyril loosened his tie as if having trouble breathing.

The audience watched with faces rapt.

"One hundred seconds left, Reverend."

Cyril flung his gaze toward the chief justice. "This is no different from a death threat!"

Judge Dunn raised an eyebrow. "You said you welcome death."

Theon leaned forward. "There's nothing I can threaten you with if you're telling the truth, Reverend. But if you're lying, you have a choice. Either hold firm and die for your lie, or come clean and live." He glanced at his watch. "Eighty seconds to prove you weren't lying when you placed your hand on that Bible."

Cyril's breaths wheezed from his constricted throat. "Can't we discuss this in private?"

"Your testimony must be as public as those you've given every Sunday for decades on your show." Theon studied his watch. "One minute and counting."

Cyril rose out of his chair, but his legs buckled. He fell to his knees with a yelp of pain.

"Forty-eight seconds to choose between religion or science."

Cyril held his hands out before him. "Please, I . . . I have a heart condition. My doctor says my time is limited—"

"Isn't that reason to celebrate?" Theon asked. "You've described the glories of the next world in great detail. I'd think your friends would throw you a party."

"I give people hope. Is that so wrong?"

"Only fifteen seconds left to choose life or death."

Tears covered Cyril's face. "Please, I—"

"Nine . . . eight . . . seven . . . six . . ."

"I don't want to die!"

"Five . . . four . . . three . . ."

Cyril's head slumped forward, and his arms fell limp at his sides. "I agree to your terms."

The alarm sounded.

Cyril jerked. His breaths came in shuddering gasps. Sweat stained his expensive white collar.

Theon silenced the alarm. "Say it again—louder."

Cyril raised his tear-streaked face to his conqueror. "I agree to your terms."

"And God?"

"Please, don't make me—"

"I will only ask one more time. Have you spoken to God?"

Cyril's face contracted in pain, and his hand clamped itself against his chest. After a moment, the spasm passed. "God has never appeared to me, and I have no proof of an afterlife."

"So you lied?" Theon asked.

Cyril's head dropped to his chest. "I lied, and I'm sorry."

"Congratulations," Theon said. "You qualify for my drug." He tossed the container of pills onto the floor.

The former evangelist scrambled on hands and knees for the plastic vial of life. The audience watched in silence as he fumbled with the lid and removed one of the white pills. He held it like a holy relic, and then devoured it. His eyes closed and his body relaxed.

Every witness in the room focused on the pathetic man kneeling in disgrace.

Cyril opened his eyes and wilted from the glares of judgment. Then he sobbed.

A few in the audience jeered, and the chief justice banged his gavel for order.

Then a gunshot echoed through the chamber.

Pain seared through Theon's shoulder. He cried out in agony, and his vision filled with a close-up of floor tiles. A sickly smell of blood flooded his nostrils, and he pressed his left hand against the wound.

The sounds of screams and a panicked stampede filtered through the ringing in his ears.

This wasn't the end I expected.

A red stain spread across the intricate pattern of tiles, moving with lazy grace.

"I order you to lower your weapon, Officer Kerns!" commanded the chief justice.

Theon raised his head with difficulty, the pain knifing through him.

Bailiff Harlan strode forward, his 9mm gun thrust before him. His face squashed in on itself. "You corrupted a blessed man of God!"

Alma stepped in front of Harlan. "I won't let you kill him."

"No, Alma," Theon said. "I can't let you do this."

But she stood her ground. "You will have to shoot me first."

"Move aside!" the bailiff shouted above the tumult as the last of the spectators dashed out the exits. "I will shoot anyone that tries stopping me from killing this evil man!"

David walked to Alma and stood beside her. Justice Dunn half-crouched behind his desk with a look of panicked outrage. Beside him was Ruth. Instead of fleeing, she'd run to the man she loved.

"Only God can judge him," Alma said.

Theon clawed across the floor, gritting his teeth against the agony.

I must give him a clear shot.

Harlan pistol-whipped David across his temple, and the boy crumpled into a heap. Then Harlan shoved Alma aside. She tripped over David, and her head hit the ground hard.

She went still.

"No!" Theon shouted.

Harlan aimed the gun at his forehead.

Cyril jumped in front of Harlan. "Thou shalt not kill!"

"You said he was the Antichrist!"

"I was mistaken—about so many things."

"I sent you money that could have put my son through college!"

Theon kept dragging his body forward, until Harlan's tormented face came into view.

"I'll repay every cent," Cyril said. "Give me the gun, and let's—"

"You sold your soul to the Devil."

"Think of your family—"

"I'm doing this for them!" Harlan pressed the barrel of his gun into the center of Cyril's wide chest. "Since your life is so important to you, I'll offer it to you in exchange for his."

"I've done things I'm not proud of, but I will not be an accomplice to murder."

Harlan's finger tightened on the trigger.

Cyril opened his arms wide and tilted his head back. "Lord, forgive my sins. I place my soul in your hands."

"Drop the gun!" commanded a voice from the main entrance.

Harlan jerked his head to the side, toward a group of police officers. Their semi-automatic rifles were pointed directly at him.

"Drop it, or we'll—"

Harlan pulled the trigger, and the reverend collapsed.

A dozen bullets tore through Harlan in a horizontal rainstorm of lead. By the time his body hit the floor, he was dead.

The Supreme Court police rushed into the room and formed a defensive perimeter. Walkie-talkies blared.

David rose and stumbled toward Alma, blood streaking the side of his face.

"She's unconscious, but breathing," the monk said.

The judge and Ruth rushed to Theon's side.

"Take me to him," Theon said.

They helped him to his feet. Blood soaked his right sleeve, but the wound wasn't life-threatening. When he reached Cyril, he knelt beside him.

A police officer was attempting to slow the bleeding pumping out the reverend's chest with each weakening heartbeat.

"Why sacrifice your life for me?" Theon asked.

Cyril coughed up bloody foam. "By saving you, I've saved millions, isn't that right?"

Theon took the evangelist's hand in his own. "That's right. You'll be remembered as a hero."

Cyril's lips moved, but the blood bubbling from his flooded lungs subsumed his words. In another instant, the hand went limp. Cyril's head rolled to the side, his blue eyes staring at nothing.

Theon gently closed the eyelids of the man he'd set out to destroy.

"I killed him," he said.

The chief justice placed a hand on his shoulder. "You gave him a chance to redeem himself."

A muffled explosion sounded in the distance, and a slight tremor set the chandeliers swaying.

Everyone froze, listening.

"Code one," said a voice through every officer's walkie-talkie.

"Everyone take cover!" shouted the commanding officer.

A second explosion shook the room. Plaster and concrete rained down.

More explosions sounded one after the other, like a giant marching toward them. The building vibrated, and parts of the sculpted figures above crumbled. Hammurabi's head crashed onto the empty benches and exploded into shrapnel.

Then silence.

"What was that?" Theon asked. "A car bomb outside the building?"

Theon's shoulder throbbed as he struggled to regain his feet. The monk lifted Alma in his arms and followed David through the debris toward him.

Above, the blinking red lights of the cameras glowed demonically.

The world is still watching.

A faint buzzing reached them. It sounded like a swarm of bees heading toward the courtroom.

The first of the drones appeared in the entryway and launched forward. They were off-the-shelf models costing a few thousand dollars a piece. Strapped beneath each were four sticks of dynamite.

"Run!" the commanding officer shouted, and opened fire with his assault rifle. The first two drones exploded in midair. The shock wave knocked Theon off his feet. Dozens more of the flying bombs followed and advanced in ever-increasing waves.

"They're flying in formation!" the judge shouted.

"It's a swarm algorithm," Theon said as he struggled to his feet. "One remote operator flies the lead drone, and the rest follow independently."

David and the monk ran toward them. Alma lay unconscious in the arms of the giant.

"Follow me!" shouted a sergeant as the drones headed in their direction. The judge and Ruth ran through the gap in the curtains. Theon and the others struggled to follow as the Supreme Court Policemen formed a skirmish line and fired on the approaching swarm. One after the other, the drones exploded.

A wounded drone slammed into a support column and detonated. The column came down on two officers. Their screams were buried in rubble.

Another drone flew out of control into the ceiling and exploded on contact. Weakened, the entire structure groaned and buckled inward.

Theon reached the curtain as several drones exploded above the officers.

The gunfire fell silent, leaving the eerie buzzing and screams of dying police.

The sergeant pulled them through the curtains into a long room.

Judge Dunn yanked open a trapdoor in the center of the floor. "In here!" he shouted.

Ruth descended the stairs and the judge followed.

The sergeant struggled to change a jammed ammunition clip. He posted himself halfway between their escape hatch and the curtain.

The lead drones hit the heavy fabric and their rotors tangled. They blew themselves up, creating holes.

"Look out!" Theon pointed at a drone flashing toward the monk.

Vadic yanked a pistol from his waistband and half-turned, keeping Alma and David shielded by his body.

He must have picked up Harlan's gun, or maybe one of the fallen officers.

The monk fired with the grace of an expert marksman. The drone exploded ten yards away, the shock wave sledgehammering him into the ground.

The giant surged to his feet, still cradling Alma's unconscious body. David dragged Theon toward the emergency trapdoor behind the monk, and the others followed.

A drone flashed through the hole in the curtain and headed for them.

I'm their primary target.

"Leave me!" Theon shouted to David.

David ignored him and kept dragging him toward the trapdoor.

The drone dived toward him.

I've killed them all.

The sergeant unjammed his rifle and snapped a fresh cartridge into place. He fired at the drone's rotors. It veered upward as if yanked by a string, then fire-balled into the ceiling, raining debris on them.

The building screeched as steel supports hidden in the structure deformed.

"It's collapsing!" Theon shouted.

The officer rapid-fired at the kamikaze drones coming through the curtains. They exploded into the sides of the building, further weakening the walls. One by one, the support columns gave way.

The monk dived into the escape hatch, followed by the judge.

Theon and David pushed through the increasing deluge of debris. As they reached the trapdoor, a slab of marble fell across it, blocking the way.

The sergeant fired his final shot, and then charged to block the approaching swarm.

David and Theon yanked at the marble slab, but to no effect.

The swarm coalesced into a V formation and flew toward them.

The sergeant shouted, "For God and Country!" and charged the drones.

"We can't move it!" David shouted.

The officer planted himself directly in the path of the drones and hefted his rifle like a baseball player preparing for a fastball. As the lead drone reached him, he swung the rifle. The drone exploded and set off a chain reaction of explosions in the rest of the formation.

The shock wave knocked David and Theon several feet from the blocked trapdoor.

Then silence.

"I think those were the last," David said.

And then the ceiling sagged in the center, groaning with the strain.

"It won't hold much longer." Theon yanked at the chunk of marble.

Shrieks of tearing metal mingled with the roar of higher floors buckling.

"It's hopeless," Theon said, and slumped to his knees.

Then the slab of marble inched upward.

"It's moving!" David shouted and got his fingers under one edge. Theon did the same and heaved. The pain shot through his shoulder, but he kept pulling.

One side of the slab rose higher and higher, until the hunched form of the monk appeared beneath it. He leaned his back against the slab as he lifted. His face contorted into something inhuman, but he kept pushing while they lifted.

The roar rose in volume, and the debris from above became a torrent.

Finally, the marble slab toppled to the side. It hit with a thud and cracked in two.

"Go!" shouted the monk. He led the way, and they followed.

Theon threw himself into the stairway after David. The roar became a sustained explosion as the levels above sandwiched. He descended in a tight spiral. The corridor shook and came apart piece by piece.

"I can see a light!" David shouted.

The stairway filled with dust as it shook itself apart. Theon leapt the last flight in near free-fall. Just as he approached the hazy light of the doorway, rubble knocked him flat.

"Shut the door before it's too late!"

David grabbed hold of his arms and yanked him free of the debris.

Theon screamed in agony as a wave of debris came sliding down the last of the passageway.

"Shut the door before it buries us alive!" Theon shouted.

The monk shut the thick steel door with a clang. The debris hit and it dented inward, but held. The roar settled, and then went silent.

When his coughing fit passed, Theon looked at David. It was the third time in a matter of minutes a Christian had saved his life.

Is God messing with me?

A filtration system whirred to life, and the dust cleared.

The room was the size of subway car, with nine cots lining the left side, and a series of metal storage compartments on the right. A computer screen, keyboard, and phone sat at the far end of the narrow room.

"Who was behind that attack?" the judge asked from the nearest cot. His arms encircled Ruth, who clung to him as if in shock.

"Hard to guess," Theon said. "The list of people who want me dead is long. Is Alma all right?"

The monk lifted her from the floor and set her on one of the cots.

David regained his feet and joined him in checking Alma's injuries. "She's still unconscious, but okay, I think."

Theon glanced at the monk's back. His robe hung in shreds, along with the flesh beneath it. Through the mass of crimson, a few of his shattered ribs poked out like broken twigs. A pool of blood surrounded his feet.

"My God," the judge said as he gazed at the monk's wounds. "I'll use the phone on that wall to call for help. It's a secure link to the surface built to survive a nuclear attack."

"I'm sorry, but I can't allow that," the monk said. Backing toward the phone, he drew his pistol. He reached the lone chair in front of the computer and collapsed into it with a grunt of pain.

"At least let me get the first-aid kit from the storage bins," Ruth said.

The monk shook his head. "If anyone moves before I've completed my mission, I will be forced to kill them."

"What mission?" Theon asked.

"I think you already know the answer to that." He raised his gun and took careful aim.

"As I said, the list is long . . ."

Chapter 16

"If you wanted me dead, why didn't you leave me to die when the building collapsed?" Theon asked.

The giant gestured toward David. "I saved him, not you."

An assassin with a conscience.

"You're not really a monk, are you?" Theon asked.

The assassin appraised him with a perfect poker face. Despite the pool of blood expanding beneath him, he showed no signs of pain. The gun remained rock steady.

"I am Dom Vadic Markovich," the monk said. "I took my vows after the Croatian War of Independence."

"So God sent you to kill me?"

"Through his representatives on Earth, God has sent me," Vadic said.

"So not God himself, but the head of your order, or maybe even the pope?"

How many attempts does it take God to kill one person?

The judge and Ruth watched in silence, while David positioned himself on the edge of the bed so his body shielded the unconscious Alma.

"I was sent to stop you from destroying the church I love."

"So you found my granddaughter to prove God's existence and win the case?" Theon asked.

"Yes."

"But then I announced I would proceed regardless of the decision."

"You left me no choice."

"Yet you endangered your divine mission to save Alma and David."

Vadic lowered his gun slightly. "I lost my wife and daughter as well. At the time, I wondered what loving God allows such a thing."

"The Problem of Evil," Theon said. "Even Epicurus struggled with it."

"I realized there's no contradiction if Heaven and Hell exist. God left me behind to atone for my sins. If I prove myself worthy, I will join my Raiyana and Tatyana in paradise."

A comforting delusion. If only I could believe that.

"Thank you for saving Alma's life."

Vadic took careful aim. "I'm sorry," he said.

Theon closed his eyes. If one doesn't fear their nonexistence before birth, why fear a return to that same peaceful oblivion?

Then why am I trembling?

"Wait!" The voice was Alma's.

Theon opened his eyes.

David helped Alma sit on the edge of the bed. She touched her head and winced.

"God sent you as my messenger," she said to Vadic. "And now he's sent you a messenger."

The monk's eyes narrowed. "You claim to speak for God?"

"Not me," Alma said. "I am only the conduit. Your wife and daughter are standing in front of you right now."

Vadic's brow tightened. "What do they look like?"

"Your daughter is clothed in a blue dress with a white sash around the waist, and your wife is wearing blue jeans and a white T-shirt."

A sob wrenched itself from Vadic's chest. "That's what they wore when I found their bodies in the rubble." Still, the gun remained steady, ready to complete its divinely appointed mission.

"Your wife says the first time you made love to her was behind the church at midnight."

Vadic's eyes widened. "We told no one about that. It would have been a scandal if anyone knew Naeda wasn't a maiden when we married a few weeks later."

"Your daughter says her name means *fairy princess* in your language. She wants me to say she misses you."

Tears bloomed in the monk's eyes. "Where are they standing?"

"They're two feet in front of you, your wife on the right."

Does she believe what she's saying, or is her mind creating a hallucination to save me? But how could she know those secrets about his family?

Vadic lowered the gun and gazed hard at the space before him. "I think I see a shimmer in the air."

"That is the earthly reflection of their souls," Alma said. "Until you visit the realm of the dead, as I have, that's all you can see."

Vadic's spoke to the empty space in front of him. "I miss you both more than you know, and I'm doing everything I can to return to you."

Alma swayed, but David held her steady. "Like Abraham, you've passed the test of faith. Your wife says God has rescinded your orders to kill Theon, since he still has a role for him to play in the Lord's divine plan."

"I hear you, Oh Lord, and will obey," Vadic said. The gun slipped from his hand. It hit the concrete and went off in a deafening explosion. The bullet narrowly missed Theon's head and ricocheted off the steel door behind him, then off the metal wall, and finally bounced onto the floor.

Ruth screamed.

The judge hugged her until she calmed. Then the chief justice walked to the monk and picked the gun up off the floor.

The giant swayed, his eyes glazing. The pool of blood at his feet covered a wide area.

"I can see them," he said. "I'm here Raiyana and Tatyana. . ."

He toppled off the chair and lay still.

The judge knelt beside him and searched for a pulse. Looking toward Theon, he shook his head. "He's dead."

Alma threw up.

Theon forced himself to his feet. "We've got to get Alma medical attention as fast as possible."

"I'll take care of that," the judge said, and walked to the phone.

While the chief justice contacted the outside world, David tended to Alma. Ruth bandaged Theon's shoulder with an emergency medical kit from one of the storage lockers.

"You'll need surgery to remove the bullet fragments from the collar bone," she said.

The judge hung up the phone. "They say it will take at least four or five hours to reach us through the rubble."

David and Alma knelt beside the monk and prayed.

"Please Lord," Alma said. "Reunite him with his wife and daughter."

How odd to lobby God. Did they think God ran the universe like a television talent show where the audience votes? But there was no denying the good intentions behind Alma's words. Maybe that was the point.

When the prayer finished, Ruth gave Alma a pain killer and anti-inflammatory. "Do you mind if I ask you a question?"

Alma nodded.

"How did you know so much about his wife and daughter?" Ruth asked.

"They told me."

Ruth frowned, but left her to rest, with David sitting in vigil beside her.

"I take it you're not a believer?" Theon asked Ruth as she handed him two pain tablets.

She sat beside the judge and smiled. "Since I signed the Immortality Contract, I'm not allowed to discuss this subject publicly, remember?"

He laughed. "Well played."

They settled onto their cots and waited. Every fifteen minutes, the phone rang with an update.

After three hours, a faint odor of decay marbled the air.

"How would you have ruled on the trial?" Theon asked the judge.

"I was wondering that myself."

"You can't possibly believe my granddaughter's near-death hallucination is proof of God?"

"Can you explain how Alma knew those things about Vadic's wife?" the judge asked.

"I know there must be a natural explanation."

"You can't know for sure that it wasn't a miracle," Ruth said.

Theon remained silent for a few moments, then gazed at Alma lying next to David. She wasn't far enough along in her pregnancy to show a bump, but soon he'd have a great-grandchild.

"While giving birth to my younger brother, my mother's uterus ruptured," Theon said. "Our parish priest was called into the delivery room to administer Last Rights."

Ruth placed a hand on his arm. "I'm so sorry."

"The doctors stopped the bleeding just in time to save her."

"So it was a miracle," Ruth said.

"That's what my parents believed," he said. "The doctor told my mother and father that if she became pregnant again, the scar tissue would burst, and both she and the baby would die. He strongly advised that my mother have her tubes tied."

"Your parents were Catholic?" the judge asked.

Theon nodded. "When the doctor left, Father O'Malley told them all forms of contraception were forbidden by God. He pointed out that they'd just witnessed a miracle, and the Lord would provide another if he desired her to have more children."

"They couldn't have ignored the advice of doctor?" Ruth asked in a whisper.

"They chose to place their trust in God," he said. "My mother became pregnant three years later. Father O'Malley sprinkled holy water on her belly, mumbled his magic spells, and led the congregation in prayer during each service. My mother assured us God would protect her."

Ruth's eyes filled with tears.

"I remember Mom lying on the kitchen floor in a pool of her own blood." Theon's eyes drifted toward the monk's body in its own crimson pond. "At the funeral, Father O'Malley told us her soul had ascended to Heaven. My father never forgave himself. He left the church and taught his children to place their faith in doctors and scientists rather than priests."

"That priest was evil," Ruth said.

"No." The judge shook his head. "That priest honestly believed in miracles, so he did what he thought was in her best interest. The legal term is *mens rea—the act is not culpable unless the mind is guilty.*"

Theon looked at Ruth. "The fact that you consider the priest's advice as wrong, shows your trust in medicine over miracles."

"I suppose that's somewhat true," she said, "but isn't Alma proof that miracles do happen?"

Theon glanced at his granddaughter's peaceful profile. "Her transformation is as close to a miracle as I've ever seen."

"To be perfectly honest," the judge said, "I don't know how I would have ruled, but you're playing with fire."

"Helena tried to warn me."

"Lucky she wasn't in the courtroom when the attack came," Ruth said.

The memory of Helena's final words echoed in his mind. "*You won't see me again until you abandon this madness.*"

Where was she now? Waiting with the rescue team above, alongside Lamarr and Kyoko?

Am I willing to give up my plan even now?

He glanced at the judge. "I suppose you'll be signing the Immortality Contract now that the trial is over?"

The judge gave Ruth a quick kiss on the lips. "The moment we're out of this infernal box."

When the rescue crews hoisted them out, Theon insisted on going last. Before leaving, he took a final look at Vadic Markovich rotting on the floor.

Another life lost because of me.

And yet, the monk died believing his sins forgiven—believing he was about to reunite with those he loved more than life.

Am I certain he's wrong? Yes, I'm certain.

When he reached the surface, bile rose in his throat.

The Supreme Court had vanished.

At least a thousand military personnel manned a wide perimeter of barricades. Beyond them, the media hyenas waited for the scraps of flesh. Next came the sea of ordinary people determined to get a smiling selfie with the ruins in the background. They would post their trophies on the Web like arctic explorers planting a flag to stake their claim.

When the rescue team unstrapped him from the harness, Judge Dunn shook his hand, and Ruth gave him a hug.

Theon watched the surviving Supreme Court police officers lead the two away. Their weapons were drawn in case of attack.

"Justice Dunn," a reporter shouted from the perimeter, "what is your ruling in the case?"

The judge came to a stop, but remained silent. Finally, he straightened and spoke in a commanding baritone. "I rule in favor of Doctor Theon Torano. He's earned the right to distribute the product of his labors as he sees fit."

The Chief Justice of the Supreme Court inclined his head in Theon's direction and stepped into a military Humvee.

There was no sign of Helena or anyone from Amara Pharmaceuticals. Maybe they couldn't get past security. He tried his phone, but there was no service.

A police officer took his arm and led him toward a tent with a red cross emblazoned on the top. "We're blocking wireless signals to disrupt more drone attacks."

Inside the tent, a medical team treated Alma and David. His granddaughter smiled at him as a doctor strapped her into a bright orange stretcher.

He smiled back. "I thought I'd lost you forever."

"Thanks to the Lord I'm still here," she said. "And Mamma and Gran are in the next world, waiting for us both."

Can I blame her? A mind can only take so much reality.

A doctor removed the bandages on his shoulder and examined the wound.

"An excellent field dressing," he said. "You'll be fine for transport to the base hospital, where we're better equipped to handle this, both from a medical and security standpoint."

"I'm ready," Theon said.

The medics carried Alma's stretcher to a helicopter. Once they secured her, David helped him climb in.

The doctors strapped them all in for takeoff.

Theon lay back and closed his eyes.

It's over, and Alma is safe.

A needle pricked his arm, and he opened his eyes.

"A sedative to make you more comfortable," the doctor said.

Theon nodded. Two figures in dark suits sat behind the doctor. One was tall and thin, and the other shorter and stocky.

Poncho and Cisco.

"Let me out of here!" Theon shouted. The two secret service officers betrayed no hint of emotion.

His vision blurred. The whir of the rotors faded, and his eyelids closed.

Chapter 17

A scent of antiseptic came first. Next was the sour odor of sweat—his own. The choking aroma of cigar smoke ruled out a hospital.

A guttural moan—also his own.

The ache in his shoulder competed with the bite of straps cutting into wrists and ankles.

A metallic taste filled his dry mouth.

Theon opened his eyes.

The blinding room might have been a dentist's office—except for the security cameras mounted in all four corners. Even the seat he was strapped into resembled a modified dental chair.

The president puffed on a cigar with the steady rhythm of a steam engine stoking its boiler. A somewhat ridiculous Smith and Wesson .44 Magnum hung from his belt—the same gun made famous by Dirty Harry.

The most powerful gun in the word for the most powerful man in the world.

Behind President Kane, Poncho and Cisco stood at attention—just following orders, as usual.

"Where is my granddaughter?" Theon asked, despite the pain in his raw throat.

Puff, puff, puff. "Do you know what happened when Richard Lawrence attempted to assassinate President Andrew Jackson in 1835?"

Theon frowned. "His gun misfired, but what does that have to do with—"

"The assassin took out a second gun and pulled the trigger at point-blank range."

"It also failed to go off," Theon said, "but I've got that beat, since I survived three assassination attempts today alone. I suppose this is the fourth?"

"People at the time took it as proof that God watched over our nation. But you and I know better. Call it coincidence, or bad planning, or not meant to be."

"Like my Immortality Contract?"

No reply. Just puff, puff, puff.

"Were you behind the Supreme Court attack?"

"Of course not. You're far more valuable to me alive."

"I already told you that I couldn't reconstruct my drug on my own, even if I wanted to."

Kane exhaled a ring of smoke. "I don't believe you, but we will find out one way or the other."

Theon sighed. "You're right, I was bluffing. If you want my drug that badly, you can have it."

President Kane took the cigar out of his mouth. "After all your tough talk, you'd surrender that easily?"

"I'm sorry if I'm spoiling your fun, but what's the point? You'll threaten to torture me. I'll say I'll never allow someone like you to use my drug to subjugate the world. You'll tell me all the great things you can accomplish with such leverage. You might even mention Plato's assertion that the best government is an enlightened dictator."

"I hadn't considered that last one, but it's a good point."

"If I still refuse, you'll drag my granddaughter in and prepare to take her apart piece by piece unless I cooperate. I'll ask myself if one life is worth the enslavement of billions."

"You're definitely on target," the president said.

"The simple truth is that Alma's life is more valuable to me than a trillion others."

"I admit I'm disappointed," the president said. "But not for the reason you think. Creating your drug took intelligence, but you neglected to plan for the obvious."

He's right. I was naïve, just as Helena said.

"How does this work?" the president asked. "Do you know the formula by heart, or do you need to issue instructions to someone in your company?"

"I want to see Alma first."

"Proof of Life it is." The president motioned to Cisco, and the officer opened the door. Two more secret service officers holding assault rifles entered the room, but instead of Alma, they escorted Helena.

"Not that one," the president said. "The granddaughter."

Helena must be his backup hostage in case there was some problem with Alma. The man certainly thought ahead.

"Alma is resting," Helena replied. Tucked into her waistband was her Ruger Mark III, with its left-handed grip.

The two officers aimed their assault rifles at the center of the president's chest.

What the hell?

The leader of the free world blanched. His hand froze with his cigar halfway to his mouth. The smoke curled past his face like some whimsical creature vying for his attention.

Cisco drew his Glock and pointed it at the president's face, while Poncho unstrapped Theon from the chair.

"You're behind this?" Theon asked her.

"It's the brainchild of Lamarr, Kyoko, and several of your more practical-minded employees. They expected problems."

Poncho helped him to his feet. "They recruited us seven years ago."

"Along with others in key government agencies," Cisco said. "There's tons of secular humanists in public service, so it wasn't hard finding supporters of your cause. Most of us are volunteering for free."

A lump formed in Theon's throat. "Why didn't you tell me?"

Helena shrugged. "You were so obsessed with secrecy, your employees feared you'd veto the idea."

"I probably would have," he said.

"You'll never get away with this," the president said through clenched teeth. His hand drifted toward the gigantic gun at his hip.

The four secret service officers tensed. Helena settled her left hand on her pistol. "You portrayed yourself as a tough guy to win the election—a sort of John Wayne gunslinger. Well, here's your chance to prove it."

The officers stepped out of the line of fire and lowered their weapons.

Dalton Kane stared at her with the intensity of a cornered badger.

Helena waited, the embodiment of calm.

The president's jaw flexed.

"What are you waiting for, Kane?" Helena asked. "As a Born Again Christian, you must welcome this chance at martyrdom. Oh, wait, I forgot—you lied about that. You still might outdraw me and get revenge before you die. I'm only a girl, and you're a big, strong man who went to a military boarding school."

Kane hesitated.

She met his gaze coolly—waiting.

Then he looked away. His fingers uncurled from his gun, and his hands rose in surrender.

"A rational choice," Helena said.

Poncho removed the .44 Magnum, patted him down, and affixed handcuffs.

"You can't kidnap the president," Kane said.

Helena smiled. "Have you forgotten your advice when we met in your office?"

"What advice?"

"You said you never apologized for doing what it takes to win."

Helena shook her head. "All the stress you've been under has caused a severe mental breakdown. Not surprising, given the circumstances. The vice president and the secretary of state are at this moment signing the official papers declaring you unfit to perform your duties. They'll make sure you get the professional help you need."

"You bitch," the president said.

"I'd watch that mouth," Helena said. "Many in your condition are at risk of suicidal depression."

The officers marched the deposed president out of the room.

"Why let him bring me here in the first place?"

"I wanted to see what you'd do when he threatened Alma."

He averted his gaze. "And I failed the test."

"You passed."

Theon looked at her in confusion. "I agreed to let him enslave the entire world to save one person."

"And that's the reason I love you," Helena said.

A wave of vertigo hit him, and he swayed. She grabbed hold of his arm and helped him toward the door.

"What now?" he asked.

"I suppose you're still determined to go ahead with the Immortality Contract?"

"I'm afraid I am."

Helena sighed. "Then I suppose we have some major security overhauls to make, to ensure something like this doesn't happen again."

Theon stopped and stared at her. "You're going to help me?"

"I'm still skeptical, but I'm willing to give it a try."

He stared into those wondrous green eyes and took her in her arms despite the pain. Then he kissed her.

She melted against him and kissed him with equal abandon.

When she pulled away, tears glistened on her cheeks. "Maybe, together, we can make this work."

Chapter 18

Pope Stephen sat at his desk, staring at the pile of resignations. They ranged from priests, nuns, bishops, and cardinals, to volunteers.

All had signed the Immortality Contract.

Many probably still prayed at home, but they'd traded church and the promise of Heaven for a return to youth.

Can I really blame them? Maybe I would do the same, if I had anything else to live for.

As collection plates fell empty, donations to secular charities grew exponentially. Orphanages, food banks, scholarship funds, and Third World aid benefited directly from the switch.

Would Jesus have been displeased?

Of course, churches employed millions of workers in construction and maintenance. Wasn't redistributing wealth by creating magnificent art and architecture better than simply handing money to the poor?

Now who's rationalizing?

His office was a simple room in the papal apartments. A plain cross on a bare wall. A small bookshelf. A desk and two chairs—one for him, and another for visitors. With the overwrought opulence of the rest of the Vatican, the simplicity of this place echoed his childhood home.

The news of Vadic's death lingered in his gut like an indigestible piece of rotten flesh. If the reports were true, the monk spared Theon at the last moment. What could cause the former soldier to fail him?

Or was it the opposite? Maybe his friend saved him from committing a sin no absolution could wash away.

He wouldn't be the first Pope Stephen remembered as a monster. In 897, Pope Stephen the Sixth exhumed the corpse of his predecessor, Pope Formosa, and put him on trial. Known as the Cadaver Synod, Pope Stephen ordered the corpse tied to the Papal Throne to face his accusers. A deacon crouched behind the chair and answered on behalf of the deceased pontiff.

When Pope Stephen the Sixth asked the corpse why he'd done his wretched deeds, the hidden deacon shouted, "Because I'm evil!"

With such a defense as that, the guilty verdict was assured.

Stripped of his vestments, the dead pontiff had the three fingers of his right hand—the ones used for blessing—hacked off. Then his naked body was dumped into the Tiber River as a final insult.

But was that worse than allowing the entire Catholic Church to vanish?

A knock interrupted his melancholy.

"You may enter," he said.

Archbishop Nsedu Makgobo entered. As always, his personal secretary wore a black suit jacket over his traditional purple shirt and ivory cleric's collar. A simple metal cross hung from his neck. Nsedu's dark skin framed the whites of his eyes so they seemed to glow.

"I'm sorry to bother you, Your Holiness, but we cannot ignore the situation any longer."

Can I not find a moment of peace?

"Come back later, when I call for you," he said with a dismissive wave of his hand.

"I will wait here until you're ready, Your Holiness."

"You dare defy the successor of Peter with such insolence?"

Nsedu's black face was a mask of determination. "You've put this off for months. It's time to decide on a course before it's too late. If you want to remove me from my position, that is your choice, but I won't stand by and watch the church I love destroyed out of neglect."

It took bravery for his loyal assistant to defy him.

Things must be worse than I thought.

Stephen rose from his chair with a groan. Damned arthritis. Soon he'd need a cane. "Walk with me," he said.

Nsedu held the door as they passed into the hallway of his gilded cage.

Many saw Nsedu's elevation to papal secretary as a stepping stone to becoming his successor. With one-sixth of all Catholics living in Africa, and a large proportion of new priests African, a black pontiff was overdue.

That was before Theon won his case, of course.

Will there even be a two hundred and sixty-seventh pope?

"You're only ten years younger than I," Stephen said. "Have you considered leaving the church and signing the contract?"

"My father used to say that those who live for this world alone, have lost sight of the purpose of living. It's the reason he sacrificed his life in the fight for Nigeria's freedom against our Colonial oppressors."

How ironic that Nsedu now served the God of those oppressors. Theon would probably say he traded one conqueror for an even more powerful one.

Was that what religion amounted to—another form of power and control?

"Tell me the news," Stephen said.

"Aside from the critical shortage of staff," Nsedu answered, "a single year of property taxes on our real-estate holdings would wipe out our reserve fund. I advise selling the majority of our properties until conditions change."

"What is a church without churches?"

"Think of it as a temporary retreat to the catacombs to outlast our enemy."

"And the Vatican? St. Peter's Basilica?"

"As a sovereign country, this one hundred and nine acres faces no tax threat. As a symbol, I think maintaining it is worth the expense."

"The situation is that bad?" Stephen asked.

"Church attendance has fallen nearly to zero, and revenues are less than two percent of operating expenses. If we don't consolidate, the Catholic Church will collapse under its own weight."

"Shouldn't we fight this evil head-on?"

"This situation is unprecedented. Even the Protestant Revolution is mild in comparison."

Yes, the lure of eternal youth is a powerful temptation, indeed.

They entered the hallway to the Sistine Chapel.

Tourists had vanished overnight, since the entrance fee was deemed a violation of the Immortality Contract. Nsedu had closed the museum under the guise of renovations, fooling no one.

"Did you know I was once an African missionary?" Stephen asked.

"In Tanzania, if memory serves."

"That's right. I headed a mission and school for the Maasai near the Ngorongoro crater."

"A beautiful place," Nsedu said. "Can we discuss the details—"

"The farmers surrounding the preserve hated the Maasai with a passion. As much as I tried preaching fellowship and tolerance, the farmers insisted the Maasai were Devil worshipers."

"I understand the problems of tribalism," Nsedu said. "If we could please—"

"One day I came across a group of Maasai men stealing one of the farmer's cows.

"Through my interpreter, I asked him why he would steal his neighbor's cows.

"One of the men stepped forward, his long spear glinting in the sun. 'When Enkai created the sky and the earth,' the man said, 'he gave all his cows to his chosen people, the Maasai. It is the sacred duty of the Maasai to look after Enkai's gift. Since all cows belong to the Maasai, we are not stealing, but reclaiming what was stolen from us in previous generations. It is the will of Enkai that we do this.' "

"I am familiar with the self-serving myths of the tribes of my homeland," Nsedu said.

"Let me ask you this," Stephen said, "what's the difference between the Maasai's belief that God gave them permission to take their neighbor's cows, and the ancient Hebrew belief that God ordered the Jews to take the land of Israel from the tribes already there?"

"Your Eminence, are you having a crisis of faith?"

A good question, indeed.

Stephen inclined his head to the colorfully dressed Swiss Guard at the entrance to the Sistine Chapel. The clean-cut young man snapped to attention, his anachronistic spear held in his right hand, and a sword hanging at his side. If there was any real danger, a modern submachine gun was close at hand in a hidden compartment of the wall.

Most of the guards had resigned, leaving only a handful of the most devoted. It was a wonder there hadn't been a robbery yet with such sparse security.

They stepped inside the famous chapel, and Stephen drew in a breath. His fellow cardinals had elected him pope in this very room. Had he known what was coming, he might have turned the honor down.

Nsedu gazed up at the image of God imparting the spark of life to Adam. "Their fingers don't quite touch," his assistant said. "I wonder if this is a reminder that we can never comprehend God fully or attain his perfection?"

"Perhaps," Stephen said. "Did you know that Leonardo despised Michelangelo's Orthodoxy? He said it betrayed the humanist ideals of reviving Greek science and philosophy."

Nsedu nodded. "Da Vinci's illustrations of the human body treated it as a complex machine. His championing of reason over faith may have been the first steps toward atheism."

"I wonder what he'd have thought of Theon's contract?"

"There's no doubt the world would have benefited from extending Leonardo's life several centuries, but at a terrible cost to his soul."

"Okay, my African financial wizard, what is your plan for saving us?"

Nsedu handed him a folder. "The church officially owns 271,602 physical churches, not including missions. I propose closing all but twenty-nine."

"You can't be serious?"

"If we don't act quickly, tax defaults will trigger thousands of expensive lawsuits in international court, followed by foreclosures. Best to pull the Band-Aid off quickly before the equity in these holdings disappears. With the money raised from the sale of so much prime real estate, we can survive into the foreseeable future."

"Survive as what?" Stephen asked. "If everyone leaves the church except a few of the clergy, we become an opulent nursing home for a bunch of childless old men and women. Without new converts, who inherits our piles of treasure when the last of us dies?"

"We have no choice, Your Eminence."

"There's always a choice!"

Nsedu said nothing.

The uncomfortable silence flooded him with dread. Could one drown from a lack of hope?

A faint sound wafted through the room.

Is my mind playing tricks on me?

There it was again.

A woman's voice? Could this be the sign from God I've prayed for?

"Do you hear that?" Nsedu asked.

Not a voice within his head, then. "I think so."

The voice called out, "Sebastijan . . ."

The hairs on the nape of his neck prickled.

"Sebastijan . . ."

That name—a whispered memory.

"Can you hear me, Sebastijan?" The ethereal voice might have been a lost soul seeking escape from purgatory.

"It can't be," Pope Stephen whispered.

"Isn't that your given name before being elected pontiff?" Nsedu asked.

Despite the pain in his joints, the pope stumbled to the doorway and ran. "I'm here!" he shouted.

He ran along the main corridor, his name echoing from the right. He entered the Rafael galleries and passed *The School of Athens* without so much as a glance. Nsedu struggled to keep up, despite his relative youth.

"I'm here!" he called out again.

"Sebastijan!" came the reply from somewhere behind him.

He sped through the maze of paintings and burst into the Gallery of Maps, ignoring the pain in his knees. Between gasps, he called out, "I'm here!"

She appeared at the other end of the room. "Sebastijan!"

It's her. It's Mira.

His long-lost love rushed past the panels depicting the regions of Italia.

She looked the same, even the plain skirt and white blouse. Her brown hair spread behind her like the wings of an angel.

A Swiss Guard rounded the corner behind her. In place of his spear, he held one of the emergency assault rifles.

He must think she's trying to assassinate me.

"Stop or I'll shoot!" the soldier shouted.

"No!" the pope screamed at the same instant a thunderclap echoed through the canyons of the hall.

Mira fell and slid several yards before coming to a stop.

"Hold your fire!" the pope shouted with all the command he could muster. He ran to the collapsed figure and went to his knees.

"Please, God," he prayed. "Let her live."

Mira groaned as he helped her to a sitting position. He searched for a wound.

The Swiss Guard reached them, his young face flushed. "I only fired a warning shot, Your Holiness."

Mira gasped for breath. "I dived for the floor"—she gulped air— "when I heard the gunshot."

Sebastijan pulled her into an embrace. "My love, you're really here."

Nsedu halted beside them. "Are you okay, Your Holiness?"

Sebastijan held Mira's soft face in his wrinkled hands. She looked the same as when he left her crying by the ocean's edge so long ago.

She's signed the Immortality Contract.

The Swiss Guard stepped forward. "We told her it was impossible to see you without an appointment, but she slipped past us and outran everyone."

"I've found you at last, Sebastijan," she said.

"Can you ever forgive me, my love?"

"My children are grown, and my husband has passed into the next world, but I've never stopped loving you," she said. "Isn't it time we lived the life denied us?" She leaned forward and pressed her miraculous lips against his.

I've waited a lifetime for this moment.

When he caught his breath, she helped him to his feet. There was no need for words.

She took his hand and led him toward the exit.

"Your Holiness," Nsedu said, "where are you going?"

Sebastijan stopped and faced his loyal deputy. "I'm making the choice I should have long ago." He removed his papal ring of office and handed it to his secretary. "You're free to choose what you want to do with this."

The Swiss Guard blocked his way. "You can't desert us in our time of need." He pointed his rifle at him. "I'll kill you before I let that happen."

Nsedu stepped in front of the gun so the barrel touched his purple shirt.

"Stand aside, or I'll kill all three of you!" the guard shouted.

Nsedu held the papal ring before the guard. "The church is no one person." He put the ring on his finger and straightened. "I command you in the name of God to return to your post."

The guard hesitated, his face contorted with emotion. Finally, he lowered his gun and went to one knee. "Forgive me, Your Eminence." Then he kissed the ring and retreated down the hall.

When the guard had gone, Mira exhaled. "You are our savior."

Nsedu seemed taller, somehow.

"What will you do?" he asked.

Sebastijan looked at Mira and smiled. "We will live."

Chapter 19

It was being called the Age of Youth.

Has it only been a year?

Helena wandered through the streets of New York just as she had when she was twenty, except now the entire city resembled a vast college campus without professors.

But one young man was absent.

Where are you, my love?

Had bad weather delayed his jet?

The UN summit on immortality started tomorrow. The diplomats would resent a delay, but would wait if necessary.

A smile flitted across Helena's lips. *Could anyone else have talked me into such a scheme?*

And yet, he'd been right. It had worked.

Ninety-five percent of those over thirty had signed the contract. In cities, the percentage neared a hundred percent. Without death, religion had lost its most potent means of persuasion.

Earlier in the day, even Pakistan passed a secularization amendment. Shipments of the Fountain of Youth pill would begin arriving in Islamabad next week. It seemed only a matter of time before Iran and Saudi Arabia gave in to the building demands of its citizens.

She strolled through Chinatown and into Greenwich Village. The neighborhoods had changed since her first visit to New York with her upper-crust classmates from Bryn Marr.

I suppose I've changed even more.

How desperately she'd wanted to fit in to their rarefied realm of sophistication. It took only a few hours to realize that her role was to play the amusing country hick from Iowa.

She adopted the stereotype without a struggle. Her "friends" laughed as she rubbernecked at the tall buildings. They brought her to the most shocking cafés and art exhibitions and tittered at her reaction. Then, as now, being a celebrated New York artist entailed creating the most offensive or obtuse work possible. The true art connoisseur took it in with no sign of shock, outrage, or confusion.

Each time she cringed, frowned, or shook her head in bafflement, her classmates laughed at her inability to recognize the profound "statement" of the work.

Why was beauty no longer considered worthy of a museum? What did that say about society?

I suppose I was out of date, even when I was young.

She had humiliated herself out of desperation for a place at their table, even if it was as the court jester.

Had her classmates been an inner city gang, she might have stolen cars for them, or stabbed someone wearing the wrong color, or slept with the gang leader. All to belong. Humans were a tribal species, and what was a tribe without leaders and followers accepting their appointed roles?

After the trip, she retreated even further into her books, the only true friends she could rely on.

Until I met him.

She angled through Washington Park, the site of her one triumph. The usual crowd of loiterers, street performers, and musicians dotted the square.

In one corner of the park sat the chess addicts. Though they still hunched over their plastic armies, their slim figures and wrinkle-free faces robbed them of their former gravitas.

Her classmates had goaded her into challenging one of the grizzled chess hustlers to a game. It was the single occasion she failed in her appointed role. Her analytical mind wouldn't allow her to override its ability to reason, even to please them. It was the one sacred portion of her being she never betrayed.

The look on her classmates' faces when she quickly won three games in a row and earned sixty dollars was her fondest memory of that trip.

"You're like a chess freak," Mirabelle had said, skillfully turning her triumph into a put down.

The old Russian had shouted and raged—claiming she'd cheated. The rest of the hustlers howled in laughter as he surrendered his money to a girl.

It was that table right there.

"Hey, beautiful girl, let's have a game," said a young man sitting where the old Russian had. "I'm just learning myself. We could make it interesting—say five bucks a game?"

"No, thanks," she said.

I'd feel guilty taking his money if I won. If I lost, I'd have to play again, and again, until I won.

The pull of the chessboard mirrored the lure of a scientific problem. As with so much of life, a virtue in one context can become a vice in another.

Such obsessiveness had made her wealthy in the world of venture capital. While other investors simply listened to pitches, she dived into the data until she'd mastered it. Only then would she invest and take an active role in developing the product.

"Next time," called the hustler as she left the scene of her triumph and entered the headwaters of Fifth Avenue.

The faces around her reflected the ethnic and social diversity one expected of this famous melting pot, except that every one of them looked no older than twenty-five.

Subtle clues separated most of the naturally young from the artificially young (or AYs, as they were known). There were a few distinguishing traits that set them apart. The awkward use of the newest technological gadgets was one tip off, but the most telling facto was the way AYs reveled in youth. It seemed only the old could fully appreciate the gift of youth.

How odd that the current generation might never experience a mid-life crisis, or the prospect of forced retirement, or all the other challenges of old age.

Most of the AYs she passed didn't hide their age, but gloried in the era of their first youth. Young men in WWII uniforms mixed with long-haired hippies, punk rockers, bell-bottom-wearing disco queens on roller skates, and every generation in between. It was as if a time warp brought the youth of the past hundred years together for a celebration.

She paused at a store window and gazed at her unfamiliar reflection. Her long red hair had been cut short and dyed black. Even her eyebrows had been darkened into miniature top hats crowning her eyes. Brown contact lenses completed the disguise. Old friends passed her on the street without a second glance.

Since his return to youth, Theon required no disguise at all, since the world's collective image of him was from the trial. Afterward, he never appeared on camera again. The only available photo of his younger self was the one in the old *Time* magazine article of the three of them in college. The reproduction was in black-and-white and not high resolution.

When the rare person asked if he was the famous scientist, Theon told them they were mistaken, and they accepted this without further question. The odds of running into the famed Theon Torano on an ordinary street seemed too unlikely.

Where are you?

Had something gone wrong at Alma's farm?

She pulled out her phone and stared at it, then put it back in her pocket.

He said he'd be here before midnight, and that's still an hour and a half away. I won't become the nagging girlfriend.

She continued up Fifth Avenue to The First Presbyterian Church, now a science academy for gifted grade school students. In the past year, every church in the city had changed hands—either to private developers, or to the city itself.

Madison Square Park and the Empire State Building broke the retail monotony with their timeless presence.

At Bryant Park, a packed crowd watched a basketball game on a big screen. From the cheers, it seemed the debut of a newly restored Michael Jordan and Larry Byrd was a hit with their fans.

A similar phenomenon was occurring across every profession. Actors, scientists, writers, singers, politicians, and legends from all corners of the globe were flooding back into the job market.

"Isn't Larry Byrd awesome!" a man shouted in her ear. The smell of Jim Beam hit her in the face. The guy looked young, but his ancient overcoat and threadbare trousers hinted at someone raised in the fifties. "I watched him play in person at ISU in the seventies."

"That's nice," she said.

"Bet you didn't think I was that old?"

He had an unfortunate chin. Youth was not a cure for all of nature's handicaps, but a good plastic surgeon could probably help.

"How about ringing in the New Year with me?" he asked. "I spent my social security check on a room at the Plaza, which leaves my pension for champagne! Figured I should make the most of it before congress does away with it."

He grabbed hold of her as if to dance. The undercover security detail surged forward, but she signaled them back.

"I'm meeting someone," she said, and disengaged his hands.

"Too bad, too bad," he said, and moved on to other prospects. His odds were good with all the alcohol and euphoria flowing so freely.

She resumed her trek.

The three men and two women assigned to her blended in seamlessly. She knew each of them well, since she'd taken charge of security at Kyoko and Lamarr's urging. Theon grumbled that all the tracking devices and evacuation contingencies were overkill, but how could he complain after what happened at the Supreme Court?

She passed a newsstand where *The New York Times*'s front page proclaimed: "The Pharma Six Sentenced to Life in Prison."

A woman in a sleek business suit bought a paper and scanned the article. "Imagine those drug company executives thinking they'd get away with bombing the Supreme Court!"

Was it that odd for a trillion-dollar industry to deem the life of one man of less importance than their corporate profits and the jobs of millions? Native Americans and former slaves might not find it surprising in the least.

She stopped outside Saint Patrick's Cathedral where an orderly line of people moving through the front doors. The city had acquired the building shortly after the pope's resignation and converted it to a Fountain of Youth distribution center. Tabloids claimed Pope Stephen had signed the Immortality Contract and married his childhood sweetheart. Maybe he was on these very streets celebrating right now?

In a strange convergence with the Eucharist ceremony, pills were placed directly on each recipient's tongue. Should there be a theft, the distribution center and all those it served would forfeit the next two months' supply of pills. This created a huge incentive for local officials and citizens to secure their facilities. So far, not a single pill was unaccounted for.

At 11:00 pm the doors of the cathedral would close until the next morning. In locations where the population was smaller, local authorities set the hours best suited to their citizens.

A voice from behind her said, "I went to school with a girl who looked almost as pretty as you."

She spun around and threw herself at Theon. "You made it in time!"

He lifted her in his lean arms and kissed her. "You don't think I'd miss our anniversary?"

She laughed. "Is that what this is?"

The nearness of his body sent shock waves through every nerve of her being.

I dreamed of this for over half a century.

He set her down and started pulling away, but she held him tight, and kissed him again.

"It's only been a few days," he said.

"Easy for you to say." She shoved him playfully. "I was the one stuck here dealing with this world-wide logistical nightmare you've created."

He laughed and took her hand. They strolled around the side of the church. "I think the system we've put in place can mostly run itself. We should take a vacation."

Helena stole a glance at him. His handsome features looked the same as that fateful day in college, when he changed the course of her life in Professor Kilnear's class.

"How is Alma?" she asked.

His eyes lost focus. "Her transformation never ceases to amaze me. If you'd seen her before—like some rabid animal—her face emaciated, eyes sunken. I'd lost all hope."

"And now she's a mother."

"Little Riley is an angel born to an angel."

"And the security I put in place?" she asked.

"It's thorough and unobtrusive. There's not a bear within a hundred miles that isn't being tracked by high-altitude drones."

"It sounds like the eye of God," she said. "Do they suspect they're under such absolute protection?"

"I told David and Alma, but I doubt the others know the true extent."

"That's good. The more normal their lives, the better."

"David's family is easy to talk to, as long as I avoid evolution, global warming, politics, the Immortality Contract, or anything to do with religion."

Helena laughed. "Your favorite subjects."

"We discussed farming, nature, cooking, and our favorite topic of all—sweet little Riley. I'd forgotten how entertaining a child could be. The wonder in those new eyes discovering how the world works one experiment at a time fascinated me."

"Did David's parents or grandparents seem tempted by the prospect of a return to youth?"

"Not in the slightest. Like Alma, they genuinely look forward to their eternal reward in Heaven."

They reached the end of the block and turned the corner. At the rear of the church, a continuous line of people exited, having imbibed their monthly pill.

"It sure is efficient," Theon said.

"You should see things inside. They handle as many as—"

"You can't do this to us!" shouted a man being escorted out of the cathedral by several security guards. "We haven't broken the contract. There must be a mistake."

A young woman clung to him with terror etched on her pretty face. "We're both in our nineties," she pleaded. "It's the same as murder!"

A small crowd gathered around the dramatic scene, their youthful faces troubled. The conclave resembled a group of college students witnessing the expulsion of a classmate. If this clean-cut couple could be kicked out of the program and left to die, what kept it from happening to any of them?

"You can't refuse treatment without evidence!" a woman shouted from the growing crowd.

"We have proof," said a security guard. An image flickered to life on a monitor mounted to the exterior wall of the cathedral.

A living room appeared on the oversize screen. The hidden camera showed the young couple attending a secret Catholic service with six other people.

After receiving communion, they each placed several hundred dollars into the collection plate.

The middle-aged priest rested a hand atop each of their heads. "Bless you for supporting us in these desperate times."

"Bless you, Father," the couple said in reply.

Helena glanced at Theon. "Amara uses bounty hunters?"

"We offer rewards for evidence of violations."

"Paying informants reminds me of East Germany under the Stasi."

"If you have a better way, I'm all ears."

The screen went blank. The woman cried softly, while the man held an arm around her shoulders. What could they say? The evidence was conclusive.

"Please, give us another chance," the man said. "We've learned our lesson."

"I'm sorry," the guard said, unable to meet the couple's eyes. "If I don't follow the rules, I'd violate my own Immortality Contract."

"Is that true?" Helena asked Theon.

"Without penalties, violations would erode the entire system."

The beautiful young woman fell to her knees before the guard. She clasped her hands together and extended them in a heart-wrenching supplication. "Please, I don't want to die."

"There's nothing I can do." The guard fled into the cathedral.

The man helped the sobbing woman to her feet, and they descended the stairs. The crowd parted before them—silent, as if watching condemned prisoners walking toward the gallows. Without the pill, they'd return to their natural ages at the rate of ten years per month. Before the next New Year's Eve, they would be bent with age and all its side effects.

Helena's heart ached. "Can't we help them?"

"It's unfair to make an exception for these two alone."

The crowd dispersed. No one made eye contact with the devastated young couple shuffling along the sidewalk in tears. They resembled ghosts returning to their graves.

"How can you be so cruel?" she asked.

"They knew the rules when they signed up."

"Have you never made a mistake?"

"So I should tear the contract up and let churches exploit people? Let them preach against contraception, promote Jihad, terrify children with threats of Hell?"

The last comment hit home. As a child, she had nightmares every Sunday after the Fire and Brimstone sermons. She pictured herself burning forever, with Satan's demons torturing her. Only after she realized it was all nonsense, in the sixth grade, did the nightmares end.

Theon's face betrayed his torment as the couple vanished into the crowd.

"What you've done has created so much good," she said. "They've already served as a warning to everyone who witnessed this. What further point is there in letting them die?"

He gazed at her with those compassionate gray eyes she'd loved from afar for most of her lifetime. Then the tension left his face. "As usual, you're right."

He set out after the condemned couple, his long strides difficult to keep pace with.

They reached the couple on the next block.

Theon placed a hand on the man's shoulder. The two stopped and turned. Tears streaked their faces, and the woman shivered despite her heavy coat and stylish leather gloves.

"Everyone deserves a second chance," Theon said.

The woman's eyes widened. "Do you mean . . . ?"

Theon passed his fingers across his smartphone, then extended it toward the woman. "Press your right thumb here," he said.

She pulled off her glove and pushed her trembling finger against the screen. When a beep sounded, Theon held the screen out to the man. He placed his thumb on the glass surface, and another beep signaled acceptance.

"You've been given a second chance, but this is the last one," Theon said.

Wonder filled the couple's faces.

"Our contract is restored?" the woman asked.

"You will receive an e-mail with an appointment at a distribution center in Brooklyn. You're not to tell *anyone* about this. Do you understand?"

The couple nodded vigorously, the joy suffusing every movement they made.

"If you violate the contract again, that will be it," Theon emphasized.

"God bless—" The woman stopped herself. "I mean . . . thank you. Thank you both for sparing our lives, whoever you are."

"We won't tell anyone," the husband said. "And we won't slip again."

The couple retreated at nearly a run.

Helena took Theon's hand in hers. "Thank you."

He smiled. "I'm the one who's grateful."

Their guards mingled with the crowd at strategic intervals.

"Let's give my team the rest of the night off, since they've been at it most of the evening," she said. "It is New Year's Eve."

Theon nodded and manipulated his cell phone. Five of the ten drifted away with a slight nod in their direction. One of the team, a man in a dark suit, walked past them and smiled. "Happy New Year," he said.

"And to you as well," Theon replied.

"I've never seen Joe smile before," Helena said.

They wandered the streets arm in arm, watching the colorful menagerie of youth. Glowing Ankhs festooned the Streetlamps along 7th Avenue.

Have I ever been this happy? I wonder if I should I tell him now?

A bubble of guilt rose within her chest, pressing outward with increasing discomfort.

I'll tell him later, when we're alone.

"Did you talk to Alma about her visions?" she asked. "Does she still see demons and spirits?"

Theon hesitated.

"Remember, we agreed not to hide anything for each other," she said.

I'm just waiting for the right moment to tell him.

Theon nodded. "Alma says Taslima's ghost told her that her memories of the murder are true."

"Are you so certain they're false?"

There was something more than sadness in his look. "Taslima spoke to her brothers over Skype that same day. She told me about it when I called her, since she was excited to see her youngest brother when they returned from their meeting in Dubai. This video call was the first time Alma saw the faces of her uncles. I think the two memories somehow got intermixed in Alma's memory."

"The brothers might have pretended to be in Dubai to create an alibi," Helena said.

"Two State Department officials attended the meeting with all five of the brothers. Not to mention the passport records, plane tickets, hotel security videos—"

"Okay, I get the point," she said. "False memories aren't uncommon in such circumstances. It's the mind's way of creating a rational explanation for a traumatic event."

Theon took a deep breath and let it out slowly. "Taslima's words were a great relief to Alma because . . ."

"Tell me."

He looked at her with fear in his eyes. "Alma had become convinced that her false memories were protecting her from the fact that she was the real murderer."

"But if Alma had killed them, Fatima would have known."

"Alma figured Fatima made up the story of the three masked men to protect her from being arrested."

"That's ridiculous."

Theon fell silent as they continued toward Central Park. Cars honked, and people laughed in a celebration of life renewed.

"You don't actually believe Alma could do such a thing?"

"They never found a single trace of the three masked men. No witnesses in the area, no informants in the Jihadist community, and no terrorist organization ever claimed responsibility for what would have been a major success. If not them, or the uncles, or the elderly Fatima, who is left?"

"But Alma was only twelve."

Theon stopped and faced her, his face haunted. "You didn't see her during her psychotic breaks. It took three male orderlies to restrain her the last time. If she'd had a knife . . ."

"How long have you suspected her?"

"It never occurred to me until she mentioned it. Maybe my mind sheltered me from the possibility as well." He shook his head and continued walking. "Ironic, isn't it? I started my crusade against religion to avenge the murder of my wife and daughter, and now it seems religion had nothing to do with it."

"So you believe Alma killed them?"

"We'll probably never know, but that's the most logical conclusion."

She walked beside him in silence.

As the New Year ticked closer, the crowds grew. Revelers leaned out the windows of cars and taxis, shouting in joyous celebration along with the pedestrians.

"What are they saying?" he asked.

"I think they're yelling, *Happy Year One*."

"I suppose this is the start of new era."

They passed two young lovers locked in each other's arms—kissing, fondling, and testing the line of public decency. The girl was stunning, with long blonde hair and a body almost obscene, even fully clothed.

"I want you, Zack," the girl moaned. "Let's go to my place—"

A dark-haired girl shoved the two apart. She was pretty, but not in the same league as her rival. "I can't believe you dumped me for her!" she shouted at Zack.

The boy avoided her gaze. "C'mon, Jess, it's not like we were engaged or anything."

Jess pointed an accusing finger at the blonde and shouted, "She's my grandmother!"

Several people stopped to watch the spectacle.

Zack looked around as if seeking escape.

Jess turned to her grandmother. "How could you do this to me, Grandma?"

"I'm sorry, dear," the blonde bombshell said. "I couldn't resist."

"This is *my* time!" Jess screamed at the top of her lungs. Then she ran off in tears.

"You go, Granny!" a woman shouted. The two lovers hurried away hand in hand, to the delight of the crowd.

Helena shook her head. "I suppose the world has gotten a lot more complicated."

Rather than answering, he pulled her into an embrace and kissed her.

A wave of desire flooded her. "I have a room at the Waldorf," she whispered in his ear. "Why don't we—"

But his eyes drifted toward a group carrying a banner proclaiming *Theon is our true Savior!*

"Thanks be to Theon!" they chanted.

As the banner passed through the street, car horns honked approval, and people shouted their own acclamations: "Thanks be to Theon!" or "Theon rules!"

His mouth fell open.

"You saved their lives," Helena said. "Are you surprised that they worship you?"

"I guess I am."

She kept a firm grasp on his hand as they followed the crowd toward Time's Square. One by one, more people with signs of praise joined the flood of celebrants heading toward the city's epicenter.

"I'm not sure if this is a good idea," she said, but he kept walking.

As they neared Time's Square, their progress slowed. Theon gripped her hand tighter and pushed his way forward. Their five bodyguards pressed close around them.

At two police checkpoints, they flashed their Amara credentials, and passed through without question.

The famed crossroads of American culture resembled nothing less than a science fiction movie set.

The pulsing miasma of light, sound, and commercialism merged in joyous abandon. It was a rave, block party, and rock concert combined. A celebration of the human mind's triumph over the despotism of nature. What more appropriate place to declare victory over death?

A giant plasma screen displayed a series of time-lapse photos of elderly faces morphing to youthful vibrancy.

On a platform in the center of the square, a young Chuck Berry blasted out a guitar solo of his famous "Johnny B. Good," while thousands danced with the abandon of a mosh pit. A young Tina Turner, Bruce Springsteen, Tony Bennett, and Loretta Lynn cheered him on.

When the final chord struck, the crowd erupted in cheers. Many sported hats with the words *Happy Year One* emblazoned across them.

A man held his daughter on his shoulders beneath a prismatic snowstorm of confetti. She wore a pink winter coat, with a *My Little Pony* stocking cap on her head.

Fire dancers perched atop platforms suspended above the crowd—twirling flaming objects in spectacular arcs.

A few wore nothing but body paint and headdresses reminiscent of Mardi Gras queens. These virtually naked men and women maintained a continuous gyrating dance—as much to keep warm as to revel in their restored bodies.

At the end of his song, Chuck Berry raised a hand into the air and quieted the audience. "If you're listening to this broadcast, I want to give my sincerest thanks to you, Doctor Theon Torano, for granting me this rare encore performance in the recording session we call life."

An eruption of adulation rose from the square. Soon a chant of *Theon, Theon, Theon* split the night like a battle cry.

Helena squeezed his hand at this validation of his efforts.

He deserves this.

"Theon, Theon, Theon . . ."

More than one naked torso displayed the words *Theon is my God!*

A young Olivia de Havilland and Kirk Douglas ascended the platform. The crowd stilled as the woman they all knew from such film classics as *Captain Blood, The Adventures of Robin Hood,* and *Gone with the Wind* leaned toward the microphone.

"Thank you, Chuck, for your music and your words," Olivia said with a nod to the singer. "I must say that 1926 makes you a baby to Kirk and myself, since we were born ten years earlier than you."

Someone from the crowd shouted, "I've got you beat, since my birthday is 1912!"

The crowd laughed.

Kirk Douglas leaned close to Olivia. "My only regret is that so many of my friends and family passed away before this miracle of science."

Quiet settled over the square as these words sank in.

"I'd like to add my personal thanks to Theon Torano and the scientists who create every wonder surrounding us in this square. We've emerged from a world lit only by fire, to this!" Her gesture encompassed the towering skyscrapers, the crowd, and the city itself.

She'd been a Christian. Maybe she still was, in private. Signing the Immortality Contract could not have been easy.

Or maybe it was. Maybe that's Theon's point.

Not a hint of regret tinted that clear voice known across the globe. "The world salutes you, Theon Torano!" Olivia said.

Cheers erupted.

A young Tony Bennett claimed the microphone and launched into a rendition of his first hit song, "Because of You."

"Hey, you two love birds!" shouted Lamarr. Kyoko grasped his arm to keep from being swept away in the crush of bodies.

Both were slim, young, and stunning. Lamarr was clean-shaven, and his hair bloomed upward in a lush black Afro. He wore jeans with a peace sign on the right thigh, a leather jacket with dangling fringe running the length of the sleeves, and a pair of battered old cowboy boots. He could have been mistaken for Jimi Hendrix.

Kyoko wore a silk kimono decorated with hand-painted flowers. A series of butterfly pins corralled her lush black hair into an elaborate bun, and her bright eyes transformed her into a princess straight out of a Kurosawa epic.

"How did you find us?" Helena asked.

Kyoko held up her phone. A red and a blue dot labeled T and H blinked on a map of the city. "Your implanted bio-trackers, of course."

I'll never get used to those damn things.

"Look at what Lamarr gave me!" Kyoko extended her left hand. A pink diamond engagement ring—ten carats at least—graced the third finger.

Lamarr rolled his eyes. "Caught me in a weak moment, I guess."

"What do you mean?" Kyoko said indignantly. "You chased me for three weeks. Oh, please, Kyoko, I love you so much. Please marry me. I'll be miserable forever if you don't."

Lamarr scrunched his face as if trying to recall. "Doesn't ring a bell."

"What does that mean, ring bell?" Kyoko asked. She'd never mastered American slang.

"It means I'm taking you to the room for a quickie!" Lamarr hoisted her in his arms with ease.

"You're terrible!" Kyoko slapped him playfully and then kissed him.

"I hear congratulations are in order," Lamarr said, setting his bride back on her feet. "This must be a record at your age!"

Kyoko pinched Lamarr's arm through his jacket.

"Ow! What was that for?" Then he looked at Helena's tense expression. "In the immortal words of Governor Rick Perry—oops."

"You are such an idiot," Kyoko said, and dragged him away.

"At least I had the brains to marry someone smart," Lamarr said. "Unlike you!"

They disappeared into the crowd, and Theon turned to her with a raised eyebrow.

Damn, no more putting it off now.

Tony Bennett began another ballad.

A hive of anxiety swarmed in her gut. Would he be happy, upset, scarred?

"I'm pregnant," she said.

His brow contracted as if faced with Zeno's Infinity Paradox for the first time. "How can that be?"

Not the reaction I'd hoped for.

"I didn't plan it, if that's what you're implying. If you didn't want children with me, you should have—"

"That's not what I meant. I'm overjoyed, of course!"

"You have a funny way of showing it."

He lifted her above the crowd and spun in a tight circle. "I'm going to be a father!" he shouted to the sky. Those nearby cheered and blew their noisemakers.

"Let me go, you barbarian!" she said through her laughter.

He obediently returned her to the ground.

"I don't understand why you were so surprised?" she said.

"Women are born with all the eggs they'll have their entire lifetime," he said.

"And I lost the last of mine when I reached menopause."

Of course! Why hadn't I thought of that?

"I assumed all women past a certain age would remain infertile despite the Fountain of Youth pill."

"Life finds a way," she said.

"I'm not sure it's a good idea to quote *Jurassic Park*. My miscalculation could result in equally dire—"

He stopped and looked around.

Tony Bennett had gone silent.

She glanced at the giant screen mounted above the stage. On the left half of it was the famous black-and-white photograph of her, Theon, and Taslima at MIT. On the right side of the screen was a live shot of them standing in the middle of Times Square.

"It's them!" someone nearby shouted. "It's Theon Torano and Helena Mueller!"

Oh, shit. One of the camera operators must have recognized us.

Ryan Seacrest pointed at them. "Ladies and Gentlemen, please welcome Doctor Theon Torano and Helena Mueller!"

A spotlight pinioned them, and the crowd cheered.

There was no hiding now. Helena took Theon's hand and waved.

The cheers rose to a roar.

"Join us on stage," Ryan called out.

A human corridor opened through the crowd. Their security team followed close behind, but Helena motioned them to keep a low profile. A few people patted their shoulders and backs as they passed, but most recorded the historic moment on their phones.

"Thank you for saving my life," a girl in a flapper dress called out.

"You're the greatest scientist that's every lived!" shouted a man in a World War II bomber jacket.

They mounted the stage, and each of the celebrities shook their hands. Olivia de Havilland knelt before Theon and kissed his hand as if greeting King Richard the Lionheart as Maid Marian.

Theon blushed at the display, but a million people roared their approval.

Helena smiled.

After so much suffering, he deserved this.

Ryan Seacrest stepped forward. "There's a couple of minutes before the countdown. I can't think of anyone more suited to say a few words to close out this extraordinary Year One."

Silence enshrouded the gathering as Theon took the microphone. Tears streaked his face as he gazed at the thousands upon thousands of young faces. "I must say that you're all looking quite well."

The audience laughed.

"One year ago, I appeared before you as an old man, my body twisted and wheelchair-bound, as many of you probably were. I cannot claim credit for this great achievement. I stand on the shoulders of giants, not the least of which is my deceased wife, Taslima."

Theon reached a hand toward Helena, and she took hold of it.

"I hope I've nudged the world toward a better path. A path of peace and prosperity. A path of environmental restoration. A new era of science and reason that can lift us to achievements that will dwarf my contribution."

Cheers bathed them in gratitude.

Theon put his arm around her shoulders and handed Ryan the microphone.

"One minute to go!" Ryan called out. The digital clock passed the one-minute mark, and the giant globe began its descent.

The crowd chanted the countdown. With each second, the globe pulsed a new color.

"Here we go!" Ryan shouted as the ball neared the street. "Ten, nine, eight, seven . . ."

The volume grew.

"Six, five, four, three, two, ONE!"

The crowd roared and confetti filled the air. Horns blasted, and everyone kissed those nearest.

Tony Bennett sang, "Should old acquaintance be forgot . . ."

It was too loud to hear, but Theon's mouth formed the words, *I love you.* Then their lips met, the life inside her snuggled between them.

When Tony Bennett switched to a rendition of "New York, New York," all the legendary singers and actors on the stage accompanied him.

A giant balloon of Marilyn Monroe appeared between the buildings high above the gathering. It depicted her in the classic pose, holding her dress down as it exposed her long legs. A fan attached to Marilyn's back kept the balloon on course.

As it drifted above the square, the crowd looked up her skirt and cheered.

Suddenly, the iconic sex symbol exploded in a blinding flash.

Theon pulled Helena to the ground and covered her body with his own. The cheers transformed into screams and then a stampede.

Bits of shredded rubber rained down, but there was no shrapnel. The propeller plummeted to the street, but those beneath it managed to dive aside before it hit the pavement.

"It appears the balloon simply burst," Ryan Seacrest announced.

Theon helped Helena up.

Above, a cloud of what looked like leaflets fluttered toward them. As they reached the crowd, people grabbed them out of the air.

Theon plucked one of the papers from the platform and held it before them both.

The first line was in red Arabic characters. Below that was an English translation, also printed in a deep crimson.

It read: *The Mahdi has Risen.*

Chapter 20

Reza settled into the straight-backed chair and arranged his robes as the cameraman fine-tuned the lighting. A makeup artist trimmed the dark beard he'd grown in the past year.

Iran's Supreme Leader, Ayatollah Ali Khamenei, had presented the black clerical robe to him personally.

The memory of Khamenei embracing him after hearing the story of his death and rebirth filled him with awe at the power of Allah to reveal his truth to even the most powerful of men.

Most important of all, the Ayatollah gave him unrestricted access to the Setad, the secretive conglomeration of businesses under the direct control of the Supreme Leader. This shadowy organization had amassed over a hundred billion dollars since its founding in 1989. By pledging his personal wealth to his cause, this descendant of the Prophet Muhammad declared his complete acceptance of Reza as the true Mahdi.

The room was little more than a concrete box filled with computers, video cameras, and everything needed to connect with the outside world. Naked florescent lights hung beside pipes carrying electricity, water, and high-speed fiber optic cable.

It resembled a submarine that had plunged five stories beneath the earth. No bombs could reach him here, even if his enemies guessed his location.

"Three minutes to broadcast," his director of propaganda announced to the dozen people in the room. Everyone remained focused on his assigned task—except the two young men chained to the wall opposite him.

The prisoners wore the same white, buttoned-down shirts his brother and father used to wear. The shine had gone from their shoes, and the knees of their dark trousers were torn and bloody.

Both looked college-age, but the resemblance ended there. The taller one had a long, angular face with three days' growth of stubble. The shorter had close-set eyes and a jaunty mustache, though the tips had drooped.

In contrast to the eager faces surrounding them, the two men sat tense and frozen in place. They hunched in on themselves, as if willing their bodies to vanish. The shackles on their legs and wrists were threaded through iron rings set into the concrete walls, making escape impossible. Their unnatural stillness suffused every bit of their countenance except for their eyes, which darted like cornered rats seeking a way out of a trap.

Reza drew in a breath and let it out slowly. His entire being ached with a profound exhaustion extending through mind, muscle, and into the marrow of his bones.

He'd crisscrossed the back roads of every nation with a Muslim majority. He'd met with Jihadist organizations, government ministers, Imams, Islamic scholars, military commanders, as well as hundreds upon hundreds of tribal elders. His team traveled only by car, under assumed names, and with the help of his growing network of loyalists.

The revolution to end all others was planned and disseminated in person, face-to-face, and strictly through word of mouth. He'd forbidden his name's use in any electronic medium. Cell phones and computers were the realm of the Shaytan and shunned as if declared haram by Allah himself.

His efforts had taken their toll, but produced stunning fruit. In little under a year, every Islamist group in the Muslim world had sworn allegiance to him—both Sunni and Shia alike. ISIL, al-Qaida, Boko Haram, al-Nushrah, Ansar al-Shari'a, al-Mulathamun, the Haggani Network, the Army of Islam, the Taliban, al-Shabaab, the Islamic Jihad Union, Ansar al-Islam, Hizballah, HAMAS, and dozens of other smaller organizations. His reach extended into every Islamic government, military, and mosque across the Muslim world.

The direct assault on Islam had bound the followers of Allah into common purpose for the first time in a thousand years.

The Immortality Contract had proved a valuable resource. Since the list of those who had signed was publicly posted on the Internet, it made it easy to identify who was trustworthy and who was not, especially among older Muslims.

Reza frowned. *If only I could join my men on the front lines this glorious day.*

But the honor of dying in battle and returning to his seventy-two Houris would have to wait. He'd been chosen by Allah for a task vastly more important than his personal pleasure.

"Mahdi," the director said with a deferential bow. "We are ready."

Reza nodded and turned toward the camera. Within its wide lens, his own face stared back at him. Behind his reflected double, the black flag of the Mahdi acted as a backdrop. White Arabic script ran across it like the trails of comets, reading: *Together—Unbreakable.*

A red light on the camera blinked to life, signaling that the feed was streaming live across the Internet.

"I am the Mahdi," he said. "A few of you already know the story of how I died in the service of Allah—of how I made the ultimate sacrifice in putting to death my own brother and grandparents when they deserted our Creator.

"During my sojourn away from this world, I experienced the pleasures of glorious Jannah. I've caressed the jasmine-scented skin of my seventy-two Houris—tasted the fig, honey, and fruits no earthly garden can match. I have met Allah face-to-face."

Reza paused, his brow furrowing to convey his sadness at leaving such a place. "I yearn to join the brave martyrs in this glorious moment when we take back our lands. It is with envy that I watch each martyr claim their reward in Jannah—a realm I so desperately wish to return to. But Allah will not allow me to go until I face the Dajjal and his evil army alongside the best of our warriors in the final battle before the Day of Judgment.

"Mohammad tells us that this deceiver will be blind to the light of Allah and all spiritual insights, but will glory instead in worldly attainment. I tell you now that this servant of Gog and Magog is the great deceiver known as Theon Torano."

Reza stared into the camera's lens. The fiery battles of Armageddon danced within it, and his heart pounded in anticipation.

"I, the Mahdi, chosen by Allah, will battle this demon face-to-face in Dabiq. There, I will slay him in fulfillment of prophecy. Afterward, I will earn my martyrdom alongside the bravest warriors of Islam."

Reza motioned to the guards. They unhooked the prisoners from the wall and led them to chairs beside him.

Long Face sat trembling, while Mustache stared at the ground at his feet.

"For both of you," Reza said, "your personal Judgment Day has arrived."

"Forgive me, Mahdi," Long Face said through tears. "I've realized my error and want to repent." The man struggled to hold his hands upward, palms open and facing Heaven in supplication. He remained motionless in this pose of contrition for several seconds. But the weight of his shackles gradually pulled his outstretched arms downward until his muscles gave out. His hands fell to his knees with a clank of metal.

As Long Face gasped from the effort, Mustache continued staring at the ground as if unaware of his surroundings.

"What is your profession?" Reza asked Long Face.

"I was a nuclear physicist. I worked under Abdul Qadeer Khan in developing the first nuclear bomb for Pakistan."

"May I ask how old you are?"

Long Face twitched, and he averted his eyes. "I'm seventy-two." He gazed at the Mahdi with desperation. "I wanted to be young again so I could continue my work. I wanted to help other Muslim nations achieve what Pakistan has. To give us the same weapons the West . . ." He trailed off.

"And so you left Pakistan and moved to Sweden the day after Theon's announcement?"

"I still pray five times a day in private. I'm a devoted Muslim. You must believe me."

"You understand we're broadcasting live?" Reza asked. "Your public declaration of faith violates the Immortality Contract."

"I was wrong to sign it. I know that now." He began sobbing. "There is no god but Allah, and Muhammad is his Prophet! Please, forgive me—please don't let me die an apostate."

Without Allah, death is terrifying. I can almost hear Ahmad's screams echoing from the fires of Ladthaa.

Reza gently placed a hand on the man's shoulder. "What is your name?"

The man looked up. "My name is Munir Siddiqui."

"Do you understand why signing the Immortality Contract is blasphemy?"

Munir nodded vigorously. "Yes, Mahdi, I understand."

"Good," Reza said with a smile. "Allah is compassionate and forgiving, so maybe he will have mercy on your soul."

"Thank you."

Reza stood. "Are there any other sins on your soul you need to confess?"

"I have sinned," Munir said. "I confess it."

Reza drew a curved knife from within his robes.

Munir's eyes widened.

The florescent light shimmered across the blade.

"What was your job in Sweden?" Reza asked.

The prisoner's head slumped forward. "Because of my education, I oversaw one of the Amara distribution centers in Gothenburg."

Reza walked behind the prisoners and seized Munir's hair in his left fist.

Munir thrashed like a fish on a hook until the edge touched his throat. Then he went still, though his mouth kept opening and closing as if unable to breathe.

The sour smell of sweat and fear filled the air.

"I might have pardoned this man for signing the Immortality Contract, but I cannot overlook treason. For working in the service of the Shaytan, I herby sentence Munir Siddiqui to the eternal punishment awaiting him in the next life."

The curved knife was as long as his forearm. It cut through skin, muscle, and tendon in a horizontal arc around the neck. Blood spurted in every direction.

Only the spine kept the head connected. Keeping hold of Munir's hair with his left hand, Reza stepped back and swung the blade like a sword. It hit the vertebrae and sliced through it.

Reza held the severed head before the camera. "This is the fate of all who desert Allah."

The faces of those in the studio stared, their eyes wide as if witnessing a miracle.

Reza took his seat and laid the decapitated lump in the second prisoner's lap.

Still, Mustache did not move. Splattered blood covered his face and dripped off the ends of his mustache.

"What is your name?" Reza asked.

"My name is Abdul Bari. You might as well kill me now. I was ninety-four and on the verge of death when I signed the Immortality Contract, so the result will be the same once I stop taking the pill."

"Are you so afraid of death?"

Abdul looked up, his brown eyes puzzled. "I was a devout man. I observed each of the five pillars of Islam without exception. Completing the Haj in my youth was the highlight of my life. I looked forward to my reward in Jannah when I died."

"Why did you leave for the West?" Reza asked.

"The devil Assad destroyed our village. I fled with my children and grandchildren to a refugee center in Germany, where I've lived for the past three years. At my age, it was hard."

The prisoner's eyes lost their focus. "It was only when I learned of the possibility of a return to youth that my doubts began. Knowing death was inevitable had made it easy to believe. What other hope was there? Maybe my faith was based on fear? I thought youth would make me happy, but I've been haunted by that choice ever since."

Abdul pressed his fists against his forehead, his shackles clattering like wind chimes warning of an approaching storm. "How could I have been so stupid? How could I have turned my back on Allah and everything I held dear my entire life? And now I will pay the price for eternity."

Am I to condemn this man because of a single moment of weakness?

Reza gently pulled the man's fists from his face and cradled Abdul's hands in his own. "What if I offered you the chance to use your remaining days for redemption?"

Abdul looked at him with eyes wide. "But how?" His gaze drifted toward the headless body chained to the chair next to him. "Just as you said, I have betrayed Allah. It is too late for me."

"Have you assisted the Shaytan by volunteering at the Amara distribution centers?"

I will know if he lies.

"Never," Abdul said without hesitation. He didn't offer alibis or other forms of proof. He seemed content to let the Mahdi judge him by his word alone.

"You are telling the truth," Reza said. "Remove his bonds."

Two soldiers unlocked his shackles.

Reza used a towel to wipe the blood off his face and mustache. Then he took the head sitting in Abdul's lap and tossed it aside.

"You are free to go," Reza said.

"Thank you, Mahdi," Abdul said. "But how can I cleanse such sins in the short time left to me?"

Reza motioned, and one of the soldiers walked over with a heavy vest. Sewn around it were metal pipes with wires connected to a small handgrip with a red button on top.

Abdul's eyes widened. "Is that . . . ?"

"A suicide vest," Reza said. "It is not a requirement of your release. You may use your remaining months however you see fit, but I'm offering you the opportunity to die as a martyr if you choose."

Abdul fell to his knees and looked up with tears overflowing his eyes. "It would be the greatest honor to give my life in the service of Allah. Surely you are the Mahdi to have pity on someone as unworthy as me."

The man prostrated himself before him, but Reza pulled him to his feet. "Bow before none but Allah."

Abdul nodded and took the heavy vest. He cradled it as one might a newborn child, smiling from ear to ear in joy.

The soldiers led him away.

How I wish I could trade places with him.

Reza faced the camera and picked up his bloody knife. "The time has come to prove your devotion to Allah. Take to the streets immediately. You will know my commanders by this flag you see behind me. No longer will the West divide and conquer us. Together, we are unbreakable!"

Adrenaline surged through him, and he felt his exhaustion shedding. He pointed the knife at the camera, his eyes glaring into the lens with the ferocity of a thousand years of oppression.

"Every true Muslim must prove their devotion this day. Whatever your sins, this is your chance at redemption—but only if you act. Tear down the buildings defiled by Amara Pharmaceuticals. Put to death the Muslim collaborates of this Western devil, even if it be the leader of your own nation.

"The godless Westerners fear death. That is their great weakness. But we, Allah's faithful, do not fear the next life. We give our lives in service to our Creator, knowing our reward in Jannah will be better than anything in this world. So go forth, my brothers and sisters, in Allah, and prove yourselves worthy."

Reza paused and took a step toward the camera. "To the great deceiver, Theon Torano, I issue this challenge. Gather your godless army with all of its man-made technology, all of your bombs, missiles, planes, tanks, your cowardly drones, and your nuclear weapons. Meet me face-to-face with your forces of evil in the town of Dabiq at the time of your choosing. Then we will see whether your science is a match for Allah."

Chapter 21

Their helicopter landed on the lawn of the White House forty-five minutes after midnight.

Theon followed Helena out the door, and they ran toward the two waiting secret service officers.

What have I gotten us into?

They had watched the Mahdi's live broadcast on their cell phones during the flight. He'd vomited into an airsick bag when the Mahdi decapitated the Pakistani scientist.

Cisco and Poncho met them at the door and led the way toward the situation room. Their continued presence on President Campbell's personal secret service team spoke volumes of the trust he had in their joint project.

"Why are we here?" Helena asked. "We're not government officials or military."

"The president requested it," he said.

"This could be a very slippery slope."

"I agree, but I don't think we have a choice."

They reached the elevator at the same time as the president, who'd been attending a New Year's Eve event at the United Nations. He looked young and fit—more like a Yale upperclassman than the leader of the free world.

The Director of the CIA accompanied the president. "The uprisings started after the Mahdi's live broadcast."

"What the Hell is a Mahdi?" the president asked.

"Islam's version of the second coming of Christ," the CIA chief said. "Muslims believe the Mahdi will bring about the final battle between good and evil before the Day of Judgment."

"Well, that's just great. Things were going so well." The president glanced at the elevator. "You'd think I wouldn't have to wait for my own elevator."

"They say it's on its way up," Cisco said.

"I thought the Mahdi was prophesied to arise after the battle in Dabiq?" Theon asked.

"The Mahdi's new website claims the prophecy was mistranslated," CIA said, "and that he's received the corrected version from Allah himself."

The president scowled. "He has a website?"

"Also Instagram, Twitter, and YouTube. Every time we block one, a dozen take their place under different names."

The elevator opened and they entered. Cisco and Poncho stayed as guards. The doors closed, and the president rested his thumb against a touchpad. It beeped and the elevator descended.

"Which countries are we talking about?" the president asked.

"Saudi Arabia, Turkey, Egypt, Syria, Yemen, Iraq, Oman, Libya, Tunisia, Indonesia, Bangladesh, Afghanistan, Nigeria and—most troubling of all—Pakistan."

Theon exchanged a glanced with Helena. Her left hand rested on her abdomen.

"Goddammit, Alan," the president said. "How could every intelligence agency miss this?"

The CIA chief shook his head. "They avoided electronic communications, and we lack HUMINT in Muslim regions these days."

The elevator doors opened, and they emerged into a room packed with analysts monitoring several dozen screens.

Signs of interrupted New Year's Eve parties were everywhere— bits of confetti clinging to hair, the lingering odor of champagne, and the festive clothing so out of place in a room reserved for the most sober national emergencies.

"The Turkish parliament is under siege," a young woman in a bedazzled cocktail dress called out.

"Baghdad has fallen to the Mahdi's forces," another analyst shouted, his tuxedo covered in the remains of silly string and glitter.

Images of mayhem and violence filled every screen. News outlets streamed on-the-spot cell phone videos of street battles, while grainy feeds from satellites and drones added a black-and-white bird's eye view. With the constant flashes of explosions, the room resembled an arcade.

The CIA chief pulled the president toward several analysts for a private update.

Theon stood with Helena near the elevator doors.

What use can we be here?

General Tilton, the commander of the Joint Chiefs, monitored the chaos with a gruff calm. Aids thrust reports into his hands and he scanned them—then issued curt orders in reply.

Theon frowned. He'd avoided the general as much as possible. The sixty-year-old career soldier refused to sign the Immortality Contract and made no bones about the fact that he never would. His gray hair added a certain gravitas to his commanding stature.

The general resembled Bulldog Rooney, the political boss who once ruled his Chicago neighborhood. Every election, Bulldog knocked on their door—rain, sun, or shine.

"I can count on you voting a straight Democratic ticket, can't I, Mister Torano?" the burly precinct captain would ask his father. He always brought a bag of groceries as a gift. It would have been a kind gesture, if it hadn't been a bribe.

Had Bulldog actually cared about the struggling family with no mother, he could have given Dad one of the well-paying patronage jobs under his control. But those were reserved for mobsters and Bulldog's own relatives.

Dad always nodded, took the groceries, and voted Republican, no matter how much he despised the candidate. "I haven't taken a bribe if it doesn't buy my vote," Dad reasoned.

They especially enjoyed the Twinkies and Little Debbie's Bulldog included with the groceries.

When the general's close-set eyes spotted them, the corners of Tilton's mouth twitched into a snarl. "You caused this."

"Islamic terrorism has existed long before the Immortality Contract," Helena said.

"But he's unified them."

"Isn't it better to face the threat sooner than later?" Theon asked.

The general motioned to a sergeant stationed at the elevator. "Escort these civilians out—with force if necessary."

The sergeant didn't move. Was it fear of removal from Amara's list?

Not fear, something else.

It was the look Lamarr got when he spoke of Martin Luther King or Harold Washington. It was hero worship.

"I gave you an order, Soldier!"

"Sir, this man saved my parents' lives," the sergeant replied.

The general flushed. "Are you aware that disobeying a direct command from a superior officer in time of war is punishable by death?"

The soldier snapped to attention, but made no move.

"We were just leaving," Theon said, and guided Helena toward the elevator.

"They're here at my request," the president said, as if reminding everyone who the Commander in Chief was. "What is our plan, General?"

The general glared at the soldier, but finally turned to the president. "This is a revolution. There is no buildup along any borders, and no columns of tanks for us to target."

"I asked you what you planned to do, General."

The general ground his teeth. "There's nothing we can do, *sir*."

"Are you telling me the entire region is falling to radical Islamists and we're standing by and watching it happen?"

The CIA chief said, "There's little threat to us, unless—"

"Unless they gain control of Pakistan's nuclear arsenal," Helena said.

"At least one of you has brains," the general said.

It was the nightmare scenario—religious fanatics with nukes.

"What are Pakistan's nuclear capabilities?" the president asked his CIA chief.

"In late 2006, the Pakistanis constructed a new reactor at Khushab to produce enough plutonium for forty to fifty nuclear weapons a year. By now, they have at least a hundred, but the most troubling are the smaller plutonium bombs spiked with tritium. This increases the yield by three to four times. At only twenty pounds, they can be carried in a backpack or hidden in the trunk of a car."

A chill crept down Theon's spine. "Do we know where they are?"

"Ever since the Bin Laden raid, Pakistan sees their arsenal as a deterrence against an attack by the US," the CIA chief said. "Since then, they've tried to hide a good deal of it from us."

"We can't wait for the government to fall," the general said. "We must go in immediately."

"I agree with the general," the CIA chief said.

But still the president hesitated. "Get me the Pakistani prime minister on the phone."

The president walked to a side desk and spoke into a land-line phone while they waited. When he returned, he looked more positive.

"The prime minister says they're making progress against the rebels, and their nuclear arsenal is secure."

"Of course—he has to say that!" the general said.

"If I send our forces in too soon, Pakistan could launch a retaliatory strike on Europe."

"Which is better than radical Islamic terrorists getting hold of nuclear weapons and putting American cities in danger," the general said.

"It's my call," the president said, "and I want to see how things play out before crossing a line of no return."

General Tilton spoke through clenched teeth. "We should bomb every one of those damn Hajjis into the Stone Age."

"Not all Muslims are terrorists," Helena said.

The general turned on her with the fierceness of a bull elephant protecting its herd. "Nowhere else in the world do you see people blowing themselves up for their god. Islam is a cancer, and we must cut it out before it metastasizes. The only solution is wiping out the source once and for all."

Theon pointed to the street battles on the television screens. "Those Muslims fighting the Mahdi are not radicals. They have families and the same dreams for freedom as we do. They deserve our help."

"The typical bleeding-heart liberal," the general said. "You caused this mess by trying to force your ideology on the world, and now won't take responsibility for the consequences. It's left to realists like me to clean up your mess."

He's right. I am hoping he will come to the rescue.

Helena got in the general's face. "It wasn't liberals that dragged us into Iraq and created the conditions for radicals like this to metastasize."

"This is pointless," the president said. "Let's deal with the situation before us and leave the blame for later."

"President Kane would never have hesitated to act when American lives—"

"General Tilton," the president said. "I am your Commander in Chief, not *former* President Kane. If you don't like that, submit your resignation now."

A vein in the general's temple pulsed. For a moment, he seemed ready to attack the president. But then he saluted. "Yes, sir, you are my Commander in Chief." The general walked away and continued monitoring the situation.

With nothing else to do, everyone watched the screens in silence. One by one, governments fell, but no one in the room paid much attention. Only Pakistan mattered now.

Al Jazeera aired live images of the Mahdi's supporters charging directly into machine gun fire, shouting *Allah Akbar!*

Helena averted her eyes. "How can they throw their lives away so easily?"

"Words are the most powerful mind-altering drugs humans have ever created," Theon said. "The Mahdi has convinced them that death is a reward."

An analyst shouted, "I'm getting reports that large portions of the Pakistani military are defecting to the Mahdi."

"Turkey is teetering on the brink," another analyst said.

CNN and the BBC lost contact with the region.

Al Jazeera broadcast gruesome street executions of scientists and university professors. Some were beaten to death, some beheaded, and a few doused with gasoline and set on fire atop piles of science textbooks and equipment. It was the Islamist version the Florentine Bonfire of the Vanities. In 1497 the Dominican priest Girolamo Savanorola had sought to cleanse Christian society for the glorious Day of Judgment just as the Mahdi was attempting to accomplish for the Islamic world.

Is history nothing but a repeating cycle of stupidity?

"Truck bombs are attacking Syria's Presidential Palace in Damascus," an analyst called out.

"What about Pakistan, dammit!" the president asked.

The general held a phone to his ear. "Our teams are in place, awaiting the order to go."

"The Israelis are screaming at the delay," the CIA chief said. "They will act without us if we wait much longer."

"No, they won't," the president said. "They have even more to lose from a nuclear counter strike than us."

"The Pakistani military claims their sites are secure," the National Security Advisor said with a phone pressed against his ear.

"Do we have eyes on their installations?" the president asked.

A dozen screens' satellite views of the installations came up. Gunfire flashed along the perimeters, and clouds of smoke billowed from burning vehicles.

Now and then a car separated from the encircling mass of attackers and rammed the defenses. The resulting explosion whited-out the screen for several seconds, then cleared to show the resulting crater.

"They've blasted through most of the checkpoints with car bombs," the general said. "Once they load those bombs into trucks, there's no way we can track that many."

"How can you deal with so many facilities?" Theon asked.

"We'll prioritize those closest to falling and move on to the next most critical once those are dealt with," the National Security Advisor said. "But we have to start soon or there won't be time."

A wave of trucks suddenly poured out of one of the facilities. The encircling horde parted, letting the defenders leave without resistance.

"They're running for their lives," the CIA director said.

"It's exactly what happened when ISIS struck in Syria and Iraq," the general said. "Those men want to live, while the Mahdi's forces seek death as martyrs. One suicide bomber is equal to a hundred soldiers."

"If they get even one of those bombs . . ." Helena said.

"Inform the Pakistanis that we're going in." The president turned to the general. "Order JSOC and Central Command to attack."

General Tilton put the phone to his ear and said, "Mission Render-Safe is a go."

Real-time feeds from attack helicopters appeared on screens around the room. Pakistan crowded out every other country's newsfeed.

Helena gripped Theon's arm as two of the screens flashed and then went dark.

"Bravo Six and Delta Two hit."

"Take out their radar," the general ordered.

Fighter jets crossed the border, their progress displayed on a digital map of the region. White numbers represented the squadrons of helicopters making their way toward their targets.

One after the other, the jets launched their missiles, and the Pakistani air defenses vanished.

"We're officially at war with Pakistan," the general said.

Al Jazeera broadcast a live feed of the Pakistani parliament besieged by mobs.

"There won't be a Pakistan for much longer," Theon said.

"Any sign of a ballistic counter?" the president asked.

"No launch detected."

"They're either unwilling or unable to respond," the general said.

"Foxtrot Five initiating assault," came a voice through the speakers.

On one screen, ten helicopters hovered above an installation.

"Team on ground," said Foxtrot Five. "Initiating cover fire." The helicopters fanned out from the drop point and fired on the wave of attackers flooding through the breached perimeter.

"Can't we just bomb them instead?" Helena asked.

"They're buried too deep for conventional weapons," Theon said. "It would take a nuclear strike."

A surface-to-air missile connected with a helicopter. It fireballed and plummeted to the ground.

"Air support requested," Foxtrot Five said.

"Cover is on its way," said the general.

When the fighter jets arrived, a ring of destruction erupted on the satellite image.

"How's that, Foxtrot Five?" the fighter pilot asked.

"Much obliged. That'll give us some breathing room."

The helicopters hovered as the ground teams disarmed, dismantled, and evacuated the fissile material.

A second column of Jihadists neared. This time, they lobbed mortars and rocket-propelled grenades ahead of them. Most troubling were the columns of tanks.

Five more teams reached their targets at different facilities. The calls for air cover exceeded the number of jets in the air, so the general left it to the commanders on site to triage resources.

"Material secure," Foxtrot Five reported.

The helicopters extracted the surviving soldiers and headed for the border.

"Clear for cleanup," said Foxtrot Five.

The cruise missiles launched from an aircraft carrier patrolling the Arabian Sea. Theon watched with everyone else as the blue icons inched across the map of Pakistan, then turned red at the target. When the smoke cleared, nothing but a massive crater remained. It had been *rendered safe*.

"Delta Seven reporting mission complete," said a voice over the intercom.

Everyone cheered—except Theon and Helena.

"I've lost the line to the prime minister's office."

A shaky video from Al Jazeera displayed the front entrance of the massive Secretariat building in Islamabad that served as the official residence and workplace of Pakistan's leaders.

Mobs looted furniture, computers, and anything of value. Flames danced within the windows, but the most disturbing image was a body hanging from the roof.

"That's the prime minister," the president said. "It's time to take out the reactors and centrifuges."

"Won't that cause radioactive fallout?" Theon asked.

"Leaving them for the Mahdi would be worse," said the CIA chief.

Cruise missiles launched and sped to their targets.

Soon, two dozen battles raged at once. When one site was cleared the teams moved to the next.

"Air support requested!" came the repeated call.

"We're down to the last five sites," The National Security Advisor said.

"All jets are dry," said an analyst.

"Goddamn it!" the general shouted. "Get them rearmed!"

"That's our last cruise missile," reported another analyst.

The teams completed their missions until a final site remained.

"It's a big one," the National Security Advisor said. "Forty cruise missiles armed with plutonium cores."

"What's the delay?" the president asked, his lips a thin white line of tension.

"They're holding us off with hardened air defenses," an analyst said.

"Why didn't we take those out with airstrikes?"

The general scowled. "Because we had more pressing targets in danger of falling to the Mahdi."

"No one's attacking that site," the CIA chief said. "We can take our time until the jets are rearmed and refueled."

"Why the hell are they even firing at us?" the general asked. "Do they want their nukes in the hands of the Mahdi?"

"I think they already are," Helena said, and pointed to the soldiers loading equipment into trucks.

"Christ Almighty!" the general said. "The other attacks were diversions so we'd have nothing left for their real target."

"Their commander must be a collaborator," Theon said.

"How long before we have air support back?" the president asked.

"Twenty to thirty minutes."

"It's too long," said the CIA chief. "Those trucks will be gone by then."

"We have to nuke them," the general said.

"Wouldn't that detonate all forty bombs at once?" the president asked.

Theon shook his head. "It's unlikely, but not impossible."

The color drained from Helena's face. "If forty plutonium bombs exploded at the same moment . . ."

"The dust cloud would blot out the sun for years," Theon said. "We're talking a nuclear winter with ninety-nine percent of life on the planet extinct."

The room went still.

"Then we can't risk it," the president said.

"Would you rather those bombs go off one at a time in our cities?" the general asked.

The president got to within inches of the general, his face flushed with anger. "I don't like either possibility, but total extinction seems worse."

"I warned you about this damned Immortality Contract from the beginning," the general said.

"It will take time to dismantle those warheads," the National Security Advisor said. "By then we should have fighters back in the area to take out those air defenses. Then our assault teams can do the rest."

"It's possible the trucks are a decoy to buy time," Theon said.

"Time for what?" the president asked.

"Their ultimate goal is Armageddon," Theon said. "Maybe they're planning on detonating all forty of the nukes right where they are?"

"The ultimate suicide bomb," the president whispered.

"Wouldn't they have done that already?" Helena asked.

"They'd need the codes from the prime minister," the CIA chief said. "And he's dead."

"How long would it take to rewire the warheads?" Theon asked.

The National Security Advisor frowned. "Depending on the safeguards, I'd estimate one to two hours."

"It's been an hour and a half already," the CIA chief said.

"Order Seal Team Four in."

"It's pointless without air support. They'd be cut to pieces."

"That was an order, General!"

The general's face tightened, but he gave the command.

The two dozen helicopters attacked the target. Surface-to-air missiles streaked upward, and half the video feeds went dark.

"Alpha Ten down. Foxtrot Three hit. Charlie Six down—"

Fifty Army Rangers fast-roped from the hovering choppers. Once on the ground, they threw aside their leather gloves and returned fire.

Those are brave men.

Four more helicopters crashed.

The remaining helicopters retreated to a safe distance, leaving only the grainy satellite image of the battle.

"It's no use," the team commander said over the radio link. "We can't get in without air cover."

The president seemed frozen in place. The left side of his face twitched.

Is he having a stroke?

The CIA chief gripped the president's shoulder. "If we give them time to set all forty off at once, it's game over for the planet."

"Mr. President!" the general shouted.

The president shuddered as if coming out of a dream. He looked at Helena, then Theon. "What do you think I should do?"

Theon swallowed. "Mr. President, it's not our place to—"

"You got me into this, goddamn it! I want to know what you think."

Theon glanced at Helena. Her lower lip trembled.

"Tell me," the president said.

Everyone in the room watched him. The vein in the general's forehead looked ready to burst.

"I agree with the general," Theon said.

The president turned to Helena. "And you?"

"Leave her out of this," Theon said.

"I'm not doing this unless everyone agrees."

Helena straightened. "We have no choice."

"Evacuate Seal Team Four and bring me the football."

"Mission abort," General Tilton said into his phone.

A secret service officer placed a black suitcase on a table and unshackled it from his wrist. The president pressed his thumb against a square on the front. After it flashed green, he typed in a code. It snapped open. Then the president removed several folders.

"What assets are in range?" the president asked.

"I've got a sub with a plutonium bunker-buster," the general said. "There will be less fallout than a conventional nuke."

Helena's grip tightened on Theon's arm. Her eyes were wide with horror. "Is this actually happening?"

"How long to evacuate our men?" the president asked.

"There's not enough time for that," the general said.

"How long, dammit!"

"About ten minutes until they're outside the blast zone, but we can't—"

"Prepare the sub for launch on my command," the president said. He opened a folder and read a series of numbers and letters into a phone.

Helena buried her face in Theon's chest, but then looked back at the screen.

"Codes received and verified," came the voice of the submarine captain. "Awaiting orders to fire."

"Stand by, Echo Three," the president said.

The dots representing the helicopters crept across the large map on the main display. A red circle appeared around the target site.

"That's the blast radius," the general said. "They need to be halfway before we launch for them to be clear by the time the missile detonates."

The dots crept along the map with excruciating slowness. No one in the room said a word.

Finally, the dots reached the halfway point.

"Do I have the okay to launch?" the general asked.

The president said nothing.

"Mr. President!"

The president waited two more heartbeats, then said. "Fire at will, Echo Three."

"Missile launched," said the submarine captain.

A red number appeared over the Arabian Sea. It crept across the map like a ladybug. The white letters of the fleeing helicopters inched toward the edge of the blast zone.

"I hope to God they don't figure out what we're doing," the general said. His knuckles blanched as they clutched a small metal cross hanging around his neck.

"Ten seconds to impact."

A digital readout at the bottom of the satellite feed counted down: eight . . . seven . . . six . . . five . . . four . . .

The helicopters neared the edge of the blast radius.

"They won't make it in time," Helena said.

Helena covered her ears and moaned.

. . . three . . . two . . . one

The screen flashed white.

From one of the rear helicopter cameras, the rising mushroom cloud was surreal.

Every muscle in Theon's body trembled.

I caused this.

The blast wave expanded toward the fleeing helicopters. "Hold on," said the strike force commander. "This might be rough."

Helena pressed against him.

The screen went blank.

For a moment, nothing,

"This is Seal Team Four," the commander's voice said over the radio link. "Ran into a little turbulence, but we made it."

Everyone cheered.

"Seismic signature shows no secondary detonations," shouted an analyst over the noise.

Theon exhaled.

The sun would rise tomorrow, after all.

Chapter 22

Theon sat beside Helena as they gazed across the valley at the Sangre de Cristo Mountains. A herd of elk skirted the river, their mating cries mixing with the gentle breeze.

He breathed in the fragrant summer air as a wine connoisseur might sample a rare vintage. Evergreen scents of Blue Spruce and Douglas-fir intermixed with the flowers Helena had planted in the garden below the deck.

Have I ever been this happy?

He pointed across the valley. "I was thinking of building a retreat on that ridge for children from the hospital."

"That's a wonderful idea," Helena said. "We could get Anna to organize it."

He laughed. "As long as she can keep her swearing and dirty jokes under control in front of the kids."

"Coming from her, I doubt they'd mind."

"One week until you're due," Theon said. "It might be safer to move closer to the hospital in Denver."

Helena patted her belly and took a sip of lemonade. "We prefer it here."

"But what if something goes wrong?"

"You did build a fully equipped delivery room, as well as hiring a doctor and two nurses to stay here at the ranch full-time. Besides, it's only a twenty-minute flight to the hospital in the helicopter."

"I want to make sure you're safe."

"Stop worrying," she said. "We're retired, remember?"

"I've never been good at relaxing. My father sold peanuts at Cubs Games, and he sneaked me in once. I spent the entire game reading chemistry. It drove him nuts."

She laughed. "Before you take up baseball, tell me the history of this place."

"It was originally part of the Sangre de Cristo Land Grant in 1844."

"So it was in Mexico?"

"That's right. It became a US territory after the Mexican-American War. The fight over whether or not the new additions would allow slavery sparked the Civil War a few years later. Afterward, Kit Carson was assigned command of Fort Garland at the head of the valley. It protected settlers and prospectors from the Ute Indians, who were not happy with having their land taken. After Congress passed the Ute Removal Act in 1880, the fort was abandoned, having served its purpose."

Helena shook her head. "So we live on land twice stolen."

"Stolen, conquered, purchased—all names for the same thing."

"Buying is very different from stealing."

"Tell that to the Indians that sold their lands under threat of having it taken by violence. Even my purchase of this property is backed by force of law and the government, which is a form of force. I'm sure the mining company I outbid wasn't happy, nor the hunters that lost use of it when I turned it into a wildlife preserve. I think both might say I stole it from them."

"I suppose only Indians have any true claim of ownership."

"The Ute language originated in California a thousand years before, so even they took this land from its previous occupants. I imagine this process goes back to the first hunter-gatherers who crossed the land bridge from Asia over twelve thousand years ago."

"It sounds like you're justifying conquest."

"Simplifying history into a morality play of good versus bad is an illusion. The truth is, it's all gray. Every single person on the planet descends from a long line of conquerors."

Helena gazed toward the last light bathing the tops the mountains. "Oh, Sun, thou who has said let there be Cuzco and Tampu, grant that these children may conquer all other people, since it is for this that thou has created them."

"Is that from your time in Peru?" Theon asked.

"It's the Inca's invocation of the sun god," she said. "Maybe the Spanish preserved it as justification of their own conquest."

"Evolution is built on competition. It's why humans are so drawn to sporting events. We even make baking cakes into contests. Recognizing our own nature is the first step to building a new paradigm."

"Says the latest conqueror."

Leave it to her to call me out on my hypocrisy.

He chuckled. "I suppose no one owns anything. Even the molecules of our bodies are recycled. Good and bad will be up to the next generation to decide."

"No doubt they'll judge us by standards we can't imagine."

In the darkening valley, the headlights of a jeep appeared and bumped along the road toward the house.

Helena held a pair of binoculars to her eyes. "It's Kyoko and Lamarr. Odd they didn't call first."

By the time they parked in the gravel driveway and headed up the porch stairs, the last of the sun outlined the tops of the mountain in a red fringe.

"Damn, that's beautiful!" Lamarr said.

Helena stood and hugged them both. Theon handed Lamarr a beer.

"Much obliged, partner," Lamarr said in a bad imitation of a Western accent. He tipped his wide-brimmed hat back and downed the beer in an uninterrupted swallow.

"He's gone native," Theon said.

Lamarr set the bottle on the table and smiled. "My great uncle, Captain Charles Boyde, served in the Tenth Cavalry at Fort Lewis not far from here, so I'm as much a cowboy as anyone."

"I didn't realize we had a genuine Buffalo Soldier among us," Theon said. "We have several horses in the stable, if you're up for a moonlight ride later."

Lamarr glanced at Kyoko. "I'm not exactly allowed on horses."

Kyoko shook her head. "No horses, no way. Too dangerous!"

"A Buffalo Soldier that doesn't ride?"

Lamarr shrugged. "Some battles aren't worth fighting."

"Is everything okay at the lab?" Helena asked.

"Things are fine," Lamarr said. "We're here because I got a strange call on our way home and we wanted to break the news in person."

*   *   *

Theon sat on his favorite couch with Helena at his side. Lamarr and Kyoko occupied chairs next to the fireplace.

"I love this!" Kyoko said, craning her neck at the hand-carved logs of the cabin's enormous living room. Twenty-foot ceiling-to-floor windows faced the deck and the moonlit valley.

"You rich folks sure live high on the hog," Lamarr said.

"Rich folks?" Theon said. "You're a billionaire."

"Still poor compared to you," Lamarr said. "White folks always keeping the black man down!"

Theon laughed.

Helena bit her nails and fidgeted. "Five of the most powerful leaders in the world flying here, and they won't say why?"

"Could it be the Middle East?" Theon asked.

"I wouldn't think so," Lamarr said. "The world coalition has the Caliphate bottled up tight. Without nukes, they aren't much of a threat to anyone."

"Do they realize you and Kyoko are in charge of Amara?" Helena asked.

"We told them," Kyoko said, "but they only want to talk to Theon."

"Call them and say we won't see them," Helena said.

Lamarr shook his head. "They were in the air when they called, and wouldn't take no for an answer."

"They're coming, Mrs. Helena," Kyoko said. "Whether we let them past the security gate is another matter."

Helena grabbed Theon's arm, her eyes wild. "Let's leave. We could go to that hospital in Denver like you wanted."

"I should at least hear what they have to say."

"I have a terrible feeling about this," Helena said. "Please don't let them in."

Theon frowned. *Her instincts were right before. Maybe we should leave.*

Lamarr's cell phone buzzed, and he glanced at the screen. "They've arrived at the security gate. What should I say?"

"Tell them they're not welcome," Helena said, wringing her hands.

Theon took Helena's hands in his. "What are you afraid of?"

"I'm afraid they'll convince you to leave me."

Theon laughed and pulled her into his arms. "There's nothing they could say to make me leave you."

Helena looked up at him. "You promise?"

"I promise," he said.

It took another fifteen minutes for the single black SUV to reach the house.

Helena's frown deepened. "The leaders of China, Germany, India, South Africa, and the United States are riding in one car without even a police escort?"

"They must not want anyone to know they've left the summit for this meeting," Theon said.

When they came in, Kyoko and Lamarr showed them to their seats.

Theon nodded to President Campbell, and he returned the greeting.

Kyoko and Lamarr sat on the same couch as Theon and Helena.

"Welcome to our home," Theon said.

The Chinese Premier inclined his head. "You're aware of the summit, I assume?"

"I find the accord bold and comprehensive," Theon said. "You tackle climate change, population growth, environmental protection, poverty, and even warfare. It's what I hoped for when I removed the shackles of superstition from humanity."

The German Chancellor leaned forward. She was in her seventies, but looked unchanged from the Olympic champion skier she'd been in her first youth. "My contribution was the progressive worldwide tax to fund a guaranteed minimum income for every person on the planet. Such a redistribution should get the world economy moving again."

"And allow the poor better opportunities for themselves and their children," said the Indian Prime Minister.

Theon nodded. "I fully support your GMI proposal. The wealthy will grumble, but everyone benefits in the long run."

"You've said the magic words," the South African President said. *"Long term."*

"The problem is how to sell all these changes to our people," India said. "Even China did away with its One-Child policy under pressure from its people, and that was in an authoritarian regime. How are democracies to restrict pregnancies, let alone all the rest of these measures?"

President Campbell nodded. "If I bind the United States to this accord, I guarantee I lose reelection."

Theon searched each of the leaders' faces. "You won't vote for an accord you know will save lives because you fear losing your positions? Are you that cowardly?"

Several of the leaders tensed, but Germany held up her hand to preempt the angry words. "It's the same problem we've faced for decades with Climate Change or nuclear disarmament. Every nation must agree or it falls apart."

"Russia already announced it will not sign the agreement," China said.

"As well as half the other leaders at the conference," South Africa added.

"We are here, not because we're afraid to act," India said, "but because it won't succeed no matter how we vote."

"Why come here?" Helena asked. "What do you expect my husband to do?"

My husband. The words sent a thrill through him.

China stood. A year and a half before, he'd been a portly old man nearing the end of his life—the perfect temporary placeholder until the National People's Congress decided on a more permanent replacement. Now, he was slim and exuded the energy and wisdom necessary to guide his people into the future.

"Here, in the United States, you have five percent of the world's population, and twenty-five percent of the word's arable land. China has twenty-five percent of the world's population and only five percent of the world's arable land. We import food as it is. What happens when our population doubles? Do you think a nuclear power will watch its own people starve?"

China sat.

"Are you saying we should stop distributing the Fountain of Youth Drug?" Theon asked.

"What we are begging you to do," India said, "is to force us to accept the accord."

"Force you?"

Germany spoke. "We want you to announce that any nation that rejects the accord will lose access to your drug."

The other leaders nodded.

"Only by adding the terms into the Immortality Contract can we achieve universal compliance," South Africa said.

Helena gripped his hand tightly as she replied to them. "You'd make Theon the target of the world's hatred because you won't do your jobs?"

"I'm sorry," President Campbell said. "If there were any other way."

Do they realize what they're asking?

"I refuse to become a dictator," he said.

"You'd let the world burn to maintain an illusory moral high ground?" Germany asked.

"Throughout history," India said, "people have craved strong leaders. A pharos, king, pope, or dictator—the label is irrelevant. Even apes have hierarchies. It's probably biologically programmed into us as primates."

"If you don't fill the void, someone else will," President Campbell said, "and the odds are, they won't be as well-meaning as you."

It's the same argument President Kane made for himself.

"No!" Helena said, her hands trembling. "You won't force him into this."

The South African President straightened. "Without the accord, eternal youth will destroy the world."

Theon turned to Lamarr. "What do you think?"

Lamarr rubbed his chin. "Martin Luther King taught me that sometimes people need a nudge to do the right thing."

"And they killed him for it," Helena said. "Are you trying to turn Theon into a martyr?"

"That's not what I'm saying."

"Maybe the world isn't ready for immortality," Kyoko said.

The German Chancellor stood, her fists clenched. "So after all this, we tell people: Sorry, we've changed our minds, you have to grow old and die after all?"

"Stop it!" Helena shouted. "I know what you're trying to do!"

The German Chancellor sat.

The five leaders exchanged tense glances.

Helena took his hand just as she'd done at the start. "Please don't do this. There has to be another way."

His heart ached.

"How can I stand by and watch the world collapse?" he asked.

"You promised you wouldn't leave me."

He caressed her cheek. "I have no choice."

She pulled back, the betrayal filling her eyes. "You'll be despised. How could we raise our child in the shadow of such hatred?"

"I'm doing this for our child, you, and every person on the planet."

Helena's eyes narrowed. "You expected this, didn't you?"

The words cut to the center of his being. *Did I know? Did I subconsciously crave the power to mold humanity into a perfect, rational form? To play God? Am I no different from every megalomaniacal dictator that's ever lived?*

"Maybe I did," he said. "I honestly don't know."

*   *   *

Theon flew to New York and spoke to the world's leaders. His speech wasn't long. He explained that any nation rejecting the accord would forfeit their Amara Distribution Centers.

The Russian President called it an act of war, but Theon held firm. It took two days for every leader to speak in response to his ultimatum. By the third day, the tide turned. Millions of online petitions urged their leaders to put the health of their citizens first.

Privately, most thanked him for the political cover necessary to vote yes on the measure.

The Immortality Contract grew from one page, to two. The most controversial provision stated that any man or woman with a living child could have no more. The only exception were those already pregnant—like Helena.

Free universal contraception was made available across the globe.

The accord also covered everything from trade, the environment, a global guaranteed minimum income, and a world court with actual teeth for enforcement.

In the end, it passed unanimously.

Afterward, he stood with Lamarr atop the UN, gazing at the New York skyline. Lamarr handed him a cigar, and they lit up. The setting sun bathed the city in an orange glow.

"Ever imagine something like this when we were in high school?" Theon asked his old friend.

Lamarr laughed. "No one could have imagined this."

Theon puffed on the cigar. "All we have to do now is make this agreement work, and hopefully save the world."

"Nothing to it," Lamarr said.

As the last of the sun's rays vanished beneath the horizon, his phone rang.

Kyoko reported that Helena gave birth to a healthy baby boy. Theon asked to speak to her, and Helena came on the line.

"Congratulations on the unanimous vote," Helena said, the exhaustion clear in her voice.

"I so wanted to be there," he said.

"Yeah, well . . ."

An awkward silence followed.

"I'm glad you're both okay," he said.

"I thought of naming him Francesco, after your grandfather."

Theon blinked back tears. "I'd like that."

How could I have missed the birth of my own son?

"I'm going to stay with Alma and David for a while."

"Good idea. I'll be there as soon as I can."

"Sure, okay."

The phone went dead. He stared at the word *END* on the screen, but didn't press it.

The screen eventually went black.

Chapter 23

Lamarr acted as gatekeeper in the hallway outside their White House office. Most visitors he dealt with himself. Only a few required an audience with the unofficial ruler of the world.

"This is urgent," said the French Ambassador. "I must see him now!"

Amazing how they thought they could do better in person. Some tried flattery, some used carefully rehearsed arguments—a few cried.

Lamarr sighed. "It's your funeral, but don't say I didn't warn you."

He led the way through the outer office, where secretaries fielded calls, sent directives, and prepared documents.

The ambassador was a slim, foppish sort, with an expensive Armani suit and purple leather shoes. He looked to be in his early twenties, of course.

Lamarr knocked and entered.

His friend sat hunched at his desk with the look of a galley slave chained to an oar and forced to row until he collapsed. His eyes peered out of sunken sockets rimmed by dark circles.

The office looked oddly temporary, despite their six months in residence. Decorating would admit they were here to stay.

Theon was on the phone, his face tense. "Have you tried local police to end the strike?"

For the past six months Theon had slept on a cot in an adjoining room. Did he fear another assassination attempt, or the emptiness of an apartment without his family?

"How does this local issue qualify for United Nations troops?" Theon said into the phone.

Now and then, Theon threatened to stop taking his monthly pill. *Suicide by old age*, he called it. But the desire to see Helena and his newborn son drove him forward.

After the first month, Helena blocked his calls altogether, but Alma and David gave him updates on little Franc's progress.

"Tell the union leaders if the strike continues another day, I will revoke their Immortality Contracts. If that doesn't work, we'll consider sending troops."

Theon hung up. At the sight of the French Ambassador, he sighed. "This better not be about taxes, again."

The Frenchman wrung his hands nervously. "Well, actually—"

"No more excuses!" Theon slammed a fist onto his desk, causing the ambassador to jerk. "The GMI tax is essential for redistributing capital to those in need. The poor and middle class are the ones jump-starting world trade, not the wealthy with more money than they can spend in a hundred lifetimes. You don't see me complaining about the two billion dollars I've paid into the GMI fund, do you?"

"But, sir," the Frenchman said in a tone of abject fear, "if we collect this tax in addition to the no-child policy, the government will fall."

Theon thrust his index finder toward him. "France has one week to start paying into the global fund, or I will suspend the Immortality Contracts of every member of Parliament that opposes these measures—including you and the president."

The French diplomat bowed and scurried out of the room as fast as possible.

Lamarr chuckled. *I warned him.*

The phone rang, and Theon picked it up. "Yes? . . . Okay, put him through."

In theory, the global accord would solve the world's social and economic problems, but fully implementing it was no bowl of kittens.

The first crisis occurred days after signing the agreement.

Layoffs from obsolete industries had depressed spending, leading to more layoffs in a self-reinforcing feedback loop that eventually froze the movement of capital.

Added to this, the tripling of oil prices after the Mahdi uprising made it impossible for farmers to run their tractors. Why plant crops that cost more to bring to market than they could be sold for?

Theon sent soldiers and unemployed workers into the fields to help with the planting. Farmers received vouchers for fuel, along with no-interest World-Bank loans to bridge them through harvest.

As the Guaranteed Minimum Income checks went out, new spending jump-started the economy.

To everyone's relief, crops made it to market and averted a worldwide famine.

It was a temporary fix. The population was growing at an unsustainable rate. Eighty million people who would have died without the pill added to the two hundred sixty million born in the past two years.

If that wasn't bad enough, an extra one billion women were fertile again. Half of these became pregnant in the exuberance of their restored youth. By autumn, the tsunami of newborns stressed food supplies to the breaking point.

To avert disaster, Theon instituted strict rationing and a five-year moratorium on new pregnancies. Enforcement fell to each nation.

Protests erupted across the globe, but what other option was there? Every time Theon averted one crisis, another sprouted.

"Tell the North Koreans we won't give in to threats," Theon said into the phone. "If they give up their nuclear weapons, we'll send food aid." Theon listened. "Yes, if they comply, I will send Kim Jong-un the Immortality Pill, as long as he signs the Immortality Contract like everyone else."

Theon hung up the phone and rubbed his eyes. "Do they think protests will change the math? Do they want me to give in to their excuses and let their own people starve next year?"

"You won't last much longer at this pace," Lamarr said.

"Who's next?" Theon asked

Lamarr got two beers out of the mini-fridge and settled into a chair beside his friend.

"I don't have time to rest."

Lamarr sighed and set the unopened drinks on the desk. "I think we need to consider an exit strategy."

Theon stared at him with a look of betrayal. "I never thought of you as a quitter."

"The no-child policy has failed," Lamarr said. "Even church attendance is growing as the desperate turn to God for help. The collapse will be worse the longer this drags on." .

"I'll cut more people off from my drug as an example, and they'll fall into line."

"Do you remember when you told me it's easy to see other people's delusions, but hard to see our own?"

"So now I'm delusional?"

How can I destroy his dream? But if don't tell him, who will?

"Expecting everyone to act rational is a delusion. It's why pure communism and libertarianism fail. We wouldn't need government at all if humans were perfect."

"If you think I'll just give up and let the world implode, you don't know me."

"Humanity isn't ready for immortality."

Theon stood. "I won't let Taslima's dream die. I'll keep fighting, no matter how long it takes."

Lamarr stood and faced him. "Isn't it time you focused on your living family? It's been six months, and you haven't met your son."

He could have dodged the punch, just as he did when they fought in Golden Gloves so many years before. But he just stood, watching the fist come toward him.

There was a crack of bone on bone as bare knuckles slammed into his cheek.

A good, solid hit for someone who'd become a walking skeleton.

Lamarr stumbled back, shook his head, then straightened. He'd received far worse, both in the ring, and during the barroom brawls that came after Harold Washington died. Taking punishment for a lost cause was nothing new.

Theon raised both fists defensively, ready for a counter attack.

Lamarr stepped forward, his hands at his side. "If you want to hit me, I won't stop you. Maybe that's all I have left to offer."

The rage melted from Theon's face, and he slumped into his chair. Then he cried.

Lamarr sat beside his friend and put an arm around his shoulders.

Theon leaned into him and let his bottled-up emotions out.

After a minute, Theon's tears stopped, and he pulled away. "You really think there's no hope?"

Lamarr opened both bottles of beer and handed one to Theon. "Remember that priest who asked if you wanted a blessing before our Golden Gloves match?"

Theon took a swig of the beer and chuckled. "I told him not to waste prayers on a boxing match, since I volunteered at the children's hospital, and miracles seemed in short supply."

"That priest looked at you like you were the Devil himself!"

"After the match, he claimed I lost because I'd refused God's help."

Lamarr took a drink and then shook his head. "I remember, but your comeback is what floored me."

"You'll have to remind me," Theon said. "Things were pretty fuzzy after that left hook of yours."

"Without missing a beat, you turned to that smug bastard and said, 'I suppose I deserved it, then, but what's God's excuse for all those crippled kids?' "

Theon laughed. "I was kind of an asshole, wasn't I? The guy was only trying to help."

"I was still going to the Baptist church every Sunday. That preacher bled my Mamma dry with all his fundraising for mission trips. Mamma never had a vacation in her life, but that preacher traveled the world." He took a long swig of his beer. "I hadn't told a single person I thought God was bullshit. Watching you confront that priest in front of everyone was the bravest thing I'd ever witnessed. You became my fucking hero."

"I thought you were brave—or nuts—to come into my neighborhood the next week to find me. You could have been killed."

Lamarr laughed. "After getting to the state Golden Gloves finals, I was as close to a celebrity as a black high school kid could get. Even in your Wop neighborhood, people wanted to shake my hand."

Theon gazed at the floor. "What are we going to do?"

"All I know is that it's time to change strategies before we pass the point of no return."

The door burst open, and the president's chief of staff ran toward them. "You're needed in the Situation Room!"

*　*　*

Lamarr's cheek throbbed as they stepped off the elevator into the communications bunker.

I wonder if there's ice down here?

He followed Theon and the chief of staff to the circular table in the center of the room. The president sat with the CIA chief and General Tilton, their expressions grim. The fact that they'd removed all but one technician was ominous.

The president glanced at Lamarr. "This is need-to-know only."

"Cut the shit and tell us," Theon said.

The president hesitated, then nodded to the communications tech.

A video appeared on the main screen.

The Mahdi stood behind three metal spheres the size of a basketball—each cradled in an individual case.

Reza smiled and said, "The components for these tritium-enriched nuclear devices were en route between facilities when your attack came— Praise be to Allah."

Three black-robed soldiers closed the cases and loaded them into lead-lined crates.

"Could this be a bluff?" General Tilton asked.

The CIA director shook his head. "They included detailed photos of the interiors of the bombs, so there's no doubt they're genuine."

The crates were sealed, and the Mahdi continued. "It took some effort to assemble these, but I'm happy to say that they will be ready in time to celebrate the one-year anniversary of the Caliphate."

Lamarr glanced at Theon, who sat transfixed, his breathing coming in staccato jerks.

The video dissolved through a montage of shots tracking the progress of the three crates. The eerie chant of the Muslim call to prayer acted as a soundtrack.

Each bomb traveled different back roads—to Turkey, Russia, and Algeria. Then each were transferred to ships. Near the coast of the United States, small fishing boats offloaded the three crates to obscure docks— one in Maine, one in Oregon, and another in South Carolina.

They traveled to their final destinations by car—Los Angeles, Chicago, and New York.

The closing shots were close-ups of the arming codes being entered into the digital display of each device. Once completed, the cases were closed and set back into their lead-lined crates. A single wire extended from each to a radio receiver.

The soundtrack ended, and the Mahdi reappeared on the screen.

"Should you locate these bombs and enter any of the buildings, I will detonate all three of them. If you attempt to evacuate Chicago, Los Angeles, or New York, I will detonate all three. If their existence leaks to the media, I will detonate all three."

The Mahdi smiled. "I'm told that each of these bombs are several times more powerful than those you dropped on Hiroshima and Nagasaki. How fitting that the technology that has allowed you to oppress others for so long, will now be your downfall."

Lamarr's stomach tightened. How wonderful it would feel to drive his fist into that demented creature's face.

"The good is, no civilian needs to die," the bearded zealot said.

The Mahdi spread his hands wide. "I will provide you with the precise locations and codes necessary to disarm these weapons—under one condition."

Chapter 24

Theon sat in the passenger's seat as Poncho piloted the car through a mix of Ponderosa Pine, White Alder, California Oak, and even a few Arroyo Willow trees. On his last visit, Cassie had carefully drilled him on their names, and would no doubt continue his botanical training if given the chance.

How could I have waited so long?

He glanced at Poncho. The secret service officer sat as stoic as ever.

"What made you join this harebrained crusade?" he asked his driver.

Poncho didn't take his eyes from the road. "I grew up in Canyon County, Idaho, in the Pentecostal Followers of Christ."

"The faith-healing sect?"

Poncho nodded. "My parents believed medicine was the resort of those unworthy of the Lord's grace."

"It's not illogical, if one believes in an all-powerful, all-knowing, and all-loving Supreme Being."

"Logical or not, I watched my little sister die in my arms as Mom and Dad rubbed rancid olive oil on her chest while praying in tongues."

Poncho's grip tightened on the steering wheel. "I begged them to take her to a hospital, but they refused. When she died, my parents blamed my lack of faith for killing her. That was the moment I stopped believing. In retaliation for my doubt, my father drove me to Boise and dropped me off on a random corner.

"I was sixteen, had no money, no education other than Bible study, and not even a social security number. My first stop was the police station to report the murder of my sister. You can probably guess what happened."

"It was John Ehrlichman and H R Haldman that inserted the religious exception into the Child Abuse Prevention Act in the 1970s."

"No shit?" Poncho said. "The men jailed for Watergate?"

"They were both Christian Scientists and believed in faith-healing. They wanted to protect parents who chose prayer over taking their children to a doctor. Idaho is one of six states that never repealed the religious shield law, even in cases where the child dies from neglect."

A tear slid down Poncho's cheek. "I still miss her."

"What did the police do?" Theon asked.

"They were sympathetic, but said local officials don't make the law. Without an autopsy, I never found out what killed Mariah."

Theon leaned forward and placed a hand on his shoulder. "I'm sorry."

"I was placed in foster care and eventually graduated high school, joined the military, and made my way into the secret service. When Kyoko approached me, I signed up instantly and suggested Cisco, since he grew up Mormon and has an intense de-conversion story as well."

"This is close enough," Theon said. "I'll walk the last half mile."

Poncho stopped the jeep on the forest road. "I'll pick you up in an hour."

"I haven't thanked you for saving my life, Matt"

"You remembered my real name," Poncho said. "I kind of like Poncho better. Sounds more gangster." He grew serious. "I guess you know the Immortality Contract forced a repeal of the shield law?"

"It was one of my specific demands of Congress."

"Think of all the Mariahs you've saved," Poncho said.

"I hope it was worth it," he said, and set off down the path.

The moonlit snow crunching beneath his boots recalled wintery days walking his paper route as a kid. Heavy snows transformed the neighborhood into a pristine netherworld. One became so accustomed to the constant sound of automobiles, their absence felt surreal.

On such days, he skipped school to shovel sidewalks for twenty-five cents apiece—a half-dollar for corner houses. His teachers understood the reason for his absence and never marked him tardy.

During summers, he delivered telephone directories, washed cars, and other odd jobs alongside his younger sister and two brothers.

His father wrote them IOUs on slips of paper for the money they earned. The extra income kept them from losing their house.

By the time he won his scholarship to college, the overstuffed cigar box with his promissory notes required three rubber bands to keep it closed.

Theon stopped on the wooded trail and removed a yellowed slip of paper from his wallet. Its edges had frayed, and the writing faded to near invisibility on the yellowed surface. He unfolded it with care and read aloud by the light of the coming dawn.

"I, Curtis Torano, owe my son, Theon Torano, the amount of forty-four dollars."

It was the last IOU before he left for college. His father had looked him in the eye and said, "I will someday repay every cent I've borrowed."

When he got his first real job teaching molecular biology at U of I, he sent his father money every month. After his biotech startup made its first profit, he paid off his father's third mortgage on the modest corner house he'd grown up in. Neither of them ever spoke of it. For his father, it must have felt like failure.

I, Curtis Torano, owe my son . . .

Theon cried.

I'm the one who can never repay you, Dad.

He stood on the moonlit trail for a long time, his tears making hollows in the snow at his feet.

What kind of father doesn't meet his own son until he's half a year old?

So much time wasted chasing illusions of utopia, when the real thing waited at the end of this simple trail.

He wiped the tears from his face and shredded the piece of paper—as he should have done the moment his father wrote it. The remnants fluttered to the ground and lay forgotten amidst the snow.

The pathway continued through the woods for a hundred yards farther before opening into an expansive clearing ringed by the Sierra Mountains.

Despite the charm of living in such a remote place, he'd marveled that anyone would spurn such basics as electricity, indoor bathrooms, and the wonders of modern technology.

Minister Gerhartz counseled the congregation to immerse themselves in God's creation directly and to distrust the barriers erected by science between the source of life itself.

I have to admit they seem happier than most people I know.

In freeing humanity from the effort of living, had something fundamental been lost?

The first touches of dawn outlined the tops of the peaks in cantaloupe orange, while the fresh snow wiped the signs of man and beast clean. As he passed the livestock barn, a rooster asserted its claim as herald to the dawn. Within the structure, several cows, goats, two oxen, and a few horses lazed away the coldest months of the season.

A second barn held two tractors and a thousand-gallon tank of diesel—a grudging exception to technology.

In a matter of days, their preacher would likely credit God for sheltering his followers from the coming apocalypse.

Smoke drifted out the stone chimneys of the two cabins. Warm lights flickered in the windows of each.

He set a course for the smaller of the two.

The closer he came to the pile of freshly joined logs, the faster his heart pounded.

What if Helena refuses to see me?

He climbed the three stairs to the porch and paused.
Helena's voice filtered through the door as she sang a lullaby.

"Roses love sunshine, violets love dew
Angels in Heaven know I love you
Know I love you, dear, know I love you
Angels in Heaven, know I love you."

The words transported him to his childhood and the face of his mother singing to him.

He raised his hand to the door, and knocked.

"It's open, Alma," Helena's voice called out.

Theon opened the door, took a step inside, and closed it to keep the cold from following.

Helena sat in a rocking chair, gazing at the sleeping child cradled in her arms. She wore a woolen green dress and winter boots. Beside her, a wood stove with a glass front illuminated them both. The smell of fresh-cut logs transformed the room into a forest.

"I was just about to come over for breakfast," Helena said and glanced toward him.

She went silent, her smile fading.

The heat of the room brought beads of sweat to his temples.

His eyes moved from Helena to the sleeping form cradled in her arms. The baby's chest rose and fell with the trusting surrender of childhood.

"Come and meet your son," Helena said.

He walked forward, his boots loud on the floorboards, then knelt beside them. Was there anything more miraculous than a baby's sleeping face?

Helena lifted Francesco from her lap and placed him in his father's arms. The child's blue eyes opened and stared at him with a universe of possibility.

Theon smiled. Francesco's mouth widened in a toothless grin and made a series of random sounds.

"I agree completely," Theon said.

His son giggled, then held his arms out to his mother. Helena gathered him up and stood.

Francesco launched into a babbling soliloquy that ended with him pointing at his father.

"He's curious about the strange man in his house," Helena said.

Her eyes held a wariness that broke his heart.

Can I blame her?

"Helena, I—"

Helena spoke to little Franc. "Why don't we visit Auntie Alma and cousin Riley?"

"Technically, he's Alma's great-uncle and Riley's great-great-uncle."

"We don't like know-it-alls, do we, Frankie?" Helena said in baby talk.

Theon chuckled.

She wrapped a blanket around their son and headed out the door.

He followed the short distance to the main cabin. Before she opened the door, he gently turned her to face him. Tears glistened on her cheeks.

"Helena, can you ever forgive—"

"Shut up, you idiot," she said, and kissed him.

Then she took his hand and led him inside the cabin. The morning rituals of dressing children, preparing breakfast, and stoking the fire whirled about them like a circus.

Riley shrieked with laughter as David's fourteen-year-old sister, Cassie, played peek-a-boo with her on the sofa. Maya and Jacob wrestled by the woodpile.

"Look who's here," Helena said above the tumult.

"Grandpa!" Alma shouted. She threw her arms around him and leaned her head against his chest.

A lump of emotion constricted his throat as he returned her embrace.

Her braided hair smelled of smoke and pancakes.

How could this be the same creature he'd seen in that psych ward? Any drug causing such a dramatic improvement would be a billion-dollar blockbuster.

I suppose it was a blockbuster until I came along.

When Alma released him, David shook his hand. "My parents are setting the church up for Sunday mass. You're welcome to join us if you'd like."

"I'd love to come," he said, "except I have to leave before then."

Helena shot him a sideways glance and frowned.

"Blueberry pancakes are ready," Alma said, and waved everyone to the table.

Once everyone was seated, Alma turned to him. "Grandpa, will you say grace?"

After a moment's hesitation, Theon lowered his head, and everyone joined hands.

"I give thanks for being here with those I love. If God does exist, I pray that he will keep my family safe."

"Amen," they said in unison, and then attacked the pancakes.

"That was a first," Helena said.

196

He shrugged. "When in Rome."

The family joked, chatted, and laughed as they shared the fruits of their labors.

Will this be the last time I see them?

"Did you know the upper and lower eyelids of chameleons are connected with a hole in the center?" Cassie asked him. "And that geckos have no eyelids at all?"

"I didn't know that," he said.

Cassie was an encyclopedia of every creature living in the vicinity, and she seemed determined to remedy his distressing gaps in knowledge. Now and then, David reminded her to let someone else speak. She would nod obediently, gobble more food, and then launch into the next story of the habits and mating rituals of an obscure insect she'd found in the barn, woods, or outhouse.

She's just like Alma was before . . .

Alma fed Riley tiny pieces of pancake while she sat in her lap. His great-granddaughter chewed halfheartedly, not having picked up the habit yet. Her gaze rarely left him, making it hard to follow the conversation. Those chestnut eyes gazed across the table as if through a hole in time.

After breakfast, David used the kitchen pump to fill the sink with water, and everyone pitched in cleaning and drying the dishes.

"Can I show Mr. Torano Terrance?" Cassie asked.

"Not now," Alma said, "but I bet Riley and Frankie would love meeting your turtle."

Cassie perked up. "That's a great idea! I'll show them what turtles eat!"

Alma and Cassie carried the two babies upstairs.

David, Maya, and Jacob dressed in their winter gear and headed out the front door. The children dashed toward the barn with shrieks of glee. Feeding animals, milking cows, collecting eggs, and cleaning out stalls was the equivalent of a video game here.

Once they were alone, Helena turned to him. "What brings you here for such a short visit?"

"I'm on my way to a meeting," he said. "I'm sorry it's taken me so long."

Alma returned, and they chatted about the children.

Halfway between a sentence, Alma stopped talking, and laughed. "I still can't get used to how young you both look," she said. "I mean, my eighty-nine-year-old grandfather and his wife have a newborn baby younger than mine."

They sat quietly for a time, listening to the muffled sound of Cassie lecturing the two babies on the eating habits of turtles.

"Alma," he said, "do you mind if I ask you something personal?"

"You can ask me anything."

"Ever since that moment in the bunker at the Supreme Court, I've wondered how you guessed those secrets about Vadic."

"How else could I have known, if not from his wife and daughter?" Alma asked.

"My best guess is that you heard him talking in his sleep on the flight from California to DC."

"Do you remember when I asked you if your story of Mrs. Thrift's dead rabbit was true?"

"The truth is that it's an urban myth started in the seventies, though no one knows where it first originated."

"It was meant to teach a greater lesson," Alma said.

"That's right. Is this what you did with Vadic? Invent a story that serves a greater purpose?"

"I wasn't lying about seeing his wife and daughter in that room, just as I'm not lying about seeing Mom and Grandma."

Theon frowned. "Do you still see them?"

"They've been here since you arrived," Alma said. "They're worried about you."

Theon's stomach tightened. "You see them right now?"

Alma nodded, then cocked her head, as if listening. "Grandma says things will work out in the end."

Goose bumps rose along his neck and arms.

Could she have stabbed them and cut their throats? Is her mind protecting her from that knowledge even now?

"You can ask them anything," Alma said. "I'll tell you what they say."

Helena's eyes watched him with that calculating intelligence he so admired.

Does she know our secret?

"Tell them I love them both," he said to Alma.

Helena's eyes narrowed.

She knows.

Alma looked past them. "They say they love you too, and will be there when you cross to the other side."

Theon glanced at his watch. Ten minutes left.

He rose from the chair. "Alma, I'm so proud of the woman you've become."

She stood and embraced him. "I love your, Grandpa."

With tears threatening, he kissed her forehead. "I love you too."

Helena followed him outside. The day was dawning bright and crisp.

Will I ever see my family again?

Helena stepped in front of him, her brows angled downward. "Do you think Alma is a con artist?"

"Not consciously."

"Why didn't you ask her the question, then?" she asked.

"Taslima told you?"

"Not the word itself, but the fact that it existed," Helena said. "She told me the idea came from reading a biography on Houdini."

"That's right. Houdini and his wife agreed on a secret word they kept between themselves. When his wife died, Houdini challenged the many famed spiritualists of his time to reveal it as proof they were talking to the spirit of his wife. None ever did."

"So why didn't you ask Alma for the word you and Taslima agreed on? If she said it, you'd have proof Taslima's soul lived on."

"Failure might spark a crisis in her psyche," he said. "What if her mind's entire façade crumbled, and she remembered . . . ?"

"Killing her mother and grandmother?"

"Yes."

"You could tell her she was right no matter what word she guessed."

"Alma is very perceptive," he said. "She might realize I was lying, and I'm not willing to gamble with her sanity."

"Are you sure you're not afraid that her answer might challenge your own carefully constructed illusion of reality?"

The faint sound of a car echoed from the forest.

Theon forced a smile. "Maybe we all need our delusions to stay sane."

"Like the idea that wiping out religion will solve the world's problems?"

"A good example."

"And what replaces that myth?" she asked.

He pulled her close. "Love. It's the one thing I know is real."

The car emerged from the woods and stopped a respectful distance away.

"What are you hiding from me?" she asked.

He kissed her and then whispered in her ear. "I'll tell you tomorrow."

Chapter 25

Theon's plane landed at Incirlik Air Base shortly before dawn. Turkey was the only Muslim country in the region to resist the Mahdi Uprising.

He glanced at his watch. Forty-five minutes before the deadline. The stop at Alma's had cut it close, but had been worth it.

The base commander rushed him to a jump plane with propellers on each wing. He'd insisted on a skeleton crew—a single pilot and a parachute instructor.

Once airborne, they flew toward the border with the Caliphate. The young soldier helped him into his jumpsuit, flight jacket, gloves, and parachute pack.

"It's slightly above freezing on the ground," the soldier said, "but it will warm when the sun rises."

Assuming I'm alive to see it.

His father used to say that every child is born with a death sentence, though the exact execution date is unknown. At least his end would be quicker than the months of cancer that took Dad.

He checked his watch. "Thirty-eight minutes."

"We're cutting it close," said the young flight instructor, "but Dabiq is not far across the border. ETA is thirty minutes."

The name *Ali Jabbar* was sewn into the soldier's uniform.

Ali followed his gaze. "To answer the question you're too polite to ask, I am a practicing Muslim but have no respect for the Mahdi and what he stands for."

Ali rattled off the speech like a waiter reciting the day's specials for the hundredth time.

"I take it from your public profession of faith, that you haven't signed the Immortality Contract?"

"I'm only twenty-two, so I don't need your pill yet, but my parents signed and are enjoying their second youth. They pray in private, but obey your rules."

"Did you volunteer for this mission?" Theon asked.

"My commanding officer chose me because I grew up in Syria and am familiar with the language if we're shot down."

"You're a refugee, then?"

Ali nodded. "Our town fell to Da'esh when I was fifteen. They rounded up all the young men and separated Shia from Sunni. I pretended to be Sunni, until our town's mayor outed me. They drove us into the desert and lined us up next to a shallow ravine. Seventy-four in all. I know because they made us count off one by one."

Ali stared out the window as they passed the fortified border. "I was sure I was going to die. All of us in that line prayed, and I remember every detail of that moment. The smells of the men next to me, the feel of the wind—even the anthill at my feet.

"When they opened fire, I tumbled into the ravine like I'd been hit. I cut my forehead with a sharp rock, rubbed blood over my face and neck, and lay still among the bodies."

He pointed to a scar over his right eye. "When they left, I was the only one alive. I found a cell phone on one of the bodies and called my parents. Thank Allah they were still alive. They found me, and we drove west until my dad's car ran out of gas. Then we walked for two weeks to the border with Turkey.

"The rest is the usual story. A raft to Greece and a series of camps in search of a country that would accept us.

"We'd probably still be in a camp somewhere in Europe, except we won the US immigration lottery before President Kane banned asylum requests from Muslims. The hardest part was leaving my friends in the refugee camp, especially a Yazidi girl named Nasima.

"Da'esh takes the Yazidi women as sex slaves. They say the Qur'an allows this because they're not people of the book, meaning Christians, Jews, or Muslims. Nasima was captured and enslaved for a month before she escaped.

"Her parents told everyone she'd pretended to be pregnant so she wasn't raped, but she told me the real story. I think she was testing me to see if I'd still love her, even if I knew. I told her it didn't matter to me and she cried with relief.

"The day we left for America, she gave me this." He reached into a shirt pocket on his flight suit and pulled out a laminated photo of a girl wearing a white shawl.

"I've tried finding her, but her parents don't like me because I'm a Muslim. I think they tear up my letters, or maybe moved to a different camp. There's not a day that passes that I don't wonder where she is."

Ali stared at the photo in silence, then replaced it in his pocket.

"And your parents?" Theon asked.

"My father was a physician in Syria, but drives a taxi now. Mom works at Wal-Mart." Ali shook his head. "I still haven't gotten used to them looking the same age as me. It will really be strange when I look older than them."

"I suppose you're a reminder that not all Muslims are terrorists."

"Most aren't," Ali said. "But you'll soon be meeting plenty of the other sort, though I don't even consider them true Muslims."

"I imagine the Mahdi's followers think the same of you."

"I'm sure that's true," Ali said.

The soldier's eyes drifted out the small window to the land of his birth. "Nasima tried explaining her religion to me, but I never could understand it. There's a Peacock Angel called Melek the Demiurge, or something like that. I suppose Islam would be equally confusing if I hadn't grown up with it."

"Would you convert to marry her?"

Ali frowned. "I'd never considered that, but yes. I suppose I'm more devoted to Nasima than to Islam. Maybe what we believe in is less important than believing in something. Maybe belief itself is what gives life meaning."

A good summation of why I failed.

"Nice of those Hajjis to gather in one place for us," the pilot called back. "I hope Allah is well stocked with virgins when our bombers show up."

"He's going down there, you know," Ali said.

"We reap what we sow," the pilot said with a scowl in Theon's direction.

"What's your problem, KT?" Ali asked, but the pilot turned his attention back to flying.

"He's right," Theon said. "I have no one to blame but myself."

The sky to the east lightened, gradually driving the stars into hiding.

Theon glanced at his watch. Twenty-one minutes left.

"You'll be using a LALO technique," Ali said, "which means jumping from a relatively low altitude—in this case, a mile up. It makes the jump safer, but leaves us vulnerable to ground fire. The higher-ups say that we've been granted safe passage, so that shouldn't be an issue."

Ali attached a rope to Theon's parachute ripcord and clipped the other end onto a thick cable running the length of the plane's interior. "This will deploy your chute automatically when you jump."

Theon nodded. He'd reviewed the procedure a few times on the flight to Turkey, but it kept him focused to go over it again. No point dwelling on the future.

Ali tested the straps a final time. "I admire your courage, though I can't imagine what could get you to go down there."

"You don't know my mission?" Theon asked.

"My commander would have briefed us if he thought we needed to know."

It made sense. The temptation to warn friends might spread like wildfire and trigger a mass exodus. Probably his commander didn't even know everything.

"When you near the ground, bend your—"

Bullets tore through the floor.

Ali screamed and collapsed.

"Hang on!" The pilot yanked the controls right, and the plane banked out of the line of fire.

Flames burst from the left wing.

"The left engine is on fire!" Theon yelled.

"Fuck!" The pilot flipped a switch and shut off the engine. Deprived of fuel, the fire blew itself out. "Radio's dead, tail shot to hell. So much for safe passage."

The plane bucked and vibrated as the pilot wrestled with the controls to keep it on course.

Theon unclipped from the rope and crawled to Ali. Blood was everywhere.

Theon yanked a medical kit from the wall and used scissors to cut open his shirt.

"Is he okay?" shouted the pilot.

Five ragged holes gaped in Ali's torso. With each heartbeat, blood spurted upward. The boy opened his mouth, but only coughed up blood. Then he went limp.

Theon threw the medical kit against the wall.

"How is he?" the pilot called back.

"He's dead," Theon said.

"Fuck!"

"I'm sorry, Ali," he said, then closed his lids.

"You hit?" the pilot asked.

"No."

"Goddamn figures," the pilot said. "The fuel tank is leaking. I'm heading back to base for another plane."

"We'll miss the deadline!"

"Let them Hajjis wait," the pilot said, and started turning.

Theon ran to the cockpit. "The Mahdi has three nuclear bombs hidden in New York, Chicago, and LA. Unless I'm there in . . ." he checked his watch, "sixteen minutes, he will detonate all three."

The pilot's eyes widened. "My family lives in New York. My kids, grandkids, and even a great-granddaughter."

He coughed, and blood dribbled down his chin.

"You're hit," Theon said.

"A punctured lung."

"Let me take a look."

"Don't bother," the pilot said, struggling to keep the plane level. "Nothing you can do for something like this." He coughed up more blood. "Tell me you why you're here."

"If I reach Dabiq by 7:00, he'll e-mail the president the locations and codes necessary to disarm the bombs."

"And you believe him?"

"He swore it by Allah," Theon said.

The first rays of sun topped the eastern horizon.

The pilot scowled. "Why couldn't you have just sold your drug?"

"Can we make it in time?"

The remaining engine sputtered, stalled, then roared back to life.

"We have to," the pilot said, struggling to keep the plane on course. Bloody foam came out of his mouth with each labored breath.

He motioned to a backpack on the floor. Theon brought it to him. On the flap, a patch read: *K T Miller.*

KT reached into the backpack and removed a small chain with a gold cross attached. He slipped it over his head and let it settle onto his shoulders.

"Wore this all through Nam. I was shot down twice and walked away. Never captured once, and I'm not going to start now." The pilot took hold of the cross with bloody fingers and kissed it. "Fuck your Immortality Contract."

The engine sputtered, stalled, then started back up.

Minutes passed. Neither of them said a word. The pilot's breathing bubbled up in wet gasps.

KT pointed toward the horizon.

A ramshackle collection of clay-brick huts and farmsteads came into view. In the surrounding fields, a vast gathering of tents, tanks, and air defenses bull's-eyed outward in concentric circles.

The vast encampment sparkled with thousands of campfires.

"Can you put the plane in autopilot and bail out?"

"Autopilot can't handle this much damage," KT said, "and I'm not letting those towel-heads get a hold of me."

The plane shuddered.

"The wing is coming apart," KT said. "Get to the jump-door now."

Theon fought his way back, but the plane lurched to the side, and he flew into the opposite bulkhead.

The engine sputtered, but kept going.

"I can't reach the door!" he shouted.

No reply.

KT's hands were off the controls, his head rolling with the bumps and jolts.

The plane rolled until the jump-door loomed above like a sealed skylight. The rope swung toward him, and he caught it.

Hand over hand, he climbed toward the door.

The plane rolled again, and he fell on top of the door.

He yanked it open. The blast of freezing air stung his cheeks.

The sparkling lights of the encampment looked like a fairy tale.

Pieces of the wing tore free and clattered against the side of the fuselage. The engine gave a final cough and went silent.

He heaved himself out the door, and the wind slammed him sideways.

His chute didn't open.

I forgot to attach the rope.

He grasped the ripcord and pulled. The chute opened and transformed him into a marionette.

The roar of wind ceased, and an unexpected solitude enveloped him. He'd undershot the target somewhat. Far below, tiny forms oozed from the edge of the encampment—too distant for any sound to reach him.

The plane hit the ground a few miles away. It tumbled and tore itself apart. Without fuel, there was no explosion.

His watch read 6:59.

His heart slowed as the disk of the sun fought free of the horizon, its surface stained red by the rising dust of the camp.

A faint sound floated past.

"Allah Akbar—Allah Akbar . . ."

The mob of people grew larger.

"Allah Akbar—Allah Akbar . . ."

The chant intensified with each second.

Well, God, you proved yourself more than a match for me.

He drifted lower, and individual faces came into focus. They varied in age and shape, but all wore beards.

"Allah Akbar!"

A circle of empty ground opened beneath him.

Men with video cameras recorded this miraculous fulfillment of divine prophecy.

The last hundred yards rushed at him with frightening speed. He landed on the hard-packed soil with a grunt that knocked the breath out of his lungs.

Four soldiers in black robes surrounded him. Except for their AK-47s, they might have been holy warriors from a thousand years past. The crowd chanted and threw shoes at him, but kept their distance. None but their leader deserved the honor of executing the Dajjal.

One soldier pulled a knife and severed the lines of the parachute, then cut him free of his harness, jumpsuit, shirt, and combat boots. At least they left his pants. The cold raised goose pimples across his body.

The soldiers marched him toward the encampment, with the mob surging alongside.

"Allah Akbar! Allah Akbar!" the millions shouted.

Within a few minutes, the bottoms of his feet were bloody. Every step became a torture. If he slowed, the soldiers jabbed the barrels of their AK-47s into his naked back with practiced brutality. When he fell, his captors beat him. At such moments, the crowd cheered and rained spittle on him. Once, an old man rushed in, lifted his robe, and urinated in his face, to the delight of the audience.

All captured by the team of diligent videographers.

Theon stumbled forward in a daze of pain. Blood and dirt stung his eyes.

Keep going just a little longer.

The faces in crowd were mostly young. They were victims as much a he. Very soon, all of them would die for a lie.

After what seemed a lifetime of agony, he reached a hill with a white tent perched on top. Its prominent placement sent a powerful message. Unlike Osama or any of the ISIS leaders, the Mahdi advertised his presence with no fear of his enemies.

Beside the tent, a plasma screen twenty feet tall displayed a close-up view of Theon's blood-drenched face as he stumbled up the hill.

The cameramen positioned themselves expertly. One crewmember held a shotgun-mic on a pole to capture every grunt and cry of pain.

A news van crouched behind the white tent, a transmitter extending skyward from its roof.

At least Alma's farm was free of televisions.

Two of the black-robed soldiers grabbed his arms twenty feet short of the tent's entrance. He gasped for breath and would have collapsed without their support. Out of the corner of his eye, a giant avatar of his bloody face mimicked his movements.

"Allah Akbar! Allah Akbar!" shouted the crowd in unison.

The Mahdi emerged from the tent, and the chanting ceased.

Blinking the blood and sweat from his eyes, Theon gasped for air as Reza walked forward and stopped in front of him. His black robe was unadorned and his beard trimmed. He was tall enough that his face was level with his.

"And so we meet, just as the prophesy foretold," Reza said in perfect English.

"Yes," Theon replied in a hoarse croak.

The giant speakers flung their words to the mesmerized crowd.

Reza turned to the vast horde and raised both his hands like a wizard casting a spell. He spoke in Arabic, the language of the Qur'an. "Sayatimm qaribaan alwafa' tanba!"

The crowd cheered and shot their guns toward the sky.

After a moment, Reza lowered his hands and his followers stilled.

He made a short speech in Arabic, no doubt promising them all a place in paradise before the day was over.

When he finished, the crowd shouted, "Allah Akbar!" for the hundredth time. Did God ever get tired of being reminded how great he was?

Theon stood shivering as his captor entered the tent. The two soldiers dragged him inside as well.

The cameramen halted at the threshold of this inner sanctum. It seemed the Mahdi desired a word in private with his sacrificial lamb.

Iranian coffee filled his nostrils with an intoxicating aroma, while the warmth of the interior eased his shivering.

As his eyes adjusted, a simple room came into focus. A desk, chair, two army cots, and several prayer rugs. A woman knelt at the back, brewing coffee on a propane stove. Her brown eyes gazed through slits in her hijab.

Beside the woman, a white-bearded man sat with legs crossed and a glass of coffee in his right hand. The left side of his face sagged in the distinctive manner of a stroke victim. He wore a purple silk robe with golden thread sewn into the hem. A traditional curved knife in a jewel-encrusted scabbard poked from the blue sash wound around his waist.

The old man stared at him with undisguised hatred.

An electric space heater hummed in the opposite corner. The sound mingled with the low chanting of the crowd outside as they prayed.

Reza motioned to the two soldiers. They released his arms, but remained alert.

"The Dajjal has finally emerged from his lair," Reza said.

The veiled woman poured coffee, stood, and brought it to Reza. In addition to her hijab, she wore black slippers and thin gloves to maintain the modesty demanded by Allah—or at least by those who claimed to know his mind.

A stain of red expanded beneath Theon's shredded feet. As the surge of adrenaline abated, his many wounds competed for his attention.

"I have come as promised," Theon said. "Now it's your turn to make good on your oath."

"What makes you think I'd keep an oath to the Great Deceiver?"

"You swore by Allah's name."

"You claim not to believe in God," Reza observed.

"I believe you believe in one, and the Qur'an condemns anyone who breaks such an oath."

The woman returned to her corner and knelt beside the old man.

"You think you can control my actions by using the words of the Prophet you so despise?" Reza asked. "Since you are such an expert on the Qur'an, you should know that one may free a captured slave for absolution from a broken oath."

Is he toying with me?

Reza walked to his desk, took a document out of the top right drawer, signed it, and then stamped it with his official seal.

"I purchased this Yazidi slave last week. Her name is Azhin."

He handed the paper to the woman kneeling on the floor and spoke a few words in Arabic. She looked at the paper, then seized his hand and kissed it.

Azhin rose, took a step, then stopped, as if expecting a trick.

Reza held open the tent's flap. "'Ant hurr lildh-dha-hab," he said. "You are free to go."

She fled, holding the piece of paper before her as a talisman of protection.

Reza shouted, "Daeuna la shay' yamnie-uha."

The woman ran at full speed through the rows of prostrating soldiers. No one glanced her way as they prepared their souls for the next world.

Reza closed the tent's flap and faced him. "My sin is forgiven. You see how merciful Allah is?"

A queasy sensation crept into Theon's gut.

"What can you gain by killing millions of innocent people for no reason?"

"The United States dropped nuclear bombs on two Japanese cities to force surrender. Are such tactics reserved for infidels?"

"It will only bring a nuclear strike against your cities."

"You forget that Allah is on our side."

He shivered despite the electric heater. "You've already detonated them, haven't you?"

Reza's expression maintained its relaxed calm. "The instant you landed on our soil, I gave the order." He sipped his coffee. "New York, Chicago, and Los Angeles have been laid waste by Allah."

All strength fled his legs, and the ever-alert guards seized his arms to keep him upright.

Millions murdered—because of me.

"You son-of-a-bitch," Theon said through clenched teeth. "You'll be dead in less than half an hour."

"That's the difference between us. You seek to hide from death, while I welcome it."

"What are you waiting for?" Theon asked. "Kill me."

"You will die at the start of the battle. It has been written."

Theon jerked forward. The guards tightened their grip and bent his arms behind his back.

"Your pathetic book is not the dictates of any god!" Theon shouted. "It's nothing but the cynical creation of an illiterate, power-hungry pervert. You've murdered millions for a reward that doesn't exist!"

Reza watched without the slightest sign of anger.

"I have tasted the rewards of Jannah," Reza said. "The food, the tender bodies of the Houris, and experienced the presence of Allah firsthand. I assure you, the next life is no illusion."

A coughing fit seized Theon.

"Did they ever catch those three masked men who killed your wife and daughter?" Reza asked.

"You know they didn't," Theon said.

"Your granddaughter told a different story."

Theon said nothing.

"With all that evidence, you assumed she was insane, or maybe that she'd murdered them herself?"

"What does it matter now?"

"You are a seeker of truth, are you not?" Reza asked. "Don't you want to see with your own eyes who killed your wife and daughter?"

Reza picked up an Ipad and held it in front of Theon's face.

On the screen was a black-and-white image of Taslima, Susan, and Alma sitting with Fatima.

"This is video surveillance of that day. Fatima removed the cameras before the police arrived to keep them from learning the truth."

Theon looked away.

"You're the great champion of truth," Reza said. "Are you afraid to face your own self-deceptions?"

Reza reached for the *Play* button at the center of the image, but Theon shut his eyes.

I won't watch Alma kill them.

The guards forced his eyelids open.

Reza started the video.

Taslima's five brothers entered the room.

"It can't be," he whispered.

There was no sound on the video, but everything matched Alma's description.

When the brothers dragged Taslima and Susan out the doorway, the video switched to a camera in the courtyard. Fatima stood leaning on her cane, encouraging her sons as they murdered their sister and niece.

Alma tried to stop them, but one of the brothers held her, even as he stabbed his knife into her mother's stomach.

When the men left, Alma stopped screaming and curled into a ball beside the bodies.

The video ended.

Theon stood supported by the two guards, his face slack, his reality stripped bare. How could one shed tears for something so impossible?

Alma is innocent. She's been telling the truth all along.

"Your mind misled you with those things you call facts. It's the same reason you reject God."

I convinced Alma her memories were delusions.

Reza walked to the old man sitting at the back of the tent and helped him stand. The entire left side of his body was partially paralyzed.

With Reza's support, the man limped to within inches of Theon.

"I am Omar bin Saud. Your wife's youngest brother."

Theon's jaw twitched, but he said nothing.

Another trick?

"My elder brothers plunged their blades into the bodies of my apostate sister and her abomination of a daughter, but I received the honor of slitting their throats with this." With his good right hand, Omar slid his curved knife out of the ornate scabbard.

Theon jerked toward him, but the guards held firm.

"How could you have faked all that evidence?"

"My brothers and I planned well. Afterward, your own government even helped us cover it up."

"The two state department men lied to protect you?"

"They also helped with the false passport stamps and faked surveillance time codes from the other surveillance videos," the old man said. "No one wanted an international incident that threatened the flow of oil. It's what you Westerners call acting for the greater good."

"Why leave a witness alive at all?"

"Allah does not allow killing one so young," Omar said. "We figured no one would believe her—and you proved us right."

Silence

"Have you nothing more to say to me, Dajjal?"

"Taslima said she sang you lullabies when you had nightmares as a child. She protected you against the bullying of your older brothers. She loved you and looked forward to seeing you again more than anyone else."

Omar's lower lip trembled, and tears formed in his eyes. But then he stiffened and raised his chin. "I carried out the sentence Allah demands."

"I forgive you," Theon said, "because it's what Taslima would say herself."

Omar spat in his face. The spittle mixed with the drying blood, dirt, and piss coating his skin.

"I seek no forgiveness from you, Dajjal."

Omar offered his knife to Reza. "Al Mahdi, accept my sacred Janbiya to uphold the honor of my family."

Reza took the knife with both hands. "The time has come for this blade to fulfill its destiny."

The soldiers dragged Theon outside, and the prayers ceased. An eerie silence blanketed the vast plain as the cameras transmitted his image onto the big screen once again.

At a motion from Reza, the soldiers forced Theon to his knees.

The Mahdi held the knife above his head in a ritualistic gesture.

The same knife that erased Taslima and Susan from existence.

A squadron of Iranian jets flashed overhead, and the crowd cheered. One of them exploded and plunged earthward a few miles distant.

Three American F35 fighters streaked after the fleeing planes, leaving sonic booms in their wake.

It marked the final proof that Reza had detonated the nuclear bombs. There would be no attack while there was still the chance of getting the codes. What was it that KT said? *I hope Allah is well stocked with virgins when our bombers show up.* Were plutonium-tipped cruise missiles already on their way to Tehran, as well?

Reza grabbed a fistful of Theon's hair with his left hand. His fingers dug into his scalp and yanked backward, exposing his neck.

The Mahdi's upside-down face was framed against morning sky. Omar stood behind him, leaning on a cane for support, his eyes hungry for blood.

Why did death so fascinate mankind? Human sacrifice was one of the oldest practices of every culture—most likely at the foundation of religion itself. Maybe the crucifixion of Jesus is a logical extension of this. In killing a god, man takes his place.

Is what I tried to do any different?

Dozens of planes flashed overhead, engaged in furious dogfights. Reza looked into the camera, speaking his perfect English. "We are ready to meet your armies in battle. Soon, the Great Judgment will be upon the world."

The knife settled against his throat.

So this is how it ends. Murdered by same blade that started it all.

The Mahdi looked to the sky. "Qabilah! I'm coming to join you!"

The knife pressed harder against his skin and drew first blood.

A bomb detonated behind them, and he was flying forward.

Everything went dark.

He awoke to fire, choking smoke, and screams of pain.

The toxic air burned his eyes, and his ears rang.

"*Always keep moving,*" his boxing coach used to repeat. "*A moving target is harder to hit,*" was Arnie's mantra.

He crawled forward, feeling his way along the ground in the blinding smoke.

His hand found Omar's body. The side of his head was gone.

Would Alma see his ghost? What would Omar tell her?

A gap opened in the smoke. Reza stood several yards away, searching. Blood covered half his face from minor shrapnel wounds. He held Omar's knife in his right fist.

He hasn't seen me yet.

The gunfire and shrieks of agony stayed just beyond him, as if he stood in the eye of a hellish hurricane of fire.

They're using my implanted tracking chip to create a zone of safety around me.

Reza turned and spotted him.

Theon lurched upright as the Mahdi charged.

The knife shot forward. He sidestepped and countered with a left hook. It landed on Reza's right temple and sent him staggering. The follow-up right missed. Reza slashed the knife at his gut.

Theon jumped back, and it grazed his flesh without hitting anything vital.

He turned and ran into the black cloud.

If I can't see, neither can he.

A breeze punched a hole in the smoke, exposing a section of the landscape below. Thousands lay dead and dying. The survivors fired anti-aircraft guns and surface-to-air missiles toward the heavens. A second wave of bombs lit the battlefield with hundreds of miniature suns.

A pressure wave knocked him off his feet.

Sunbeams reached fingers toward him through the haze.

Keep those feet moving!

Choking on the noxious air, he struggled down the hill, searching for a weapon. If his theory was right, all he needed to do was put Reza outside his protected zone, and the bombs would do the rest.

Shrieks of pain mixed with exultations of those welcoming their martyrdom.

The shadowy form of the Mahdi appeared behind him.

A soldier leapt in front of him, his gun raised. Theon broke his nose with a jab, then followed with a straight right. The man collapsed, his rifle clattering away into a fissure in the rocks

Theon turned and ducked a slash from the Mahdi's knife.

Reza lunged, aiming for his gut.

Theon jumped aside and grabbed the Mahdi's wrist with both hands.

Then, they were falling.

He held to the wrist with every ounce of his fading strength.

They slammed into water and went under. He lost hold of the wrist and struggled to the surface. The water reached his waist. Light filtered through a circular opening far above.

We stumbled into a well.

A splash sounded behind him.

Reza leaned against the side of the curved stone wall, gasping for breath. Blood seeped out of a gash in his forehead. Most important, his hands were empty.

The echoes of the battle had faded like some distant universe.

"You cannot avoid your fate," the Mahdi said.

Reza was no longer a man, but the embodiment of every religious dogma, holy war, oppressive doctrine, and small-minded superstition.

With a guttural snarl, Theon charged. Reza blocked the jab, then the straight right, but the left uppercut caught him under the chin. He fell and Theon pounced.

"Die, you bastard," Theon shouted as he held him under the water.

Reza gripped his left thumb and bent it back.

Theon screamed and let go.

Before he could react, Reza's right arm locked around his neck from behind in a military-style headlock, cutting off his air supply.

Theon got both feet on the wall and shoved. They went underwater together.

Reza didn't struggle, but kept his unbreakable hold.

My expiration date has finally arrived.

Disjointed images flashed before his mind in the usual cliché: Taslima's body arching beneath him the first time they made love in the planetarium—Dad selling peanuts at Wrigley Field—Susan's wide eyes gazing at their first captured Immortal Jellyfish—Mom reading a children's story by candlelight during a power outage—the smell of Helena's hair—Alma's smile—Grandpa Frank's masterpiece.

The internal slideshow halted on that day he got the call from the man at the embassy. *"Mr. Torano, we're sorry to inform you that your wife and daughter have been—"*

His hand settled on something smooth at the bottom of the well—the blade of a knife. The same one that had started it all. The knife that had killed his wife and daughter. Whether chance, or fate, he slid his fingers to the ivory handle and gripped it.

The last of his oxygen flowed into his arm, fueling his cells for one final burst of energy.

I'll only have one chance.

He thrust the knife to the left of his head. The blade embedded itself and jerked from his grasp.

The arm across his throat relaxed and then slid away.

Theon floundered to the surface, gasping for breath.

The Mahdi floated on his back, the knife protruding from his left eye socket and part of his brow ridge. His face stared, unseeing, toward the disk of illumination above.

The distant explosions ceased, as if the death of the Mahdi signaled the battle's end.

Theon slid lower on the wall, shivering. His vision wavered as consciousness dimmed.

How ironic if I drown in the blood of the Mahdi.

An image of the smoking ruins of the three great cities filled his mind.

Maybe this is the death I deserve.

The light flickered, and he looked up. Two dark forms descended through the circle of light.

As he slipped under the water, something grabbed him.

Are they demons or angels?

Hands dragged him to the surface.

A soldier secured a harness around his chest, and yanked twice on the rope.

They rose out of the hole strapped together, with the soldier using his feet to keep from hitting the sides.

The morning breeze cleared the smoke from a moonscape of craters and dead bodies. Here and there, the twisted remains of tanks and anti-aircraft guns poked through.

What a waste. What a tragic waste.

He sobbed and turned his eyes upward, away from the consequences of his own delusions.

Soldiers pulled him into a sleek helicopter with rounded edges.

Inside, a team of medics tended his wounds.

"Didn't expect to see you again," said a familiar voice.

Lamarr crouched next to the doctors. He wore the same uniform as the soldiers.

"How bad is it?" Theon asked his old friend.

Lamarr grinned. "I think you'll make it, but I'd suggest quitting while you're ahead."

Theon grabbed Lamarr by his flack jacket and pulled him closer. "I don't mean me," he said. "Los Angeles, Chicago, New York."

Confusion knitted Lamarr's brow. "The Mahdi sent the codes like he promised. Our teams had disarmed the bombs by the time you entered his tent."

Dizziness swept through him. *Am I dreaming? Is my mind creating an alternate reality to protect me from the truth?*

The soldiers hauled Reza's dead body into the chopper, the knife still protruding from his eye.

"Both targets secure," called out the team commander. "Let's get the fuck out of here before one of those Hajji's wake up next to a rocket launcher."

The door clanged shut, and the helicopter headed west, keeping low to avoid radar.

A couple soldiers photographed Reza's body and extracted blood samples for DNA verification.

They left the knife in place.

Why had Reza lied to him? Psychological torture?

Or maybe Reza wasn't as monstrous as he thought.

By the time they landed, his wounds were patched, and he was dressed in the same uniform as the soldiers.

"I think I can walk," he said, despite the pain in his bandaged feet.

"What the Hell were you thinking?" Helena shouted as she marched across the tarmac.

Theon shot Lamarr a hard look.

"I didn't tell her," Lamarr said, "She followed your tracking device here on her own."

Theon held his hands up in a sign of surrender at Helena. "I had no choice—"

She slapped his face, and then embraced him. "Thank Aphrodite you're alive."

Then she broke down and cried.

He wrapped his arms around her and stroked her hair.

Lamarr led the soldiers away to give them privacy.

When Helena's tears abated, she looked up at him. "Don't you know I couldn't live without you?"

"I wish I'd listened to you from the beginning," he said.

Helena glanced at a team of soldiers carrying a body bag. "You killed him?"

He nodded. "Before he died, Reza showed me a surveillance video of Taslima and Susan's murders."

"Was it Alma?"

"No," he said. "It happened exactly the way she remembered it."

"So it was a cover-up?"

He nodded. "If only I'd believed her from the start."

"Are you going to tell her?"

"There's no point. She already knows the truth."

"Because Taslima's ghost told her?"

He shrugged.

"So you're an agnostic, now?"

He laughed. "I'm always open to any new evidence you might want to present."

Helena motioned to a private jet with Poncho and Cisco standing guard beside it. "We should get going. It's best if the rest of the world believes you died back there."

"Is that an order?"

She kissed him. "You've been demoted. I'm in charge from now on."

"That's fine with me," he said.

Chapter 26

Alma held tight to her cane as the hover-car glided to a stop in front of their cabin. Normally, David greeted guests, but he'd left early to collect the out-of-town kids and grandkids at the airport.

It was best they weren't here, in case the reporter overstepped the agreement and tried sneaking additional interviews.

The homestead hadn't changed much since she arrived fifty-two years ago. David sometimes talked of adding a layer of Solar Paint to the barn for electric heaters, but ultimately decided against it. During the Great Collapse after the Mahdi's death, their self-sufficient community weathered the storm of famine and war better than the cities. Why change what had worked so well for half a century?

The reporter got out of her vehicle and walked toward her. The girl wore thick snow boots, a huge white parka, and stylish white skiing pants that showed off her athletic legs.

"I'm Faith Chang," the woman said. "It's so nice to meet you in person."

"You certainly were persistent."

"I never give up on an interview once I set my sights on it."

"*Ask her if she has it,*" her mother's spirit said.

"Mom asks if you brought the payment we agreed on."

Faith looked around. "Your mother is here with us now?"

"She's standing to my right," Alma said.

"I'm pleased to meet you," the reporter said, looking too far to the right. "I have the item in my car, and I'll give it to your daughter after our interview."

Her mother chuckled. "*I don't think she trusts you.*"

"Why don't we sit on the porch?" Alma said. "My legs aren't as strong as they used to be."

Faith followed her up the steps to wooden rocking chairs facing the shimmering amphitheater of the Sierra. Then she removed a pair of stick-on audio transmitters from her pocket, each the size of a shirt button. "Is it okay if I record this?"

"It's fine with me," Alma said.

The reporter adhered one button to her own jacket, and the other to Alma's sweater.

"Your weekly Sunday podcast is one of the most listened to programs across the globe," Faith said. "Can you explain why people of every religion admire you?"

Such empty questions were why she normally didn't do interviews.

"Maybe they find inspiration in my story. If God saved me, he can save anyone."

Faith glanced at her notes. "Tomorrow will be the fiftieth anniversary of your grandfather's death—"

"I don't believe he's passed from this world," Alma said.

The reporter's left eyebrow arched. "You're referring to the conspiracy theories about your grandfather somehow surviving the bombing of the Mahdi's camp? Of him and his colleagues starting a secret coalition of scientists intent on pursuing banned fields of research under the noses of the authorities?"

"I don't know about any of that," Alma said, "but my grandfather's spirit hasn't visited me, so my heart tells me he's alive."

"Okay, then," Faith said, as if dealing with someone who believed the earth was flat. "Many consider Theon's surrender to the Mahdi the greatest self-sacrifice the world has ever seen—except for Jesus, of course. What did your grandfather say to you before leaving on his secret mission?"

Such pointless questions. Yet, I do want what's in that car.

"My grandfather said goodbye, as if he knew it was the last time."

Faith scribbled a few notes, then looked up. "The next morning, every Amara distribution center on the planet was found empty. The company's top scientists and executives vanished without a trace. Did he tell you of his decision to withdraw his pill?"

"He never shared his plans with me, but I think he realized his invention had brought us to the brink of destruction."

"Then you support the global ban on scientific research that poses an existential threat to humanity? Things such as artificial intelligence, human genetic engineering, and self-replicating robots?"

"I'm not political," Alma said.

The door of the cabin across the field burst open, and three of her great-grandchildren ran into the snow, shrieking in delight at the fresh layer deposited as they'd slept. Their father followed them toward the barn, throwing snowballs amidst peals of laughter.

"That's my grandson, Aaron, and his kids. All told, I have seven children, thirty-five grandchildren, and seven great-grandchildren."

"*Bragging now, are we?*" Mom said with a smile.

"What's wrong with being proud of my children?" Alma asked her mother.

"Are you talking to me?" Faith asked.

"I'm sorry, I forgot you can't see my mother."

"It's fine," Faith said, though a slight frown flitted across her forehead. "It took the world several decades to recover from the famines, wars, and plagues following the collapse."

"It was tragic," Alma said.

"What would you say to the growing number of people who think we should reinvent your grandfather's pill?"

Another odd question. Does anyone care what I think about such worldly issues?

Alma leaned forward. "Do you believe in God?"

Faith hesitated.

"It's okay if you don't," Alma said. "I was an atheist before my death and resurrection. I ask because I suspect the yearning for everlasting life in this world is only possible if you don't believe in an afterlife."

The reporter spoke as if choosing each word with care. "I'd be committing career suicide to admit doubts in the midst of the religious revival sweeping the world."

"That saddens me," Alma said. "I suppose the backlash against non-believers isn't surprising, now that church institutions have rebounded stronger than before, but true belief can't be coerced."

Above them, an eagle glided past, its shadow racing over the snowy field faster than any land animal. What had once been a rare sight was now a daily occurrence. Not all species had survived. Elephants, rhinos, lions, and the American Bison had been hunted to extinction during the great collapse, as humans sought food wherever they could find it.

The opposite occurred in the oceans. With a shortage of oil to run the fleets of massive fishing trawlers, aquatic life exploded exponentially in the two-decade lull. When the world's economy rebounded thirty years later, fishermen found the seas filled to capacity.

"Are you seeing another spirit?" Faith asked with a tinge of bitterness in her voice.

What is this girl hiding?

"Everything is spirit," Alma said. "You, me, the eagle, the mountains."

"But you claim to see what others can't."

Alma studied her before answering. "Did you know bees perceive a wider range of light waves than humans? Some flowers that look white to us display colorful patterns in the ultraviolet spectrum that only bees can see."

"Were you born with the ability to see the dead?"

Why would she waste time on questions that are common knowledge?

"*Something's not right here,*" her mother said.

"My visions started after I died and met God," Alma said.

"You understand why some people might be skeptical?"

Alma shrugged. "I've done full podcasts on doubt. I'm happy to answer your question, but it might use all our remaining time."

"We'll skip that, then."

The young reporter fidgeted in her chair. "Would you be willing to take a test to prove your claims?"

"*Here we go,*" her mother's ghost said with a roll of her eyes.

"A test?"

"My sister died two years ago," Faith said. "If you summon her spirit, I'll ask a question that only she knows the answer to."

"I am not a medium," Alma said. "Those from the other side choose me. I could no more summon your sister than I could a hibernating bear from those mountains."

Faith's lips compressed into a tight line.

"It's not your sister you want me to contact, is it?" Alma asked. "My guess is that you don't have a sister."

The reporter averted her gaze and took a deep breath. "Every adult on the planet watched video of you at that trial. A prostitute and drug addict who conquered death. A beautiful, tragic symbol of God's love."

Faith's wide Asian features glowed as the rising sun topped the mountains. "My mother died from liver cancer when I was eight—a side effect of North Korea's nuclear blitzkrieg of the South in '32."

Alma's heart ached for the girl. *How well I know your suffering.*

"The minister at the refugee center played your radio address every Sunday," the reporter said. "Your story gave me hope when I was at my lowest."

Faith's eyes abandoned the sky for the distant mountains. "I prayed and prayed for a visitation from my mother—but she never appeared. I wondered why God allowed you to visit your mother in Heaven, but denied me?" The girl's fists clenched. "By the time I reached college, I realized God, Heaven, and all of it was a cruel hoax."

Faith glared at her. "After that, my goal in life became exposing you as a fraud, just like your grandfather did to that evangelist."

The young reporter stood and removed a slim knife from her jacket pocket. There's no way she could have smuggled it through the security checkpoint. She must have stopped at the hut beside the bridge where David stored his fishing gear.

"Either summon my mother, or admit you're a fraud," Faith said.

With the help of her cane, Alma levered herself out of the chair and faced the girl. "I may be one of the few people who understands what you're feeling," Alma said.

Faith grabbed her by the sweater and yanked her close, pressing the knife to her neck. "You're nothing but a snake-oil salesman with a cross."

I must not fail this wounded soul.

A vision of Sandi's bruised face appeared before her mind's eye. She had searched for her after marrying David, but her friend had vanished. Had Jojo murdered her? Or some john? Her friend's spirit had never appeared, so her fate remained a mystery.

"You don't believe I'll kill you," Faith said.

"No, I don't."

"You're right. If there is a God, he must know my threat is empty as well." She let go of her and placed the knife to her own throat. "But if God does exists, he knows this is no bluff."

The reporter leaned her head back, gazing into the blue of the sky. "If you are there, let me see my mother."

After a long moment, nothing happened.

Faith closed her eyes. "There's two possibilities. Either God is an evil monster and doesn't care if I die, or there is no God at all." She pressed the curved blade harder against the side of her throat. "It's the same either way."

"I lied about it all," Alma said.

Faith opened her eyes, but said nothing.

Alma's heart pounded. "I lied about seeing Heaven, God, spirits—all of it."

Faith eased the knife from her neck. "The one thing that I haven't been able to figure out is how you knew the monk's secrets?"

"When we flew to Washington DC on the pope's private plane, Vadic talked in his sleep."

"Of course," Faith said with a smile. "That was clever."

"My grandfather guessed the truth."

"You realize everything you say is being uploaded to my cloud account from your micro transmitter?"

"I could not live with your death on my conscience."

Faith's eyes narrowed. "It's hard to believe that someone who cynically deceived the world for so long would ruin her reputation merely to save the life of an unstable reporter she just met."

"She's got you there," Alma's mother said.

"But you might lie to save me if . . ." Faith's eyes slowly widened, as if seeing her for the first time. "If your story was true." The knife slipped from her fingers and clattered to the deck. "You were willing to let the world condemn you as a fraud to save my life?"

"Yes," Alma said.

Faith fell to her knees and gazed at her in awe. "Then you did see God?"

"Just as you will see him and your mother in Heaven if you accept Jesus into your heart without reservation."

Alma stepped forward and placed a hand on the top of the girl's head. Faith cried and leaned into her like an infant seeking comfort.

"God led you here for a reason," Alma said.

Faith looked up. "I almost forgot your gift!"

The reporter dashed to her car. The trunk opened automatically, and she removed an object wrapped in a black cloth.

When she returned, Faith leaned the package against the side of the cabin. "Finding this took some doing, and even more effort convincing the owners you should have it."

Alma removed the cloth and stared at the self-portrait of her mother. It had been over half a century since she sold it to feed her inner demon.

The brush strokes were impressionistic through most of the painting, lending the refined face a startling realism in contrast. The soft brown eyes gazed at her with a look of contentment.

"Did you paint this knowing I was growing inside you?" Alma asked her mother.

No reply.

She looked around, but Mom was gone.

"What does she say?" Faith asked.

"She's left," Alma said. "But I'm glad she saw this."

Faith wiped a tear from her eye. "Thank you for giving me peace."

The reporter turned and started toward her car.

Alma placed a hand on her arm. "Why don't you celebrate the New Year with us here at the farm? It might make an interesting article for your magazine."

*　　*　　*

Alma gazed at the Milky Way just as she used to with Grandpa.

He believed the stars and galaxies formed out of the initial components created during a thing he called the Big Bang. "Our planet is a mote of dust compared to the vastness of the universe," he'd said. "The fact that we've evolved to the point of figuring this out is the greatest miracle of all."

Her five-year-old Great-grandson—Theon Jr.—took her hand. "What are you looking at, Grandma?"

"I'm looking at the stars, Theon," she said.

"Where do stars come from?"

"They come from God."

The little boy screwed his face into a frown. "Who made God?"

Alma laughed. *A question worthy of his namesake.*

"God has always existed," she said.

The boy kept hold of her hand and continued gazing at the sky. One by one, the rest of their extended family emerged from the cabins and joined them. Cassie was there with her husband, children, and grandchildren. All told, seventy-three people stood gathered together.

David took her other hand, and she smiled at his timeworn features. The scar marking their meeting remained as a reminder of what she'd once been.

"It's almost midnight," he said.

"What happens then?" little Theon asked.

"A new year starts," David said.

Eight-year-old Kaitlin walked beside Faith, her eyes darting around like a cat searching for a mouse. The reporter had lent the little girl her camera, and Kaitlin took her job as photojournalist very seriously. She snapped everything in her path, with special attention paid to the animals in the barn.

"Time for the countdown!" Cassie called out, her eyes focused on her smart-watch. "Ten . . . nine . . ."

Everyone joined in.

"Eight . . . seven . . ."

Alma glanced around. There wasn't a single spirit, angel, or demon in sight.

"Six . . . five . . . four . . ."

Faith walked over, with Kaitlin snapping photos in her wake.

"Three . . . two . . .ONE!

"Happy New Year!" everyone shouted in unison.

David took her in his arms and kissed her with no less passion than the first time.

"What's that?" Little Theon asked, pointing toward the mountains.

A light outshining any constellation rose like a reverse shooting star.

"There's another one!" Kaitlin pointed her camera in the opposite direction and snapped away.

One after the other, more lights appeared on the horizon—all heading skyward.

"What could they be?" David asked.

"I'll see if there's anything about it on CNN," Faith said, and tapped her wrist link.

A hologram of a middle-aged man in a blue suit materialized in the air in front of her. A caption reading *Breaking News* floated beneath the disembodied head.

"We're receiving reports of hundreds of objects rising into the sky all across the globe."

The hologram morphed to a close-up of a spherical metal ball moving upward at great speed. Unlike a rocket, no flames propelled it, but the space beneath the vehicle shimmered and distorted.

"This is a view of one of the objects from a ground-based telescope," the hologram said. "Though it's hard to tell from this image, we're being told that the craft is twice the height of the Empire State Building. It seems to have emerged from underground in a remote section of Colorado. CNN's science advisers tell me there is no known technology to lift something this massive into the atmosphere.

The man paused, and was handed a paper. "I've just received a report that many of the world's most prominent scientists and their immediate families are missing."

"You can turn that off," Alma said.

Faith pressed her wristband, and the hologram vanished.

They watched in silence as the sparkling lights rose like fireflies heading toward the stars.

"He timed it for me," Alma said.

"You mean your grandfather?"

Alma nodded. "He knew I'd be watching the sky at midnight, as I did with him as a child at the start of every New Year. It's his way of saying goodbye."

Her grandson gazed at the fading lights, his mouth open in wonder. "What are they?" little Theon asked.

Alma smiled. "They are the dreams of your great-great-grandfather."

"They're beautiful dreams," the boy said.

"All dreams are beautiful," Alma said. "Goodbye, Grandpa. I hope you find your truth."

The End

Author's note:

My novels and essays allow me to let my thoughts truly run wild, so thank you for coming along for the ride. Feel free to email me at ScottBurdick.com@gmail.com with your own thoughts on the subjects I've delved into here or in my previous novel, *Nihala*.

If you enjoyed the story, I'd greatly appreciate a short review on Amazon and a mention of the book on your own social media network. As a self-published author, such reviews are my only way of reaching a wider audience.

Sincerely,
Scott Burdick
website — www.ScottBurdick.com

Acknowledgements

Our knowledge is a direct reflection of the company we keep, either in person, or though books and films. I have been fortunate to meet some of the great thinkers of our time, who so generously shared their ideas and corrected some of my ignorance (which is still a work-in-progress). There are certainly too many names to fit here, but these are a few of the highlights.

Richard Dawkins must top any list. His books have had as profound an impact on my worldview as the first time I read Darwin's *On the Origin of Species* and Thomas Paine's *The Age of Reason* while attending Jesuit-run Catholic High School. The dedication of this man to freeing humanity from the chains of ignorance and self-delusion spurred me to come out publicly as an atheist sometime after college. I am humbled and honored to have spent time with this great thinker and even used a quote from one of our filmed interviews in this book. For your writings and generous example in spreading truth and reason, I cannot thank you enough, Richard.

The *Richard Dawkins Foundation for Science and Reason* can be found at https://richarddawkins.net/

Dan Barker and Annie Laurie Gaylor of the *Freedom From Religion Foundation* have not only been generous in their time in helping me with my various projects, but are to a large extent the inspiration for much of this novel. Their tireless stance for the separation of church and state in the face of those who would push us toward a theocracy is what first got me thinking about the core concept of *The Immortality Contract*. The dream of a world where true freedom of and from religion is a universal human right is something Dan and Annie Laurie fight for on a daily basis. I sincerely hope that everyone, whether religious or not, will join them in this effort by visiting their website at https://ffrf.org

Todd Stiefel has lent his encouragement and help so many times for so many projects I've embarked upon, that it's hard to imagine this book and most of my documentaries existing without him as a catalyst. His generosity with his time and money through The Stiefel Freethought Foundation has made a real difference in spreading the principles of humanism throughout the world. http://stiefelfreethoughtfoundation.org/

Sue Kocher and all the members of the Triangle Freethought Society deserve special thanks. After making my first documentary, *In God We Trust*, it was Sue who contacted me and led me down the rabbit hole of the Freethought community. Every time Sue called me with an idea for a documentary or interview project, I would turn it down at first with the excuse that I simply didn't have time in my schedule. Somehow, her excitement would rub off and I'd change my mind. What adventures I'd have missed out on without Sue Kocher! Thank you for not taking "no" for an answer. https://trianglefreethought.xyz/

James Randi had been a major influence even before I had the pleasure of meeting and interviewing him for a few of my documentaries. His efforts to expose those claiming supernatural powers to prey upon the desperate was the inspiration for the courtroom scene when Theon unmasks Cyril as a fraud.
James Randi Educational Foundation - http://web.randi.org/

Lawrence Krauss has also been kind enough to do several interviews with me for documentaries, and his book, *A Universe From Nothing*, was an eye-opener for me.
http://krauss.faculty.asu.edu/

Ray Comfort. Though we don't agree on much regarding religion and science, it was kind of him to do an interview with me and even allow me to film him having a discussion with Lawrence Krauss for a YouTube video. Without a dialogue between people of different views, how can knowledge and society ever advance? I greatly enjoyed our discussions and look forward to many more. I used the character of Alma in the story to represent Ray's viewpoint as thoroughly as possible. My hope is that I succeeded in conveying the logic of the fundamentalist philosophy in as fair and thorough a manner as possible. Too often books on both sides caricature arguments of their opponents, and I was determined to avoid this, though I'm sure my own bias shows through in the story. http://www.livingwaters.com/

Reverend James Dunn. I met James while filming my first documentary, *In God We Trust*, and we became close friends during that process. He is truly one of my heroes, both for his tireless fight for religious freedom during his twenty years as the director of the Baptist Joint Committee for Religious Freedom in Washington, DC and then as a professor of Divinity at Wake Forest University. James passed away while I was writing this novel and I sorely miss him and our discussions of politics, religion, and all his stories. I used James as the model for the Supreme Court Justice in the novel, even down to his story of "*Bobwar*," which is one he told me during our very first meeting. http://bjconline.org/james-m-dunn-1932-2015/

Steven Hewett, the subject of my first documentary, is another hero of mine who showed me what true bravery is by standing up for our secular constitution in the face of threats and intimidation. Much of this novel was written while those events in King, NC were occurring, so the interviews I did with local evangelists while making that film had a big influence on the character of Reverend Cyril. If not for people like Steve, the tyranny of the majority would replace all the freedoms our founders fought for.

Phil Torres' book *The End: What Science and Religion Tell Us about the Apocalypse* helped shape the second half of this novel with the danger of religious extremists acquiring nuclear weapons in an effort to spark End Times. I was fortunate enough to have lunch with Phil after reading his book. He is a truly brilliant thinker on many subjects. https://www.amazon.com/End-Science-Religion-about-Apocalypse/dp/1634310403

Richard Carrier's book *On the Historicity of Jesus* (and the interview he was kind enough to grant me while he was finishing that book) informed much of my knowledge on the Biblical evidence and sources of the gospels I included in the Supreme Court trial scenes. All of Carrier's work is phenomenal and thoroughly researched and peer-reviewed. His work is a must-read for anyone interested in seeking truth.

http://www.richardcarrier.info/

Charles Campbell, a good friend who read several early drafts of this and my previous novel over several years. Charles offered many great suggestions and lots of encouragement that kept me excited to finish both works. When I get down about how things are coming out, it's important to have good friends like Charles to keep you on track!

My parents, whose tireless encouragement in all my artistic endeavors extend all the way back to my first memories of my mother teaching me to draw and my father telling us ghost stories of his own invention while on camping trips. Being a writer himself, my father's suggestions through all stages of this novel have been invaluable. There's a lot of biographical material woven into this story about my parents and my own life, but prying them apart from the fiction would be too long of a discussion, and I'm not entirely certain if my memory is capable of fully separating dreams from reality at this point. The one certainty is that everything I write, paint, and film would never have happened without the inspiration of my parents. They continue to amaze me with their energy and generosity even now.

My wife, Susan Lyon, deserves special thanks for putting up with all my obsessive scribbling's (and ruining many a dinner party with talk of subjects normally forbidden at such gatherings). We don't agree on the existence of a supreme being, but if there is a heaven, you certainly will be there. Your example in volunteering your time, be it teaching in Africa or your weekly assignments with patients for hospice, has been an inspiration to me. Knowing there are people like you in the world gives me hope for the future of humanity.